DETROIT PUBLIC LIBRARY

3 5674 05753885 3

ONE NIGHT IN
GEORGIA

D0067516

DUFFIELD BRANCH LIBRARY
2507 WEST GRAND BOULEVARD
DETROIT, MICHIGAN 48208
(313) 481-1712

AUG 0 6 2019

DU

ALSO BY CELESTE O. NORFLEET

Irresistible You

Just One Taste

Love Is for Keeps

Mine at Last

One Sure Thing

Only You

Priceless Gift

Reflections of You

A Taste of Romance

The Thrill of You

DUFFIELD BRANCH LIBRARY
2507 WEST GRAND BOULEVARD
DETROIT, MICHIGAN 48208
(313) 481-1712

AUG 0 6 2016

ONE NIGHT IN
GEORGIA

A NOVEL

CELESTE O. NORFLEET

Amistad

An Imprint of HarperCollins*Publishers*

This is a work of fiction. Names, characters, places, and incidents are products of the author's imagination or are used fictitiously and are not to be construed as real. Any resemblance to actual events, locales, organizations, or persons, living or dead, is entirely coincidental.

ONE NIGHT IN GEORGIA. Copyright © 2019 by Celeste O. Norfleet. All rights reserved. Printed in the United States of America. No part of this book may be used or reproduced in any manner whatsoever without written permission except in the case of brief quotations embodied in critical articles and reviews. For information, address HarperCollins Publishers, 195 Broadway, New York, NY 10007.

HarperCollins books may be purchased for educational, business, or sales promotional use. For information, please email the Special Markets Department at SPsales@harpercollins.com.

FIRST EDITION

Designed by Renata De Oliveira

Library of Congress Cataloging-in-Publication Data

Names: Norfleet, Celeste O., author.
Title: One night in Georgia : a novel / Celeste O. Norfleet.
Description: First edition. | New York, NY : Amistad, 2019
Identifiers: LCCN 2018058771 (print) | LCCN 2019000590 (ebook) | ISBN 9780062329912 (ebook) | ISBN 9780062329899 (paperback)
Subjects: LCSH: African Americans—Fiction. | Race relations—Fiction. | Nineteen sixty-eight, A.D.—Fiction. | BISAC: FICTION / African American / Historical. | FICTION / African American / Romance. | FICTION / African American / General. | GSAFD: Road fiction.
Classification: LCC PS3614.O735 (ebook) | LCC PS3614.O735 O54 2019 (print) | DDC 813/.6—dc23
LC record available at https://lccn.loc.gov/2018058771

19 20 21 22 23 LSC 10 9 8 7 6 5 4 3 2 1

I have a dream that my four little children will one day live in a nation where they will not be judged by the color of their skin but by the content of their character.

—DR. MARTIN LUTHER KING JR.

1968

1

BEFORE NOON THE RESIDENTS OF CENTRAL HARLEM WERE already stewing in the sweltering mid-August heat. It was the hottest summer on record, with unrelenting temperatures that tipped close to one hundred degrees. Anywhere else and this weather would have been bearable. But in New York City, the concrete sidewalks beneath our feet and the buildings towering over our heads trapped the oppressive heat and made us feel like they were holding us hostage for a ransom we couldn't possibly pay.

It was a well-known fact that summer heat and a full moon amplified anger. Fights broke out with very little provocation, and arguments erupted over something as slight as a stubbed toe. Those who had the resources to leave the city were long gone. Those alone and left behind were just that, alone and left behind.

That was me, Zelda Livingston, alone and left behind, trying to survive the next moment and the next moment after that. My entire summer had been abysmal, and I felt like I was being choked from the inside.

I stood in front of the parlor's picture window. This used to be my favorite place in the house, with the view being the best part. The window was huge, taking up most of the front wall. Each pane was symmetrically rimmed with clear leaded glass that always reminded me of fancy art deco from the 1920s.

The window with its beveled edge reflected a distorted image of myself. I saw my mother's soulful light brown eyes staring back at me, with my father's intense passion. I had her high cheekbones, and a dimple in my left cheek winked when I laughed hard. I had her height and petite stature, which gave me a graceful poise that often led people to mistakenly assume I was soft and gentle; I was not.

Some things were merely a façade. I examined my outside because it was easier than exploring inside, and trust me, that was a good thing. I used to think nothing bad could ever happen here. I would always have my father to protect me. I was wrong.

I looked down at my hands. They were trembling nervously, anxiously, and angrily.

Six weeks ago I had come back and instantly regretted it. I attended Spelman College in Atlanta, but called Washington, DC, home now, since I regularly lived with my aunt and uncle between semesters. So I didn't get to see my mother that often. It had been twenty-two months since I had seen her last. That was why being here was so important to me. I had truly thought this time together would be different, maybe even special. Whoever said it was right: you really can't go home again.

I was supposed to be enjoying myself, having the time of my life. After all, I was twenty and here in Harlem, but the home I'd once known and loved was no longer my home.

Hearing the murmur of voices above, I looked up, knowing what was coming. The last few days had been a succession of spiteful nasty rages that seethed as the heat and hostilities escalated. "Not today," I whispered. "Not today."

Memories began to swell around me as I stood in the parlor at the front window. Assaulted by every sense, I felt the wet drops roll down my face and tasted the salt of my tears. Lost in my thoughts, I heard frighteningly loud noises, one right after another, like claps of thunder. Twenty-three gunshots later, I saw a lifeless body covered in blood lying in the street.

The images cleared, and I looked out across the street at Mount Morris Park, where I had played when I was a kid. The air around me was still. The air conditioner in the room did little to ease the nervous restlessness stirring inside me. In wishful solace, I leaned my head against the window's smooth surface, hoping to feel cool relief. Instead I felt the blistering heat of the summer day penetrating the glass.

I wiped away the tears that streamed down my face and took a deep stumbling breath. I could almost hear my father's comforting voice echo in my ears, telling me to be strong. I closed my eyes. It was a perfect moment. I held on as tightly as I could for as long as I could.

A door upstairs slammed loudly.

I winced and glared up at the ceiling again.

Darnell Wilson, my mother's husband, had been yelling and shouting since yesterday afternoon. No one enjoyed the sound of his voice more than he did. The argument, steeped in angry resentment, had been brewing for the past five years. It had reached its inevitable climax last night, resulting in a tirade of accusations, disparagements, and ridicule. Then Darnell, having barely let up, had continued arguing again first thing this morning.

He stomped downstairs, still yelling. Each heavy footstep punctuated his hateful words. "We could use that money. She needs to stop being so damn selfish."

The man was an idiot.

I ignored him like I usually did and turned the radio up loud and prayed that for the next few minutes I could drown out his tirade with some good music. Thankfully, Marvin and Tammi were singing a new song called "You're All I Need to Get By." I allowed the melody and energy of the rhythm to flow through my body, and all of a sudden I was someplace else, somebody else. Calm. Relaxed. Feeling good.

"Turn that damn music down!" he yelled.

A child of New Orleans's Creole upbringing, my mother always told me to be still and mind my manners and to be a lady in all situations. And the man was always right. "Young ladies listen and obey. They don't cause trouble," she had reminded me over and over again. I had never been very good at all that obeying stuff. Today wasn't going to be any different. I turned the music up louder and chuckled to myself.

A few seconds later, Darnell stormed into the room. I turned around, and we stood there staring at each other, face-to-face. At first he didn't say anything. He just glared at me, sneering, looking mean and evil, like that was supposed to scare me. He was wrong. I smirked. Then he snorted and slipped a toothpick between his thick lips. He started chewing on it.

"All that money just thrown away, wasted, given to a damn school. Who the hell is going to hire some black girl lawyer? See, that's what college teaches you, not a damn thing, just like her dead-ass daddy."

"Darnell, leave it be," my mother said as she followed him into the room. She looked at me woefully. "There's nothing you can do. What's done is done."

"And now you're telling me there's more money for her to waste. You're her mother. You should've had some say."

She looked at me. "Her uncle is the executor of Owen's will. It's out of my hands."

"Well, it's not out of my hands. If she's going to be in this house, she needs to pay her way. This is my house," he raged. "I pay the bills here. If she doesn't pay, she doesn't stay."

I stormed out of the house and slammed the front door behind me. The door, rickety on its hinges, with its latch already weak, shut soundly and then bounced open again, slamming back against the wall.

"Zelda!" I heard my mother call out.

Ignoring her, I slowly paced on the front stoop, muttering. It was different at my aunt and uncle's house. I never felt alone or left behind while living with them. *"Seul et gauche derrière."* I said it aloud and decided it sounded better in French. But then again, mostly everything did. That's what my aunt Dorothy always said, in French, of course. She was a linguistics professor at Howard University and the one who had taught me French when I was a kid. *"La gauche derrière,"* I repeated. "Think I'll have that etched onto my gravestone."

2

MY FATHER, OWEN LIVINGSTON, WAS FROM A WELL-established DC family, but he was now long gone. He'd had everything Darnell Wilson envied if he had any sense or ambition: money, power, position, and the prettiest woman in the city. Born to upset the status quo, and raised by generations of formidable advocates for civil rights, Owen Livingston was the continuation of a long line of freedom fighters. But his future, bright and promising, ended far sooner than it should have. His death was said to have been an accident. Nobody believed it, though. I saw it with my own eyes and definitely didn't believe it.

Six short months later, Owen Livingston's grief-stricken widow became Mrs. Darnell Wilson. She had lived well and was well provided for even after my father's death. She had enough money for the rest of her days. And then she erased her husband as if he'd never existed. Darnell, a fledgling actor, had moved into my father's home and slept in his bed. They shacked up before marrying, and within a year there was no more money, except what had been left to me.

Darnell had been fuming for five long years. Then last night my mother had told him that because I recently turned twenty, I had received an inheritance from my grandfather, which only added to Darnell's ire.

The man had barely held a job in the time I had known him. All he did was pretend that he was an actor to anyone who'd sit still for two minutes with his dumb ass. He had promised my mother that he was going to be a big star, bigger then Belafonte and Poitier put together. Of course it never happened. And him claiming this was his house was a blatant lie.

This was my house. I had left, but the house was not Darnell's. I was born and raised in this house. Three stories, five bedrooms, lavishly decorated, and on one of the most prestigious streets in Harlem, Mount Morris Park, where the only color that mattered was green. I knew every inch of this house. The eighth floorboard in the parlor creaked when I stepped on it, the vestibule door swelled when it rained for more than two days, and the stained-glass windows in the dining room had never budged an inch in twenty years. This wasn't his house. It was my father's.

"Zelda Livingston, what the hell has gotten into you?" my mother fumed as soon as she stepped outside.

I relaxed my shoulders and held my head high, looking straight ahead at the park. "He needs to stop berating my father," I said plainly, deciding to hold back on everything else I wanted to say.

She sighed heavily. "Zelda, you know that's not what he meant," she stated.

I shook my head. I didn't know why my mother insisted on constantly defending Darnell's behavior. I remember the day the parasite had come into our lives. The first words out of his mouth had been to disparage my father's memory, while my mother had said nothing. Having him around was a curse. He had brought nothing but misery.

"What am I going to do? What am I going to do? Good Lord, this is such a mess. Zelda, you're not a child anymore. You're too old to act like this. You're going to have to apologize to him."

I ignored her and let her words pass. If nothing else, I had been raised well and knew now was not the time to be fresh or mouthy.

"Do you hear me talking to you? Look at me," she said.

I didn't respond and didn't turn around.

"Zelda Livingston, I know you hear me. Look at me."

After a brief pause, I slowly turned to face her. I searched her eyes and saw that they were red and puffy.

"I hear you," I said more tersely than I had intended.

"If you'd at least try to get along, to know him. He's really a good man, talented, strong, kind, and loving."

I looked at my mother, wondering if she had ever really loved my father. Marrying a total stranger just a few months after my father died hardly seemed like it.

"I swear to God I have no idea what's wrong with you these days," she said miserably. "Maybe Darnell is right. Maybe this college thing isn't working out."

"No," I said forcefully, surprising myself by my sharp tone, my eyes piercing and final. There was no way I was going to leave school. "I'm going to be an attorney like my father. I'm going to change the world and never look back."

She nodded slowly. Standing directly in front of me, she reached out and touched my arm tenderly. "You can't upset this household every time someone mentions your father's name. Try to get along." She shook her head sadly. "You're so much like your father, the same indomitable spirit. When he wanted something, there was no talking him out of it. But that determination has a double edge. Don't get so wrapped up in your ambitions that you forget what's really important."

"What do you mean?" I asked.

"The choices you make in life have consequences, not just for you but for those around you. Try to remember that. I don't want you to be like . . ." She stopped.

I looked at her as she looked away. "Like what? Like my father?"

She ignored me. "Whose car is that?" she asked, looking down the street.

I turned around and saw a flashy red convertible slowly driving down the street with kids trailing behind on the sidewalk, waving and cheering.

"What in the world is she doing here?" I waved. Two women in the car waved back.

"You know them?" my mother asked.

I nodded. "Yeah, I know the driver. Veronica Cook. She's a friend of mine from Spelman," I said. "Remember, I told you about her the last time I was here. I don't know the other girl." I hurried down the steps to the curb just as the car pulled up and stopped right in front of me.

"Guess who," Veronica said, smiling from ear to ear. She turned off the engine and raised her shades onto the wide headband holding back her long black curls.

I laughed. "What are you doing here?"

"I think she needs a hint," the passenger joked as she removed her wide-brimmed straw hat and dark shades and got out of the car. With bleached-blond hair and wearing bright red lipstick, a long-sleeved paisley baby-doll top, and shorts with flat sandals, she looked like she'd just stepped off a hippie fashion runway.

My jaw dropped. "Daphne Brooks? Is that you?"

"In the flesh," Daphne said, striking a dramatic pose.

I hadn't seen them since classes had let out almost three months ago. Veronica and Daphne were my best friends in the world. They were more than my sorority sisters. They were my sisters of the heart.

"Oh my God, I didn't even recognize you. You look like a movie star," I said, hugging her.

She seemed uncharacteristically happy and free-spirited. Normally she was shy and timid, preferring to fade into the background. Unpretentious, she usually dressed in drab, unassuming colors and always kept her mousy-brown hair pulled back and pinned up. She was easily rattled and distraught, so Veronica and I always took up for her. Being of mixed race—her mother was black and her father was white—and being very light-skinned at a predominately black women's college could be tough, and the girls at Spelman weren't always kind. One girl's clothes had been burned up, because she had a famous mother and some of the other students were jealous.

"I told her the exact same thing when I saw her," Veronica said, laughing as she came around the back of the car. "Don't you love the hair and new look?"

Daphne fluffed her wavy tresses and giggled.

"I love it. It works with your blue-green eyes. You look positively chic," I said.

We laughed and hugged and as usual began talking all at once. "Wait a minute. Wait a minute," I finally said. "Not that I'm not thrilled to see you both, but what in the world are you two doing in Harlem?"

"We were just in the neighborhood," Daphne joked.

"Since when is Harlem in the Long Island neighborhood?"

"Well," Veronica began, then glanced at Daphne, "we thought we'd go for a little drive."

"A drive," I repeated, "all the way to Harlem?"

"Sure. Why not?"

"I don't think so," I said doubtfully. I knew my friends, and I could see they were definitely up to something.

"Zelda." My mother was walking down the steps, coming toward me. "Who are your friends?" she asked.

"Mom, this is Veronica Cook and Daphne Brooks, my best friends from college. This is my mother, Gail Wilson."

"Hello, Mrs. Wilson," Daphne said pleasantly.

"It's a pleasure to meet you, Mrs. Wilson," Veronica added in her perfectly polished voice. She was the only debutante I knew, and the only black girl I knew who had been born into old money.

"Daphne, Veronica, welcome. It's wonderful to finally meet some of Zelda's friends from college. Why don't you come inside and get out of this heat. I just made a pitcher of iced tea."

"No thank you, ma'am," Daphne declined.

"We're not staying long," Veronica added.

"Okay. Well then, I'll let you girls visit. It was nice meeting you both," Gail said, then turned and headed back to the house.

"You too, Mrs. Wilson."

As soon as she left, I turned to my friends. "I can't believe you're here," I said almost tearfully, "and look at this car. It's outta sight. Whose is it?" I asked. I leaned over the passenger door to get a better look at the inside.

"It's mine," Veronica said proudly.

I turned quickly, seeing the grin on her face. "No way!"

"I said the exact same thing when she drove up to the house this morning," Daphne announced. "But her name is on the registration. Veronica Cook—I saw it myself."

I shook my head. "I don't believe it."

"Well, it is. It's all mine. Candy-apple red convertible Ford Fairlane with all the bells and whistles."

I looked at her skeptically. "Who gave it to you?"

"It's an early graduation gift from my parents."

"Isn't it just beautiful? And it rides like an absolute dream," Daphne added excitedly.

I nodded, admiring the car once more. "It is beautiful. Congratulations!"

"Thanks," Veronica said happily, then quickly glanced at Daphne.

"So we were thinking . . ." Daphne began and then glanced at Veronica. Both began smiling mischievously.

"Okay, what are you two really up to?" I asked, seeing the exchange between them.

"We were thinking . . . Feel like taking a ride with us?"

"Ah, sure, okay. Where to?" I asked.

"To Georgia," Veronica and Daphne said with big smiles on their faces.

"To Georgia. You're not serious."

"Yes, we are."

"No way," I said.

"Come on. Do something spontaneous for once in your boring life. Don't think, do," Veronica insisted.

I shook my head emphatically. "No, no way."

"Zelda, come on. It'll be a blast," Daphne added. "You know, it's okay to color outside the lines sometimes." Veronica and I both looked at Daphne. Apparently this was another one of her pearls of wisdom. She frowned. "Oh, you know what I mean."

"No. I have no idea."

"Zelda—" Veronica began.

I cut her off with a simple response. "No."

"But—" Daphne tried to chime in.

"No. Do you have the slightest notion how dangerous it is being black in the South these days? And you want to just up and drive down there like it's just a trip to the seashore? You must be out of your minds. No way. Blacks are being killed every single day, and nobody does a damn thing to stop it. Cops, lawyers, judges—they're all in on it."

"We're not fools. We're going to be careful," Veronica said.

Daphne nodded.

"Look. See? We're all packed and ready to go," Daphne said, showing me the small bags already in the back seat. "Our suitcases are in the trunk. All we need is you."

I shook my head. "There's no way I'm going," I declared.

"Why not?"

"Because," I said.

"Because why?"

"Because of a dozen different reasons."

"Name one," Veronica said.

"Because I already have my train ticket," I said quickly.

"So cash it in," Veronica countered.

"Because classes don't start for another week and a half. There's no reason to leave this early," I reasoned, then paused and looked at them questioningly. "So why are you leaving so early?"

"We're making a stop along the way," Daphne said.

"Hurry up and get your things. We don't have a lot of room, so maybe just bring two suitcases."

I shook my head again. "I can't go with you."

"Of course you can. It's a moral imperative that you come with us, and besides, you already promised you would," Daphne said, smiling victoriously.

"When did I promise that?" I asked.

"Three years ago, the first day we met on the train going to Spelman, remember? We said that we'd drive down to school our senior year and have one last big adventure before we separate and start our real lives."

I remembered. But it had been just a pipe dream. "That doesn't count. We also promised that we'd travel the country in a VW bus and backpack through Europe. We didn't do any of that."

"We still have time," Veronica assured me.

"Oh, come on. It'll be a blast. What else do you have to do next week, sit and melt in this heat?" Daphne said, then held up her pinkie finger.

I looked at Daphne's finger. This has meaning. It was something my father and I had done when I was growing up. It was a promise not to be broken.

"Don't you read the newspapers? The laws have changed, yes, but it's still dangerous driving in the South. Not everyone respects the law."

"Of course I read the newspapers. But I'm not going to live my whole life being scared of what might happen. We don't have every freedom, but let's use what we do have."

"Veronica, black people disappear, never to be seen again. Or if they're found, they're mangled beyond recognition, like Emmett Till."

I remembered in my freshman year at Spelman when I first saw the picture in the *Jet* magazine. I'm still sick to my stomach every time I'm reminded of it.

Veronica shook her head, waving it off dismissively. "No. That was more than ten years ago," she said.

"Veronica, are you really that naïve?" I asked her.

"Those things happen in Alabama and Mississippi. Everybody knows that's where the real racists are."

"Racists are everywhere, even up here in the North. Cops shoot black men, and the judges look the other way with acquittals, just like in the South," I retorted.

"She's right," Daphne said solemnly.

"Well, if that's the case, then no black person should ever leave their house. We should all just give up our lives and hide. Is that what you're gonna do, hide and be scared the rest your life? What about being a lawyer and changing the world?"

"I'm not saying hide, I'm saying don't take unnecessary risks, such as traveling in a red convertible in the South. It's like riding around in a giant bull's-eye."

Veronica rolled her eyes. "Now I know you're loopy."

"Don't call me loopy," I countered, getting more annoyed. "Ever heard of Addie Mae Collins, Carol Denise McNair, Carole Robertson, or Cynthia Wesley? My father had me memorize their names. They were the four young girls killed in the Sixteenth Street Baptist Church in Birmingham. Ever heard of—"

"All right. Stop it. Enough," Daphne said tensely, then lowered her voice again. She looked around cautiously as she always did on the rare occasions when she spoke up. "We get it, okay? We get it. The South is dangerous. But we're going to be careful, and we'll be fine. I don't know about you, Zelda, but I need to get out of this damn city. I can't be here anymore."

Daphne looked terrified. I looked at Veronica. She held up her pinkie finger. Daphne held up her pinkie finger again. They turned and looked at me. I shook my head.

"This is crazy," I said softly as I looked at my friends' dejected faces. "I'm sorry. I can't." I stepped back from the car. I hated disappointing them, but there was no way I was going to jump into a car and drive down south. "Just do me a favor and please, please be careful."

Veronica and Daphne looked at each other. Veronica opened the passenger door, got in, and slid across to the driver's seat. Daphne grabbed her hat and shades and got into the car. She looked at me and tried to smile. I mouthed the words, *Be safe*.

Daphne nodded and I headed back to the house. As soon as I did, I saw Darnell standing at the parlor window, leaning against the windowpane, his belly hanging over his belt. Sweat was dripping down his face. He was smirking like he always did when he thought he was going to get his way. I stopped in my tracks and turned around just as

Veronica started the engine. "Wait! I'm coming with you," I said as my heart pounded.

Their faces lit up instantly.

"But I need to stop in DC to see my uncle," I said. I figured I had until then to talk them out of driving down south. We could catch a train from DC to Atlanta.

"No problem," Veronica said gladly.

"I'm nearly packed. I just have to toss a few more things into my suitcases." I held up my pinkie finger. Our three fingers touched. "Wait here. I'll be ready in fifteen minutes."

3

I HURRIED UP THE FRONT STEPS AND WENT BACK INSIDE.
I heard my mother and Darnell talking and overheard my
name but still kept moving. I was thinking about everything I needed to pack. Most of my stuff was in DC. I was
halfway to the second floor when I heard Darnell call out
my name. I didn't stop. He called me again. "Zelda!"

I ignored him and continued.

Then my mother called my name. I stopped, rolled my
eyes, and sighed heavily. I slowly went back downstairs, one
hesitant footstep at a time. I knew he was up to something
as soon as I walked into the parlor. He was standing there
smiling like he'd just hit the daily street number.

I stared at him as he turned and nodded out the window. I could almost see the wheels in his tiny-ass brain turning. He wanted something. He *always* wanted something.

"Whose car is that?" he asked, speaking to me directly, which he only did when he wanted something.

"What?" I answered.

"The girls out there, whose car?"

"It belongs to my friend Veronica."

He glanced outside again. "Your mother tells me that her father is Sebastian Cook, that hotshot stockbroker on Wall Street. He's in the newspapers all the time. He hangs around all them movie stars and politicians. I've seen his pictures."

Of course, I knew all this already. Veronica didn't brag; she didn't have to. Whenever she saw pictures of her parents in *Jet* or *Ebony* magazine, she just shrugged and smiled politely like it was no big deal. The first few times Daphne and I saw them we were ecstatic. We'd never known anybody in a magazine before. Then after a while we did like Veronica and just shrugged. I didn't respond to Darnell.

"Who's the white girl?" he asked.

"She's not white. She's light-skin."

"Her name's Daphne," my mother said.

"Her father got money too?" he asked.

I ignored him.

Darnell nodded and smiled all giddy-like, then looked at my mother. She moved across the room, feigning disinterest. "So she got money too, then," he assumed. "Well, you know, I'm concerned about them standing out there in the hot sun."

"Of course," I responded sarcastically.

His eyes narrowed. "Look-a-here," he began, "you go out there and tell your two friends to come on inside the house where it's cool and meet your family," he insisted.

I could barely contain the chuckle bubbling inside me. You would think he was joking, but I knew better. I glared at him for a few seconds, then shook my head. "My friends have already met my family," I said. "We've celebrated Thanksgiving in DC together for the last three years."

"They ain't met *all* your family," he said as his eyes widened. "They ain't met me."

"No, they haven't," I said plainly, not budging. "And why would you want to meet my friends anyway?"

"I want to meet their fathers. They can introduce me to—"

"No," I replied, not giving him a chance to finish.

We locked eyes. His perpetual frown seemed to turn into a menacing scowl. But I wasn't moved. There was no way I was going to bring my friends inside to meet him.

"I ain't playing with you," he threatened. "Now go tell them girls to come on in here and get some cool iced tea. Tell them you want them to meet your father."

Father? I couldn't believe what came out of his slithering-snake mouth. He was delusional. I had been telling my girls about his foolishness for the past three years.

After I laughed, I looked at him as if he had lost his mind. Sensing no reply from me, he scowled, thinning his lips to slits of rage.

"Zelda, please," my mother said, exasperated.

"Call them in here," he demanded.

I turned and went upstairs. I could hear him cussing just before I closed my bedroom door. I flung a suitcase onto the bed and began filling it with my things. As I did, something fell to the floor. I reached down and picked up a doll my father had given me when I was seven years old. I smiled as I sat down on the edge of the bed. My heart sank. Once my sanctuary, this room was now as foreign to me as Timbuktu.

I looked up and saw my mother standing in the doorway. Suddenly I felt sorry for the woman I had grown to despise. No, "despise" wasn't the right word. I still loved my mother dearly. It was the weakness inside her I despised. Years of trusting Darnell had worn her down to the frail, pitiful woman standing before me. Once vibrant and beautiful, strong and fierce, she was now weak and pathetic. Darnell had taken her youth and her spirit.

He had sweet-talked her out of her panties and into his bed with promises of lasting love, fidelity, and good times. And after three months of auditions, it was painfully obvious that not only was he not going to be the next Belafonte, but he could barely read the scripts. So, with his pipe dreams dashed, he started working as a doorman and sometimes ushered at the Harlem Palace Theatre. It was as close as he'd ever get to the stage.

I placed the doll back on the bed and continued packing.

"Darnell wants you to invite your friends in."

"There's no time," I said hurriedly.

"What are you doing?" she asked, looking around aimlessly.

"Packing."

"I can see that," she said, sounding more surprised than distressed. She walked over to the closet and saw all my clothes gone.

"Zelda, stop," she insisted, holding my arm still. "What are you doing? Why are you leaving so soon?"

I looked at my mother, slightly puzzled. "You said it yourself. Me being here causes strife. So I'm leaving." I grabbed my big red, black, and green macramé tote bag and started stuffing clothing inside. I grabbed my doll and stuffed that inside too.

"Zelda, don't take everything so literal. That's not what I meant, and you know it."

"Your husband just told me to get out of my own father's house and you didn't say a word. You just stood there and let him put me out."

"You know he didn't mean it. He was just angry. You're so touchy about everything," she said, then rolled her eyes and shook her head. "For God's sake, you need to stop getting so upset when someone mentions your father. I'm so tired of always defending you."

I spun around, furious. "Defending me? You have never defended me. My father protected me. He saved my life." I quickly continued packing.

"Zelda, stop it. I look at you and see your father. He would never yield on anything, and that's what got him killed."

I didn't say anything. I closed the suitcase, snapping the locks. I turned and looked at her. She stood there, her eyes wide and agonizing. "Do you even know what today is?" I asked.

She looked at me, confused. I shook my head sadly. "You don't have a clue, do you? It holds no significance for you whatsoever. He did everything for you, and you can't even remember that he was handcuffed, beaten, shot, and killed five years ago today."

Her jaw dropped.

"That's okay, I understand. You're blinded by Darnell, the master manipulator."

The slap across my face was instant. It was hard and loud like an explosion going off in my head. My right eye blurred and teared up immediately. The prickling sting came seconds later, like a hundred tiny pins piercing the side of my face. I held my cheek and stepped back.

"Zelda," she began, reaching out to me.

I slung my tote bag over my shoulder, picked up my suitcase, and headed down the stairs and straight out the front door. As soon as I got outside I saw Veronica and Daphne leaning against the car with Darnell talking to them. His arms waved around in full animation. Whatever lie he was telling was a big one.

"Hey," he said, smiling at me.

I didn't answer. I walked straight to the back of the car. Veronica and Daphne hurried over and opened the trunk. We squeezed my suitcase inside and slammed it shut. Daphne climbed into the back, and I sat in the passenger seat. Veronica slid behind the wheel, and just like that, it was done. No goodbye. No farewell. No nothing. We drove off.

As we got to the corner, I turned one last time to see my mother standing midway up the front steps. Darnell was talking to her. She held her hand up to wave goodbye.

Two blocks away I was staring in the side mirror. No one had said a word. After a bit, Veronica stopped at a traffic light. She looked over at me. "Well now, that was memorable, wasn't it?" she blurted out as soon as the light turned green, and off she drove.

"Veronica, hush," Daphne said quickly.

"I'm just saying." Veronica glanced in the rearview mirror and caught Daphne's eye. "You were thinking the same dang thing I was, so don't tell me to hush."

They both turned and looked at me as I sat quietly.

"Are you okay, Zelda?" Daphne asked softly as she leaned forward and touched my shoulder.

I shook my head slowly, then closed my eyes as tears began to fall. Veronica quickly pulled the car over to the side of the street and turned the engine off. She slid close to me and took my hand as Daphne leaned over the seat and wrapped her arms around my shoulders. "Zelda, we're here for you," she whispered.

I nodded. "I know. I'll be fine," I said, my voice cracking. I lay my head back on the soft leather seat and closed my eyes. "It's just that today is—"

"We know," Veronica said softly. "That's why we came by to see you today. We thought you might need a couple of friends to stand by you."

"You're gonna be okay," Daphne said.

"She's fine, and we'll all be better than fine as soon as we get the hell out of this hot-ass city and we can start having some fun."

"I second that," Daphne said.

I smiled and nodded. "Make it unanimous," I said.

"All right, then," Veronica said, digging in her big bag. She pulled out a Polaroid Land camera and held it at arm's length. Daphne tucked between us.

"Cheeeese." We smiled and laughed as I pushed the red button. There was a flash, and after a minute Veronica peeled away the negative to reveal the print of us smiling.

"Perfect."

"Cool. Now let's get on the road," Veronica said as she handed me the camera and glanced over her shoulder, then merged back into traffic.

Daphne relaxed back. "This is going to be so boss."

"So you have any idea how to get there?" I asked.

"To Georgia, no, not a clue," Veronica said.

"Well, we know we have to go south, which means taking the New Jersey Turnpike. We can stop at a service station on the way and get a map," Daphne added.

I opened the glove compartment and fished inside and found a half pack of cigarettes, two sticks of Beech-Nut peppermint gum, and a map of Connecticut and Massachusetts. "Nothing we can use." I tossed everything back inside.

Veronica sighed heavily. "I know exactly where we're going," she assured us again. "And getting to Georgia is a snap. We just go south and follow the road signs."

"But—" I began.

"Oh, for heaven's sake, Zelda, would you please relax and let her drive in peace?" Daphne said. "We'll be fine."

I looked at Daphne, surprised by her tone. It was completely out of character. Apparently her new look wasn't the only thing that had changed. Still, I was no fool. I was not reckless. I didn't walk down a dark alley and hope no one was there with a billy club or a straight razor. I'd heard about too many heinous goings-on when people drove down south. Chaney, Goodman, and Schwerner were three names I'd never forget. They'd volunteered to register black voters. With no protection from the police, they were arrested, held, ambushed, abducted, and murdered. Unimaginably bad things happened all the time. Having no map and no plan, we were asking for trouble.

Daphne was relaxed and calm. She had replaced her wide-brimmed straw hat with a silk scarf and had put on her dark shades. She stretched out on the back seat with a smile on her face and her chin tilted up to the brilliant sun. I guessed I was the only one feeling anxious.

"If I get raped and murdered and my body is dismembered and scattered up and down the East Coast, I'm gonna haunt you both for the rest of your natural lives."

"What else is new? You do that now," Veronica said wryly as she reached over and turned on the radio. James Brown's "Say It Loud" blasted free.

4

IN NEWARK, THE RADIO STATION AUDIO WENT STATIC.
Veronica turned the radio off, and we rode in silence. The
continuous flow of ordinary people in regular cars gave
traveling the New Jersey Turnpike a false sense of America's
civility. Almost every driver we passed crawled close beside
us and stared curiously at the three of us in the flashy convertible. They gawked at us as if we were zoo specimens.
Curiosity, grimaces, scowls, and loathsome frowns seemed
to be the most popular reactions. I was amused by their
expressions.

A simple drive down a highway by three black women
should not cause this much uproar. One day maybe it
would be different, just as Dr. King had said in his March
on Washington speech. A time when we wouldn't be stared
at or stopped and harassed for the color of our skin.

"It feels like we've been sitting in this traffic for hours. What's going on? Is there an accident up there?" Daphne asked, scooting forward and poking her head over the seat.

I shrugged. Veronica removed her dark shades and leaned over the steering wheel. She cupped her hand above her brow and squinted against the brightness of the sun. "I don't see anything."

I'd been down the turnpike often enough to know that it was taking much longer than it usually did. By the time we'd gotten to New Brunswick, traffic was at a complete standstill. Stalled, overheated cars had been parked to the side of the road, littering the highway nearly every half mile.

I looked back at the slow, desperate exodus with traffic snarled in every direction. "I've never seen it this backed up before," I said.

"Me either." Veronica turned the steering wheel, then eased over into the next lane. "But it doesn't matter. We're getting off at this exit." A few minutes later, we proceeded to take Exit 8 for Hightstown and Trenton.

"Why are we getting off here?" I asked.

"You'll see."

I sighed and relaxed back against the seat. I closed my eyes and reclined my head toward the sun. The soothing warmth on my face and the untroubling breeze felt comforting.

After we got off the turnpike, we drove down a narrow road through a heavily wooded area dotted with pastures, fields, and farmhouses spaced far from each other.

Out of the blue, Veronica started laughing. "Hey, we forgot to tell you, your best buddy Darnell said he was going to send somebody to look after us."

"What? What are you talking about?" I asked, alarmed. "In Atlanta?"

"No. While you were in the house, he was acting concerned about our safety. We told him we were stopping in Cape May first and he said a son of a friend of his would meet us at Veronica's family's place," Daphne explained, leaning over the front seat.

"When did we decide to stop in Cape May and what do you mean Darnell's sending someone to Veronica's family's place?" I asked.

"It was a surprise for you, but then Darnell wanted to know where we were going."

"And you told him? And he's sending someone to meet us? Are you two crazy?" I asked them, feeling myself getting more and more angry. I couldn't believe this.

"Girl, now you know that man ain't got friend the first," Daphne stated, barely managing her screaming laughter.

"Yeah, I made him feel big and all by playing along and giving him the address. Sistas got to respect the man. You can't bring a brotha down. You know, unite, black power, and all that other stuff you say, Zelda."

I gave her a look that let her know now was not the time. "I don't want anything to do with that man or anybody he knows. And I don't want anybody he knows near me. That's all I got to say about it."

"Here," Daphne said, handing me a Pepsi cola and a big half-eaten bag of Bugles.

"Thanks." I had skipped breakfast earlier and was getting hungry. I sipped the soda and munched on a few cornucopia-shaped snacks. It wasn't a stack of flapjacks with butter and syrup and sausage links, but it hit the spot.

After a while I looked around in earnest. "Are we almost there?"

"Relax," Veronica said, smiling. "I haven't been here in ages. I thought it would be nice to hang out at the shore for a while."

"Sounds good to me," Daphne said happily. "I've never been to Cape May."

"Me either," I said, feeling bothered for no particular reason. Daphne was right. Darnell didn't have any friends as far as I knew. He was just boasting again.

"You're gonna love it. I used to spend almost all my summers down here when I was younger. It's quiet and peaceful, and the beach is amazing. It'll be a blast."

I shrugged indifferently. I wasn't much of a beach person. I could swim. My aunt had taught me years ago, but messing up my hair with salt water and sand wasn't what I considered having a blast. Unlike Veronica, who had a lye straightener in her hair, and Daphne, who had good hair, I had hair that was thick and corkscrew curly. I'd worn an Afro for years, ever since my father showed me a picture of Nina Simone. He said her Afro was her crown and made her look strong and determined. I admired her and wanted to be just like her.

Driving through Cape May, Veronica slowed as we came to an area that was dilapidated. A huge vacant lot was across the street, and beside it were long-neglected homes. Two old men with short gray hair stood looking at the site. I watched as they pointed and shook their heads. "What happened here?" I asked Veronica as she stopped at a traffic light.

"They're tearing it all down."

"Why?"

"It's called urban development," she said. "They're building new homes and businesses and making way for progress."

"I'm guessing this was a black neighborhood."

"Yeah, it was," she said, driving on when the light changed.

"What happened to all the people who used to live there?" Daphne asked.

"I'm sure they kicked them out," I said.

"No. They got compensated and moved someplace else. This area is prime beach-front real estate, and the houses were a disgrace."

"So they just chuck everybody out and call it progress."

"Don't start, Zelda. It's none of our business," Daphne said.

I turned to face her. "What are you talking about? This is everybody's business. This is how they're shutting us up, erasing us from history. They take everything from the poor, and that's usually black people. Do you really think black folks are going to be able to afford to move back to this area when they're finished building those fancy new houses? No. What happens if they want your father's house next?"

"They can have it." Daphne smirked.

"Why do you always want to make it a war? Life isn't always black versus white," Veronica exclaimed.

"That's exactly how it is, black versus white. They mean us no good. They're all alike. They're the status quo, the good ol' boys who want everything back to how it used to be. It's a hatred as old as the republic itself."

"Not all white people are like that," Veronica corrected.

"Can we please change the subject?" Daphne complained. "I'm tired of hearing about this."

"I can't believe you two. What happened to concern and care for your fellow human being?" I said, astonished by their lack of empathy.

"Zelda, come on. We're here to have fun."

"Are we going to be doing this the whole time?" Daphne asked.

"Doing what?" I asked. "Not caring?"

"Oh good Lord, somebody get her a placard and let her go picket. It's done, Zelda, there's nothing anybody can do about it. The people took the money and moved on. Case closed. You don't know what this place looked like before. It was horrible. Because of crime, you couldn't come around here after sunset. At least now it will be different. And the black people you're talking about can start over someplace else, someplace better."

"But don't you see? These were once their homes."

"You know, in the 1920s about thirty percent of Cape May was black folks and about sixty percent of the businesses were black owned. From Jefferson to Lafayette to Broad was all black."

"So they just congregated here—why?" Daphne asked.

"There was good-paying work with the railroad, and then they stayed. I even heard that this was a meeting point on the Underground Railroad."

"See? That's what I'm talking about. History. Our history. Pretty soon it'll be even less and less."

"She's got a point," Daphne said.

I nodded. "See?"

"My aunt volunteers on the community archives committee," Veronica said. "They document local black history like the Smith House. Stephen Smith was famous for being one of the richest black men in America. He had a summer house right over there." She pointed to a small two-story building with floor-to-ceiling windows and a second-floor balcony. "That's the Stephen Smith House. President Johnson saved it, so it can't be torn down."

"We've got to do for ourselves," I stated.

"There's not a whole lot we can do. We sat at lunch counters, picketed, boycotted, and then what? Nothing really changed," Daphne said.

"I wouldn't call the Civil Rights Act of 1964 nothing," Veronica said.

"Yes, but that was then. It's our turn now and we have to do it better. Yes, we sat and picketed and boycotted, but now we have to be more vocal, more out there."

"You mean like the protests and riots?" Daphne asked.

"Protests, yes, and riots, maybe, if we have to," I said.

"Things will change. It'll just take time," said Veronica.

"Time." I shook my head. "I'm sure that's exactly what the first slaves said when they got off the *Jesus of Lübeck* in 1562. It'll just take time and we'll be free."

"Oh brother, here we go, another history lesson," Daphne complained.

"I'm just trying to educate you," I said. "Change only comes when we make it."

"Can we just drop it now? Please," Daphne said.

I didn't say anything after that. None of us did. But I kept thinking about what Veronica had said and what she told us about places like Oak Bluffs, Idlewild, Sag Harbor, and Cape May years ago. Places where elite and affluent blacks could summer in peace without the need to constantly prove worthy.

I looked around sadly, seeing the lost splendor of yesteryear. Churches, dance halls, restaurants, banks, hotels, all black-owned, were gone or on the verge of vanishing. Some decimated by the ravages of time, others stolen by greedy men for profit, determined to wipe away our history and forever change the demographic.

I knew this place would soon be the end of an era, destined to fade into nothing, and nobody was going to do a damn thing to stop it.

We drove a few more miles. The heaviness of the conversation had brought down our mood, and we all three retreated into our thoughts. Of course Veronica interrupted the peace.

"Oh, I love this song," she said.

"Me too. Turn it up. Turn it up," Daphne instructed.

I reached over and turned the knob. The impeccably harmonic voices of the Fifth Dimension flowed from the car speakers. "Stoned Soul Picnic"—it was perfect in promoting a lighthearted and carefree spirit throughout the car. We immediately bobbed her heads, sang, and swayed along with the lively ballad.

"Yes. A picnic!" Daphne shouted. Veronica glanced up in the rearview mirror and I turned around. "That's what we should do. We should have a picnic." Daphne excitedly sat up on the edge of the seat and started looking around. "We're close to the beach, right? We can stop and grab some sandwiches, then have a picnic on the beach. Oh, that's perfect."

"A stoned soul picnic on the beach," I said, still singing along with the radio.

"I know the perfect spot," Veronica said as she turned the music up even louder. Daphne and I raised our hands and continued to sway with the music.

The song faded and a commercial came on, advertising a brand-new cigarette, Virginia Slims. I turned the radio down as we stopped at a traffic light. Next to us, sitting there at the light, was a sunburned man in an old beat-up truck with more rust than paint. The driver-side door panel was a different color than the rest of the truck, and the side mirror was barely hanging on. His round face was as red as the insides of a ripe watermelon. His blond hair, matted and greasy, crept out from beneath a dirty straw porkpie hat. The rest of it crawled down the sides of his face and ended in a scruffy, scraggy beard at his chin. His mouth was the barest slit, with his lips almost invisible. His eyes were dark and intently focused on us, and our shiny car.

I saw in his back seat a little girl with eyes bluer than the sky and blond hair as white as the clouds. I thought about an angel, or better yet a cherub, as soon as I saw her. Rosy cheeks, and little sausage fingers gripped an apple nearly the size of her face. She bit into it and chewed happily. Then she turned to me and stuck out her tongue.

I looked at the man again. He was still staring. I didn't know if Veronica or Daphne noticed him. They were talking about the new cigarette from the commercial. I turned and looked straight ahead. I was done with the stares.

"We're almost there," Veronica said excitedly.

Daphne leaned over the front seat. A few blocks later Veronica rounded another corner and immediately pulled into a long, narrow driveway right beside a small house surrounded by a mass of bright red rose bushes. She continued driving along the side of the house toward the rear, where I realized the enormity of the house. White with evergreen shutters, a host of windows, and a spacious wraparound porch on the ground level, it was the most beautiful house I'd seen.

"We're here," Veronica announced. "This is my family's house. My great-grandparents bought the land and then my grandparents built the house. Now it belongs to my father and my uncle Harold. That means it belongs to me too."

I knew they had a summerhouse in Oak Bluffs on Martha's Vineyard. Although I had never been there, I had seen pictures of Veronica on Inkwell beach. Looking at this house, I had to say I was impressed.

Veronica opened the car door and got out, stretching. She looked up at the house, smiling proudly. "Yep. I'm the next generation. The only one to carry on the family legacy."

"Hello! Hello! Yoo-hoo."

Two older women, both around seventy or so, hurried across the street and walked toward us. One was a light-skinned black woman wearing a floral apron and the other was a white woman with garden clippers, wearing a straw hat and cat-eye sunglasses.

"Veronica Cook, is that you?" one of the women shouted.

"See, Betsy, I told you that was her. I knew it. She looks just like her grandmother, don't she though?"

"She sure does, Sadie. Just like her."

Veronica groaned just loudly enough for us to hear. "Oh, great. I was hoping to avoid them. They're the biggest two busybodies on the planet." Then she smiled and waved happily. "Hi, Miss Betsy. Hi, Miss Sadie. Yes, it's me."

The two older women walked up and grabbed Veronica, then swallowed her in a huge hug. They laughed and hugged her again. "Look at you. You are the spitting image of your grandmother, God rest her soul," one of the women said as she quickly glanced over to Daphne and me.

"How's everything in the neighborhood?" Veronica asked.

"Fine. Fine. Quiet for the most part. Although we've got a couple of strange ones renting the Petersons' house on the corner," the black woman said. "I think they're musicians and hippies," she mouthed, barely audible. "British hippies."

"Yes, that's right. We think they're doing those psychedelic drugs too."

"They wear flowers, beads, and bells. Imagine that?"

The black woman nodded. "It's about ten of them."

"I just hope they're not having sex orgies in there. The Petersons just got brand-new living room furniture. I don't know why they would rent their home to those people."

The two women looked at me peculiarly, or maybe it was just my imagination.

"I'm sure they smoke those funny cigarettes too." The white woman leaned closer and whispered, "You know the ones that get you dizzy and drive you stark raving mad."

"You mean marijuana," I offered. Both women turned and scowled at me as if I had just divulged state secrets.

"You know about those cigarettes?" the black woman asked, looking at me suspiciously.

"No," I said quickly. "I saw it on the news. It's scary." They nodded in unison.

"So, Veronica, are your parents coming down as well?"

"No, not this time. It's just my girlfriends and me. Mom and Dad are still vacationing in the Vineyard for the summer."

"And these are your friends."

"Yes. Miss Sadie, Miss Betsy, I want you to meet my two best friends from school. This is Zelda Livingston and Daphne Brooks."

We smiled and nodded politely.

"From Spelman?" Miss Sadie asked. "My alma mater?"

"Yes, ma'am," Veronica said and then turned to Daphne and me. "Miss Sadie, her mother, and her grandmother all went to Spelman."

We talked about the weather, traffic, and the drive down. Then we talked about Spelman and college life and how things had changed over the years. Sadie, now retired, had been a nurse, like Veronica's aunt. Her husband had been an engineer. Betsy was a writer and owned the local newspaper with her husband. Veronica and I asked questions and did most of the talking while Daphne remained quiet. She was never very talkative around people she didn't know.

"Well, we can stand out here talking all day, but I've got a cake in the oven and guests coming over this evening," Sadie said, adjusting her apron ties.

"And those hedges are not going to trim themselves, although I wish they would."

We laughed at the joke as the two neighbors began walking back down the driveway toward their homes. "Enjoy the beach," Betsy said. "I hear the water is nice and warm today. But be careful. There's a near high tide with a strong current and a serious undertow. Rips will pull you over by the sewage pipe."

"We'll be careful," Veronica assured them.

"You're all welcome to stop by this evening after dinner for cake and coffee."

"Thank you," Veronica said, waving. "We'll try. Have a good day."

I looked at Veronica. "Sewage pipe in the water where people swim? There's no way I'm getting in the water with a sewage pipe spewing garbage and only God knows what else all over the place."

Veronica shook her head and waved me off. "Don't worry about it. The pipe is all corroded and slimy, and it's been shut off and plugged up for decades. It's right next to an old dilapidated pier that collapsed in a storm years and years ago. Nobody ever goes near it. But people around here still fret. It's like the boogeyman. The only people who go near it are the fools who don't live around here and don't know any better."

"Aren't there warning signs posted?" I asked.

"Yes, of course, as long as people pay attention and read them. But like I said, nobody ever goes near the pipe. As big and ugly as it looks, who would want to?" she said, then walked back to the car.

"What are rips?" Daphne asked.

"Rip currents—basically ocean waves with a shitty attitude. Miss Betsy is obsessed with listening to the weather and tide forecasts. She reads the tide predictions like the Bible, and she panics whenever they mention the words 'high tide' or 'undercurrent.' Don't worry. We'll be fine. Come on, it's time for us to start having some fun."

5

WE HURRIEDLY GRABBED OUR THINGS FROM THE CAR,
then followed Veronica up the front steps and into the
house. She dropped her suitcases in the foyer. "Okay,"
Veronica began, "I'll give you the quick five-cent tour, and
then we can hit the beach."

Daphne and I shrugged agreeably and followed her
from room to room. She called it her family's summer bungalow, but since it had four bedrooms and was just two
blocks from the beach, I called it heaven.

The downstairs rooms, even with the drapes mostly
drawn, were open and airy with dark wooden floors covered by a thin layer of sand, which made our footsteps
crunch every time we took a step. The parlor in the front of
the house had three large floor-to-ceiling windows allowing
thin slits of bright sunbeams to fall across the decorative

area rug beneath the tufted turquoise Selig sofa, matching slipper chairs, and coffee table. Most of what I could see of the other furniture was simple and modest, and not at all flashy and fancy like I thought it would be.

The kitchen was small with an old-fashioned stove, a stone fireplace, and a hot water heater beside a small refrigerator. There were no enclosed cabinets, just open shelves lined with dishes, cups, and canned goods. Beyond the kitchen was a screened-in porch, with a round wood table in the center of the room surrounded by six chairs. The porch overlooked a small backyard, a tiny shed, and a well-tended garden.

Upstairs were two spacious bedrooms and two smaller ones. All four were hot and stuffy, with the same thin layer of sand covering the floors.

We put our luggage in one of the two larger bedrooms. I thought it was Veronica's parents' bedroom because there were several pictures of her on the dresser. Since there were two full-size beds, we decided we'd all stay in one room, with Daphne and me sharing a bed.

"Hey, want to see something super cool?" Veronica asked. We had no choice but to agree since she dashed out of the room and hurried down the hall and up a narrow staircase at the back of the house. It led to the attic, packed with old furniture and storage boxes and trunks.

"This is my favorite part in the whole house," she said excitedly as she grabbed one of the boxes stacked against the back wall.

Daphne and I helped her move the last two boxes. My mouth dropped wide open. I could not believe my eyes, looking at the view. "That's the ocean."

She chuckled softly. "Yep, it sure is," she said admiringly. "My own private view of the Atlantic Ocean. Isn't it wild? My grandmother showed me this view years ago. She told me that nobody knew about it and I had to keep it a secret."

"That's so beautiful. It goes on forever," Daphne said.

"One of these days I'm going to make this my bedroom," Veronica announced. "I used to play up here for hours when I was younger." She looked around wistfully.

"What is it?" I asked.

She shook her head. "I had to play by myself back then. None of the kids in the neighborhood were allowed to play with me because I was black. But when my cousin Anthony came to visit, we would play cards and board games up here all the time."

"Sounds like you had fun."

She smiled. "I did. We did. He was two years older than me. He was like my big brother, always joking around and making me laugh. And he always watched out for me no matter what." She paused and started putting the boxes back against the wall. "Except now I guess he's not."

"What do you mean, he's not?" I asked while helping her put the boxes back in place.

She stopped, took a deep breath, and released it slowly. "Anthony's dead. My uncle Harold got word right before

I came home from school last semester. He was killed in Vietnam. He just got there and he was killed."

I stopped stacking the boxes and looked at her. "Veronica, I'm so sorry," I said softy.

"Me too. I'm sorry," Daphne said quietly.

"He wanted to become a doctor. He was a junior at Morehouse College, then he just up and enlisted in the army. He had a deferment, but he enlisted anyway." She shook her head. "How crazy is that? Why would anyone do that?" she asked, looking completely confused. "Everybody else at Morehouse is deferred and he decided to enlist. I asked him why, and he said because they needed him. Can you believe it? He actually enlisted because he wanted to go save lives. But then he lost his own. They killed him."

"How?" Daphne asked. "I mean how did it happen?"

"They said it was friendly fire. That's when someone from your own side kills you."

"That doesn't sound friendly to me," Daphne said.

"To me either," I added.

Veronica looked at us with a confused and bewildered expression on her face. Then she closed her eyes. "Tân An, the Mekong Delta region of Vietnam."

"What's that?" I asked softly.

She opened her eyes and nodded. "That's where he was killed. I remember the exact name of the place. I don't ever want to forget that name, Tân An, the Mekong Delta region," she repeated. "How can he be killed in a place and I don't even know where to find it on a map?" she said.

"I'm sorry about Anthony," I said, then wrapped my arms around her tightly. A few seconds later, Daphne wrapped her arms around us both.

After a while Veronica stepped away and continued piling the boxes in front of the window. "He always cheated. When we played Scrabble. He came up with crazy words and always swore to me they were real. And when we played Monopoly, he mixed his money in with the bank money." She chuckled and shook her head.

"It sounds like he was a really nice guy."

She took a deep breath, exhaled slowly, and quickly changed the subject. "Good Lord, it's so damn hot and stuffy up here. I can barely breathe. Come on. Let's go find some bathing suits and get to the beach."

Before we could get changed, there was a loud, urgent knock that startled us. We went downstairs and headed toward the front door. Veronica moved ahead and looked out the window, peeking through the curtains to see who it was. She turned back to us and shrugged her shoulders. We lined up behind her as she reached for the doorknob. On the other side of the screen door was a handsome guy standing there smiling.

"Good afternoon, ladies. I'm Daniel Johnson. I believe you're expecting me."

Veronica smiled. "No, I don't think so. Are you lost?"

He pulled a piece of paper from his pocket, reviewed it, and then looked at the address of the house. "I was sent by my father's friend Darnell Wilson. Zelda's father."

With my emotions leading the way, I pushed past Veronica. "Darnell Wilson is not my father. He's just the man who married my mother. I don't know who you are or what you think you're doing here, but we don't need any help from you or Darnell."

A smile brightened Daniel's face, and as he glanced down at me, I saw a row of gorgeous white teeth. "Miss Zelda, I'm an army man, and I always complete my assignment," he replied as he leaned down and picked up his suitcase. I could see the outline of his muscles through his shirt.

"Well, that settles that," Veronica said as she stepped back, indicating that it was okay for Daniel to enter. At that moment, I was certain Veronica had lost her cotton-picking mind. How could she let a complete stranger, especially someone Darnell had sent, come into the house? She looped her arm around Daniel's. "Exactly what is your assignment?"

"Just to serve and protect, ma'am. I understand that you are on your way to Georgia and need an escort."

"Well, first we're headed to the beach. Why don't you join us?"

"Veronica, are you insane? We don't know him. If he knows Darnell, he's probably a con man and a liar," I said.

He looked at me and smiled. "I'm neither. I'm merely doing a favor. Your stepfather and my father served together in the army."

"Brothers in arms," Daphne said.

"Yes."

"See, Zelda. He's okay. Come on, let's go to the beach."

"I'd like that." He turned and winked at me.

What was that about? I couldn't figure out what was wrong with him, but there had to be something if he was in any way connected to Darnell. While Veronica eagerly showed him to one of the rooms, I decided I needed to keep an eye on him.

ON OUR WAY TO THE BEACH WE PICKED UP SANDWICHES and sodas at a little deli on Beach Avenue. As soon as we reached the sand we started selecting our spot, as far from other people as we could get. We spread out the large floral blanket and had lunch. Daniel reluctantly came along, after mumbling something like, "Every time black folks go near water there's trouble." I wasn't sure, but I thought it might have been a joke that had roots in the Middle Passage. When he said it, it seemed he had leaned toward me, as if I understood what he was talking about.

At the beach, Daniel wore an unbuttoned oxford shirt and swimming trunks, which gave us an idea of what he was working with. Since none of us girls wanted to get our hair wet, we weren't actually planning to go swimming. Veronica and I splashed and played at the water's edge, while Daphne, wearing a terry-cloth cover-up, stayed on the blanket and buried her feet in the sand. The crystal-blue sky, the water, and the white sand made the shoreline seem to go on forever. Everything was perfect, except for the strange man in our presence. I still didn't trust Daniel even though he'd been quiet most of the time. We lay back, relaxed, and listened to the radio we had brought with us.

Surprisingly, the beach wasn't as crowded as I expected. Men were tanning themselves and sitting and drinking from cups, liquor or perhaps beer. Women, with big sunglasses and floral bathing caps, smoked cigarettes and sipped from Coca-Cola bottles with straws.

The crowd was mixed, but there was no real interaction between the races. A group of girls tossed a giant beach ball around, a couple of guys flung a Frisbee and several oddly shaped and ill-fated sandcastles were under construction too close to the water's edge. Everybody was in their own world, playing and enjoying the beach.

The only interaction was farther away, across the dunes. A group of young children, both black and white, were playing and tossing bread crumbs at seagulls squawking and swooping down for a late-afternoon meal. "I cannot believe I'm lying on the beach in Cape May watching kids feeding a flock of seagulls."

"Colony," Daphne said.

"What?" I asked.

"They're called a colony of seagulls, not a flock."

I chuckled to myself. "Daphne Brooks, only you would know that seagulls cluster in a colony. I swear, you must stay up at night and memorize the whole encyclopedia."

"I have a very good memory. When I read something, I remember it."

I looked around again, then squinted. "Is that a lighthouse down there?"

Veronica, who reclined on the blanket with her eyes closed and her shades on, nodded. "Yeah, that's the Cape

May Lighthouse on Cape May Point. One time Anthony ran all the way up the steps and . . ."

Just then a white guy zoomed by us and fell in the sand only a few feet away. Soaking wet and now completely covered with sand, he laughed and held up the Frisbee in joyful celebration. Daphne nearly jumped out of her skin. Her eyes were as large as saucers. He looked at us and grinned. "Sorry 'bout that, folks," he said, then stood, flicked his wrist, and sent the Frisbee sailing toward his friend. A second later he went charging after it.

Then another man walked by. He stared at us real hard, as if we didn't belong there, and muttered something disparaging as he moved on. We didn't say anything for a few seconds, then Daphne shook her head. "They're always gonna hate us."

"Don't pay any attention to him," I said.

Veronica, having opened her eyes and sat up attentively, sucked her teeth. "People like that are just assholes who teach their kids to be assholes."

Daphne turned with tears in her eyes. "He looked just like my uncle, the same dirty blond hair and the same mean, evil face. I wish he was dead."

"It'll get better," Veronica assured her. "I promise."

"Or maybe it won't. Maybe we should go back home and forget about driving to school," I said.

"No," Veronica said emphatically. "We're not going to be chased away by some jackass stuck in the past. This is 1968, for God's sake. We have every right to be on this beach."

"It's not just about you, Veronica," I began. "This affects all of us. What about Daphne? Just look at her."

"She'll be fine."

"She's a mess," I told her. "We should just go back."

"No," Veronica said again.

"Enough. Stop it. We're not going back. Let's just keep going," Daphne said. "I'll be okay. I promise. I prayed about it and I'll be fine."

"You prayed about it?" I rolled my eyes. "Please, leave God out of this. I swear I don't see how you can still believe in a God with all the monstrous things that go on in this world."

"God loves us, but sometimes we turn away from him, and that's when evil comes in."

"After everything you've gone through, how can you still believe that?"

She looked at me and smiled. "Look at all this. Isn't it amazing? It's beautiful."

I shook my head, confounded. "Yeah, it's beautiful, but look at all the ugliness, too, hatred, racism, war, killings."

"That's not God-made. That's man-made without God."

"You mean the God who was created by man to control us? Daphne, you are way too smart to fall for this."

"Zelda, you have it wrong. Man did not create God; God created man in his likeness."

"How can you believe that?"

"It's called faith."

"I can't have faith in a God who lets hate rule. How can God be God if he allows all this to go on without helping?"

"God helps us. We just don't always see it."

"My grandparents in Louisiana were devout Catholics. They went to church, read the Bible, and prayed. When I was five years old and visiting them, one night some men in white robes with blazing torches came banging on their front door. I looked out the window and saw them with their torches. They wanted my grandfather to come outside. All my grandmother did was fall on her knees and start praying to a God who didn't listen to her. She prayed for strength. What was that going to do?"

"What happened?" Veronica asked.

"They broke the door open and dragged my grandfather outside and put a rope around his neck. I ran after him and I held on to his legs, and no matter how hard those two men pulled, they couldn't pull me free. They didn't take my grandfather away that night or any other night after that, and that was because of me, not God."

"No, that was because your grandmother prayed to God."

"God didn't grab his legs and not let go. I did."

"How does a five-year-old get the strength to hold on against two grown men?"

"She's got a point," Veronica said.

"Your grandmother had faith. She prayed for strength."

I opened my mouth but said nothing. Daphne's Christian faith was unwavering and drove me crazy. She went to church, read the Bible, and prayed all the time. She was the only one I knew, except for my parents and grandparents, who believed so strongly in God. I didn't understand it.

"How can a God be so good and still be okay with so much evil in the world? Why doesn't he kill the evil people before they kill the good people?"

"It doesn't work like that. We're all God's children."

"Didn't he smite the evil people at Sodom and Gomorrah?"

"Yes."

"Okay, so then he should smite the racists and the murderers here too," I said.

"And also the politicians and rich that intentionally get us into a war nobody wants just so they can make more money. Knowing that their sons will never go over and die because they get out of it with stupid made-up medical conditions," Veronica said

"Like I said, it doesn't work like that."

"Why not?" I insisted.

"Because it doesn't. God loves all his children."

"That's just rhetoric that defies logic. How can God be so loving when someone like James Earl Ray and all the others complicit in bigotry and hate kill a good man?"

"James Earl Ray and others like him are monsters, but my religion teaches me that he is a child of God too. He needs to be saved, forgiven, and redeemed."

"My father, like his mother and father before him, believed fervently. He prayed, read the Bible, and attended church service. I did, too, until the day my prayers weren't answered. I begged and pleaded and promised everything I had if only he would save my father, but he didn't. I gave up on God a long time ago. He turned his back on me, and I turned my back on him," I said.

"That's okay," Daphne said. "When you need him, he'll be there for you. Everything happens as it's supposed to."

"Oh, please. I give up," I said, throwing my hands in the air, knowing this argument could rage on forever. Just as I thought of another point and was about to speak, Veronica changed the subject.

"I'm thinking about becoming a lesbian."

Daniel had not said a word during our conversation, but he definitely arched his eyebrow when he heard Veronica's words.

6

DAPHNE AND I TURNED AND LOOKED AT VERONICA AND burst with laughter. Veronica was the last girl on earth I would have said was a lesbian. She loved men, and men loved her. She had a flirty personality that always drew men to her.

"Why would you say that?" I asked, half chuckling.

She didn't respond.

"Oh for heaven's sake, it's a joke. Don't you see? She's just joking with us," Daphne said, still humored.

"No, I'm not joking. I'm serious," she affirmed soundly. "I can't stand men. They're sneaky, conniving, egotistical, deceitful dogs and should all be spayed."

"You mean neutered. Spayed is done to females; neutering is done to males," Daphne corrected.

Veronica glared at her. "Fine. Whatever it is," she said sternly, "they should all be neutered and castrated with a rusty butcher knife."

She had said the words with such vehement ire that it worried me. "What happened?" I asked, letting my words slowly ease from my lips.

Daniel stood. "I'm going to take a walk."

As soon as he left, Daphne and I turned our attention to Veronica. "My father told me that I was getting married. It has already been decided and arranged."

My jaw dropped. Daphne and I looked at each other and then at Veronica, who was now staring out at the waves.

"How can he do that? I don't believe it," Daphne said.

"Believe it. Just like that. 'Veronica, dear, next May, right after graduation, you will be marrying Reginald Kingston. You remember him? You met him at our Christmas party last year. He's Holland Kingston's oldest son.' And that was it. That's all he had to say to me about it. It was an order, like 'Pick up that book.' My plans to take over my own life after graduation ended right then and there."

"That's crazy," Daphne said.

"How can he just . . . Wait, what about the guy you're supposed to marry? Doesn't he have something to say about it?" I asked.

Veronica chuckled dryly. "I doubt it." Then she just started laughing her head off with a huge smile on her face. "That's how it is with blacks who have money, especially in the North. It's expected. We have to preserve and protect the family name and melanin."

"What does skin color have to do with marriage?" I asked.

"Zelda, don't be naïve," Veronica chastised.

"That's so absurd. I hate that that part of our heritage is still a part of our culture. Light-skin blacks should only marry other light-skin blacks to preserve the family melanin. Not only do we have to contend with white racists, we also have to contend with racism within our own race. The lighter you are, the better you are is slave plantation bullshit," I said.

"That's the norm among my family's ilk," she said, then laughed again.

"What is so funny?" I asked.

"Yeah, what gives?" Daphne added.

Veronica said, still chuckling, "Reginald's family has a house not too far from us in Oak Bluffs. Last week I went over there to try and talk him out of the marriage, and I walked in and found my beloved husband-to-be having sex with his best friend, Gregory, in the pool cabana."

"We'd had a neighbor like that. He was a good friend to my mother and me after my father was killed. I called him Uncle Phoenix. He used to bake cupcakes and bring them over. Then Darnell moved in and would always go on and on about him and called him 'sweet.' Eventually Uncle Phoenix stopped coming by and later moved away."

"Well then," Daphne began, "if that's the case, it's a good chance he doesn't want to marry you any more than you want to marry him. Right? Problem solved."

"No, no, no, you don't understand. Being homosexual doesn't make a difference. I'll still have to marry him. My father holds the purse strings."

"You can't marry a man who likes other men," Daphne said.

"Of course she can. Uncle Phoenix was married," I said.

"That's right. So he'll have his affairs and I guess I'll have mine. That's how it's done all the time."

"Hey, what's going on over there?" Daniel asked, pointing across the beach to the water's edge.

I could see a woman screaming for help. I jumped up and ran over in the direction of the woman with Daniel right behind me. A short distance into the water we saw three men struggling. One was punching and fighting in the water, as he went under several times. The two might have been trying to save him, but he was fighting and flailing. The woman on the shore continued screaming, looking around in desperation. She pointed farther out in the water by the sewage pipe. "I can't swim. Please somebody save my babies."

We saw two little kids struggling, barely holding on to a large pipe sticking out into the water. They bobbed on the surface of the water several times. Without hesitation, Daniel and I ran into the ocean and swam toward the pipe. We reached the children quickly.

They struggled, clutching the pipe and sliding under the surface of the water, then came up again gasping for air. Daniel tried to grab them, but they kicked us away. "Stop! Let go!" I screamed to them. They had scratches on their cheeks, hands, and arms from grabbing at the iron pipe, yet they continued to reach for it. They slid down beneath the surface again. That's when Daniel and I grabbed hold of the kids. "Swim parallel to the beach!" Veronica screamed to me. Daniel and I kicked away from the pipe and swam back to shore with the little kids in tow.

As we reached the shore, the man who had been fighting and struggling in the water came up and snatched the two little kids away. The woman who had been screaming on shore earlier stared at us, then turned and followed.

We helped each other, dragging and crawling, then collapsed onto the wet sand near the water. A wave splashed us, then receded. We got up and staggered farther onto the shore, landing in hot, dry sand, which covered us from hair to toenails. By this time a small crowd had gathered around us. Some stood in silence as others began applauding and congratulating us for saving the kids.

A few seconds later, I saw the man who had snatched the kids from us, raging forward with wild eyes. He picked up a clump of wet sand and threw it, just missing me but hitting Daphne on the shoulder and Veronica on the leg.

"Get up! Get up, you black niggas!" he shouted, staggering forward. He fell to his knees, then got up.

"I'm gonna kick your ass. Get up! How dare you put your filthy black hands on my children? Don't you ever touch a white child again. Do you hear me, niggas?" he barked.

"I guess you would have preferred for us to let your children drown?" I said.

He glared at me but didn't say anything.

I think I stunned him by speaking up.

"What did you say to me?" he asked.

"You heard her," Daniel said.

He glared at both of us. "Now get your ass up off this beach. You don't belong here with these fine white folks. Go back to Africa where you belong."

We were stunned. The crowd stopped applauding. We were surrounded by all pale faces looking at us.

"What did he call them?" someone in the crowd asked.

"Niggas," a man whispered loudly. The word repeated.

Here it comes.

Daphne quivered and trembled, praying, "Please, God, save us," over and over. Veronica looked away, staring out at the ocean. The seconds that followed seemed like a millennium. Time hung in the air like the strange fruit I had seen so many times in grainy, black-and-white photographs of men, women, and children hung by the neck during slavery times and more recently in the Jim Crow South.

My heart thundered in my chest. There was nowhere to flee. Surrounded. Trapped. Terrified. I could feel the adrenaline as I began to hyperventilate. My tears ran, mixing with the salt water from the ocean.

Silently, yet with stern presence, Daniel stepped in front of us, using his body as a barrier against what was to come.

"No, you leave, you wanker," said an accented voice in the crowd.

"Yeah, you bloody go, arsehole."

"They just saved your kids' lives, jerk," someone shouted.

"That's right," others mumbled throughout the crowd.

"You should be thanking them," someone else added.

"Jerk!"

"Pig!"

"Asshole!"

"Racist!"

The man looked around quickly, searching for anyone on his side. No one seemed complicit. The surrounding crowd had rebuffed his ignorance. He searched anxiously, appearing even more angry.

"Yo, bugger off, you bloody tosser," said the guy who had fallen near us with the Frisbee.

"Yeah, we're civilized here in Cape May. We don't do that racist shit here," a man standing next to him shouted.

"Are you okay, darling?" A large woman in a size-too-small bathing suit knelt down and protectively put her hand on my shoulder. "Don't worry, child. Nobody's going to do a damn thing to hurt any of you. I promise you that." She turned and glared up at the angry man. "He'll have to go through me first."

"Me too," said a man standing beside Daniel.

"Yeah, and me too."

"I have the whole thing on my Super 8 camera."

"Hold still," a man said, looking down with an instant Polaroid camera pointed at us. We didn't smile. We barely looked up, but he took our photograph anyway. He pulled it free, then took another. The first one he gave to us. "Here, this is for you."

I took it.

"Here, y'all take my towel, dry yourselves up," an older man with mixed black and gray hair offered.

"No thank you. We're okay. Our towels are over there."

The woman who had been screaming on the beach for help came to stand by the racist man. The two little girls followed.

He glared menacingly at the people standing around us and then stormed away, cussing vehemently. The woman and two little girls followed.

"The gall of that man. He should be horsewhipped."

"Thank you for speaking up and helping us, Mrs. James. It's good to have neighbors like you," Veronica said.

"He's a damn fool," she continued angrily.

Two other women standing nearby agreed. "He sure is."

"Thanks, Mrs. Hertzberg, Miss Lewis," Veronica said.

"Veronica, are you girls okay?"

"Yes, we're okay, Miss Lewis. Just a little shaken up."

"Well, don't you worry. You and your friends just stay as long as you want," Mrs. Hertzberg declared. "No one's going to bother you."

"That's right, Maude."

"He obviously doesn't live around here. We don't care for racist trash like him," Miss Lewis added.

"Thank you so much for your help. I'll make sure to tell my parents how kind you've been," Veronica said as the woman walked away and others spoke up.

One man wanted our names so he could put us in the local newspaper. He called us heroes. I thanked him but declined. Veronica obliged.

Veronica dried herself off, then wrapped a towel around her hair. Daphne's wet hair clung to her scalp like gnarled vines on branches. She pulled it back severely, as tight and restrained as possible. Her shoulders hunched. My hair puffed up like Jiffy Pop, looking like a giant dripping mass of riotous ringlets. I dried it as best I could. As I looked for my Afro pick in my beach bag, I saw the Polaroid photograph the man had given us. "Hey, look at this." I peeled back the negative to view the image. We weren't smiling. We were staring blankly at the camera. We passed the photo around. "We can do better than that," Veronica said, pulling her camera out.

At that moment, the guy who had caught the Frisbee near us earlier came over, smiling from ear to ear. "Hey," he said.

Daniel stood protectively.

"Hi. Would you take our picture, please?" Veronica asked.

"Sure." He took the camera from Veronica, and the three of us sat close and smiled.

"Wait. Come on, Daniel. You get in the picture too," Veronica said.

Click. "Perfect," he said, giving the camera back to Veronica. "I'm Harry. That's my mate Liam over there. I just wanted to say that you birds are bloody amazing," he said with a very noticeable British accent, and seeming to speak directly to Veronica.

"Thanks for what you said over there. You blokes are pretty amazing too." She smiled, pleased with herself.

He laughed. "Yeah, well, we should have let the bloody arsehole drown," he said, sounding more serious. Veronica grinned. He slowly fell to his knees in front of her. "So are you here in the area for long? I mean—"

"We're here for long enough," Veronica said teasingly.

He smiled, bobbing his head up and down. "Far out. So listen, a few blokes and I rented a house not too far from here. We're having a party tonight. Why don't you and your friends come by? It'll be a blast. We're right off Grant, the corner house. You can't miss it. We're gonna really groove tonight, even got a special friend coming."

"Who's the special friend?" I asked.

"Come and you'll see," he said, grinning again.

"Well then, we might just stop by."

He nodded. "Yeah? Far out. I'll see you tonight."

She nodded. "Yeah, far out."

He popped up, waved, and then ran off down the beach with his buddy, who immediately cheered and nodded. They waved at us. Veronica waved back.

"Please tell me you were not flirting with that white boy."

"And what if I was?" Veronica said, still smiling.

"That's asking for trouble," I scolded tightly.

"Zelda, you're so provincial. Don't you know it's 1968? Times have changed. People are different now."

I shook my head. "Believe me, times and people will never be *that* different. There will always be a separation of the races. Didn't you just hear what that white man called us?"

"Yeah, I heard him. I also heard about a dozen other

white people come to our defense. See? Not all white people are the same," she insisted.

I shook my head. "They are as far as I'm concerned."

"Given that logic, then all black people are the same."

I opened my mouth but said nothing.

"You are such a hypocritical cynic," she added. "You can't group a whole race in with those kind. There were white people who fought against slavery, and there were black people who owned slaves."

"Black people didn't own slaves," Daphne spoke up.

"Yes, they did. We did. My family owned slaves."

"They did not. You're lying."

"I am not. They did."

"For real, your family owned slaves?" I asked.

"It was back in the 1850s. My father's family, the Cooks, and my mother's family, the Parkers, have always lived in New York and Massachusetts. They both owned slaves."

"How can you just say it like that?" I asked. "That's cruel." I was annoyed by her nonchalance.

"Because it's the truth, Zelda," she said. "It wasn't an anomaly back then. A lot of blacks owned slaves and indentured servants. They weren't mistreated like the Southern slaves under white plantation owners and slavers. My ancestors were also abolitionists who helped runaway slaves."

Daphne asked, "How could they own slaves then help other slaves?"

"I don't know. I wasn't there, was I? But I do know from family stories, journals, diaries, that they treated the slaves well."

"It doesn't matter how well they were treated. They weren't free. They were still owned by someone," I said indignantly. "It was wrong. They were wrong. This whole world is absolutely crazy."

"You don't know what you're talking about," she snapped.

"I know that slavery was an abomination to humankind and your family got rich off it."

"Don't get all self-righteous with me, Zelda Livingston. It was a long time ago, and it's the truth of my family. They also channeled their wealth to free blacks, they funded libraries, taught slaves to read and to be self-sufficient. That's the truth of my family too. What's the truth of yours?"

I didn't answer. What did it matter? The way I saw it, we were all enslaved by our actions.

"What happened to them, the slaves?" Daphne asked.

Veronica shrugged. "They worked for my ancestors' lumber and paper mills. Eventually they were able to buy their freedom. I remember reading in a journal that most of them stayed and still worked at the mills for wages. They were free men and women, but they started out as slaves."

"You're right. It was a long time ago, a different time and a different place. I'm sorry. I didn't mean to be—" I said.

"Me either," Veronica interrupted. "Come on. Let's go."

Daphne and I were quiet.

"I need a shower," Veronica said, dusting sand off her arms and legs as we headed toward the bungalow. She and Daphne walked up ahead, and Daniel walked beside me. At first he didn't say anything. Then he thanked me.

"For what?" I asked.

"For letting me come along."

"I don't have much of a choice."

"You could have said no and meant it."

He was right. I could have vehemently said no, and the girls would have listened to me, but I didn't. "So, is this what you do all the time, escort people from city to city?"

"No, like I said, this is a favor."

"How does your dad know Darnell?"

"They were in the military together. They were friends."

"So your dad is like Darnell then."

He chuckled. "Hardly. I don't think anybody's like Darnell."

"That's for sure."

"Your mother's a nice lady."

I stopped walking. He stopped and looked at me.

"When did you meet my mother?"

"We had dinner a few times at your house. You were away at school. She talked about you the whole time. She's very proud of you."

We started walking again. I wasn't sure how I felt about what he said. He seemed to know a lot about me and I had no idea who he was.

"Come on slowpokes," Daphne called out over her shoulder.

As soon as we caught up and turned the last corner, we noticed a car parked in front of the house and saw the front door open.

My heart jumped. "There's somebody there."

"Oh good Lord, now what?" Daphne moaned.

"It's a Pennsylvania license plate. That's my aunt and uncle's car," Veronica said.

Just then a woman stepped out onto the porch with Miss Sadie from across the street. They were laughing and talking. "Ah, here they are now," Miss Sadie said, waving and smiling as we approached.

"Aunt Trudy," Veronica said, then hurried up the front steps and hugged the woman.

She was dressed in a fashionable pink-and-green floral halter sundress, with the tiniest waist ever, and high-heeled sandals, and she had pink lips, fingernails, and toenails. She was stunning. Her hair was cut short with a mass of soft wavy curls that made her look like a Hollywood movie star. She reminded me of my mother—before Darnell.

"What on earth are you doing here?" she asked Veronica. "I thought everyone was still on Martha's Vineyard for the summer."

"Mom and Dad are. I left early," Veronica confessed then turned to us. "Aunt Trudy, these are my best friends from college, Zelda and Daphne."

"Hello, ladies. Welcome," she said, smiling pleasantly. We smiled back. We couldn't help it. Not smiling at someone that pretty had to be a sin. "And who is this young man?" she asked, gesturing in Daniel's direction.

"Ma'am, good afternoon. My name is Daniel Johnson. It's a pleasure to meet you. I'm here to safely escort these young ladies to Atlanta," he responded with an uprightness that far surpassed my expectations. His words and demeanor made me freeze, as I recognized that he had the same charm as my father. There was no way this guy could be connected to Darnell, even remotely.

"Well, come on inside out of this maddening heat," she said. I could see she'd been cleaning. The sand had been swept up, the drapes pulled back, and everything looked bright and clean. "I see you've been to the beach. How was the water?" she asked casually.

" 'Threatening' might be the right word to describe it," Daniel said, amused with himself.

Our jaws dropped before a few gasps escaped. Trudy cocked her head and arched her brow curiously. "I guess we'll get back to the question later."

"Where's Uncle Harold?" Veronica changed the subject.

"He and Kimo are picking up a few things for dinner. I'm glad Sadie told us you and your friends were here or we wouldn't have brought enough food."

We heard a car pull into the driveway. Through the window we saw two men get out of a slick dark blue sedan parked behind Veronica's car. The older man was laughing loudly as he reached for a brown paper bag from the back seat. The driver, a younger attractive man, was smiling and talking as he pointed in the direction of the beach.

"Who's that with Uncle Harold?"

"Kimo Lee."

"Kimo Lee?" I repeated softly. The name sounded odd, foreign, but I liked it.

"Who is he?" Veronica asked.

"He's a young doctor at Mercy-Douglass Hospital with your uncle. He's a really nice guy. His family is from Hawaii, and his father is a renowned surgeon on the island of Maui. Your uncle Harold and I are taking Kimo to meet some friends and introduce him around at Burdette Tomlin Memorial Hospital. He has an interview Saturday afternoon. He's single and a major catch if any of you are interested," she said, winking.

"We'll think about it," Veronica said. "Come on. We should get changed."

"Okay, and don't worry about dinner. I'll cook when we get back. Unless of course your cooking has improved greatly?" she said jokingly.

Veronica smirked. "Not a chance."

Trudy chuckled. "I'll forever be hopeful. We should only be gone a short while."

"Okay, Aunt Trudy."

7

I WASHED MY HAIR FOUR TIMES AND I STILL FELT LIKE I was carrying around a sandcastle on my head. "Damn, there's sand everywhere. How does anyone ever get rid of it?" I turned to Veronica, who was sitting on the edge of one of the beds polishing her nails. Her hair was rolled up in her mother's giant curlers as she sat under a dryer bonnet. It had been on full blast for the past fifteen minutes.

"Does that thing have to be so loud?" I shouted. Of course, she couldn't hear me.

I turned on the radio. Anything was better than listening to the droning sound of the dryer. I spun the dial and stopped at Gladys Knight singing her hit song "The End of Our Road."

As the song faded, a newscast about Richard Nixon and his running mate, Spiro Agnew, came on. I shook my head. I had no idea why people were going crazy over them and their "law and order" bullshit. They were richer than God, and nobody comes by that much money honestly. "If there is a hell," I exclaimed, "we're all going there and those two rats are gonna be leading the way."

"What?" Veronica shouted, lifting the dryer bonnet.

I shook my head and waved her off. "Nothing."

I continued greasing and braiding my hair as unwanted thoughts of Daniel filled my head. I could still feel his strong thigh brushing up against my leg while we were in the water. The way he took control seemed natural. It showed his confidence. I thought about going into his room to talk but then considered my hair. Better that I get it all braided and dried first.

Daphne entered the room already showered and changed, wearing a cotton sundress. She began looking around the room anxiously.

"What are you looking for?" I asked her.

"Nothing," she said, rifling through an open suitcase.

"Oh my God, Daphne, what happened to your wrist?" I exclaimed, seeing it red, bruised, and scarred.

"Nothing," she said quickly.

"It's not nothing. What happened to you?" I insisted.

Veronica looked up and shouted. "What?"

"What?" I yelled back just as she turned the dryer off.

"Look at Daphne's wrist."

Daphne quickly put her hands behind her back. "I need my sweater. Where's my sweater?"

"Daphne, a sweater? Come on. It's a hundred degrees outside. You don't need a sweater," I said.

"Here, it's over here." Veronica held it up.

Daphne quickly put it on. "I just need to wear my sweater, that's all."

She looked at the palms of her hands. "I can't take it off. Everybody will see," she said, pulling at the sleeves to cover more of her hands.

"What's there to see?" Veronica asked.

"Daphne, what is it? You know you can tell us anything."

"Nothing. I'm fine. Just leave me alone, okay?" She backed away, looking wide-eyed and panicked.

"Daphne, we're sisters. Remember? Whatever it is, it's okay. Just tell us. You know we'll help."

"Nobody can help me now," she said softly.

She walked over and sat down on the edge of the bed and slowly took her sweater off. "I cut myself," she admitted in barely a whisper.

I sat down beside her. Veronica walked over. "Are you okay?" she asked as she sat on the other side of her.

Daphne looked at me and then at Veronica. "I don't know if I'm okay. Sometimes I think I'm going crazy like my mother. But I know I can't go back there again."

"Back where? What are you talking about?"

"Back home to my father."

"What happened?" I asked, fearing the worst.

Daphne didn't say anything. Her lower lip quivered and her body trembled as her glassy eyes stared straight ahead.

She looked terrified, like she was in a trance or something. She looked like a fragile porcelain doll.

"I'm going to hell," she stated plainly.

"What?" Veronica said.

"No, you're not," I said.

"Yes, I am. I tried to kill myself," she said, stretching out her left hand, palm side up, showing us a raised, lumpy red scar on her wrist. "I committed an unforgivable sin."

I flinched. "Daphne," I whispered, but it came out more as a breathless gasp. I threw my arms around her. Daphne's life was a misery. Passed from family member to family member, she was never really wanted by anyone. Then years later, and after her mother had committed suicide, she went back to live with her father. I suspect he felt guilty for his treatment of them.

"Why? Why did you do it?" The words tumbled from Veronica.

"I was desperate. I had to make him stop."

We knew exactly whom she was talking about. Her uncle was an evil man who had called her "nigga baby." She was the shame of her father's family. Her mother passed as white and had married a wealthy white man. After Daphne was born, the truth had come out. Her father was humiliated and had kicked her and her mother out of the house.

"So you did this," Veronica said.

Daphne hunched her shoulders and shook her head as if seeing him right there with us. "He had the devil in him the day I came home. I saw it. His eyes were red and hateful. He was drunk. Dirty. Nasty. He came at me. I fought him off. I swear I did. I wouldn't let him touch me. Not again. Never again, but he wouldn't stop coming for me," she stammered.

"It's okay." We soothed her as best we could.

"No, no, you don't understand. I had to do it."

"Do what?"

"He was all over me. His hands were all over me." She recoiled, trembling. "I grabbed a fork from the kitchen table and stabbed him. There was blood everywhere. If I'd had a gun I would have killed the son of a bitch!" she shouted.

"Shhhh, it's okay. It's okay," I told her.

"We're here with you," Veronica added.

"No, you don't understand." She began to weep. "When I stabbed him he said he was going to have me put in the crazy house like my mother. That's when I did this." She looked down at the wound on her wrist. "I took some sleeping pills and some whiskey. I lay down in a tub of warm water and used a razor blade. I woke up in the hospital."

"Did you tell your father what your uncle did to you?" Veronica asked.

She nodded. "He didn't believe me. My uncle told him that I went crazy and attacked him."

"He didn't believe you?" Veronica asked.

"That's it. He needs to be locked up. You need to tell everybody what he did to you. You need to . . ." I was just about to go off. Veronica looked at me and shook her head. "I'm sorry," I said softly.

"You're safe with us, no matter what," Veronica said.

"I remember after I did it I felt like I was floating. There was blood in the water. My father found me. After he took me to the hospital, he sent me to a sanitarium, a psychiatric institution. It was a crazy house. The same place they sent my mother before she died. I stayed in that place for seven weeks, four days, and sixteen hours. The doctors told my father that I was no longer a threat to others or myself. He agreed. They let me go. College was my escape from all of it. We need to get back there as soon as we can."

"Nobody will ever know your scars are there. I promise. And you don't need that stupid sweater." Veronica got up and quickly rummaged through her mother's drawer and pulled out a wide-cuff bracelet. "Here, put this on."

Daphne slipped it over her hand. The bracelet covered her scar perfectly.

"See? No one will ever know."

"Won't your mother miss it?"

"Nah, she probably doesn't even know she has it."

"Daphne, listen to me," I began. "If there's one thing you've always told me it's that God is love and he forgives, right? So there's no way he would send you to hell. I know he won't. You taught me that. You didn't do it all the way and you're repentant now, right? Isn't that what you always say? So as long as we repent, we can be forgiven anything, even this, right?"

"Yes, that's right," Veronica added.

"We're all together, and nobody's going to hurt you again," I said. "You don't have to go back to Long Island. You can come stay with me."

"And when Zelda starts driving you crazy, which will probably be five minutes after you get there, you come live with me. Okay?" We laughed.

An old favorite song came on the radio. It was Martha and the Vandellas' "Dancing in the Street." Veronica squealed and hurried over to turn up the volume. She whooped and hollered and started dancing. Veronica pulled three curlers out of her hair and shoved them into our hands, and together we dragged Daphne to the dresser mirror. We started singing at the top of our lungs using Veronica's big curlers as microphones. Daphne was the only one who actually had a decent singing voice, and she stood in the middle to sing lead.

We glided around the bedroom doing the jerk, the slop, the mashed potato, the twist, and the hitchhike. When the song faded into a commercial, we fell back onto the bed sweating. We talked and giggled and sang our hearts out along with the commercial jingles that followed.

"You're so lucky to have all this," I said.

"I know that I'm fortunate," Veronica said. "Lots of famous people have come to visit. I've met James Baldwin, Dr. King, Lena Horne, Eartha Kitt, and Ethel Waters. All of these people have taken risks for the race. The conversations at dinner were out of sight. But it was Langston Hughes who changed me. He died last year. He was a poet, a writer, an orator, and an amazing man. He was a genius. He once told me to live outside my glass box and to never let anyone define me. He said to dream as big as I could and with intense purpose. My life isn't filled with foot soldiers and radicals, but it's certainly filled with revolutionaries of the mind, spirit, and soul."

She was right.

"I can't believe this is going to be over soon. Us, together, at Spelman. In a few months we'll be going our separate ways. We'll get jobs, get married and have kids, and this will all be over."

"No, it won't. We'll always be friends and sisters."

"I know, but not like this."

"See? That's why this drive is so important. No matter how crazy our lives get, we have to promise to always make time for us."

"So, Zelda, you being an attorney and then a Supreme Court judge, and Daphne a college professor, and me, well . . ." She paused. "I don't really know what I'm going to be yet."

"I do," I said quickly. "You're going to take over your family business and be president and CEO of Cook Securities and then Cook Enterprises."

"Yeah, president and CEO. I like that. We, my dear sisters, are going to take this world by storm. They'd better watch out, 'cause we're coming."

AN HOUR LATER WE WERE STILL SINGING AND DANCING, although we had moved to the kitchen and Daniel had joined us. We decided to make a spaghetti dinner for Veronica's aunt and uncle. Veronica pulled out some singles and albums and turned the record player on. We cooked listening to the Supremes and the Temptations. Then she found our absolute favorite album, *United*, with Tammi Terrell and Marvin Gaye.

As we cooked, we debated whether to attend Harry's party. Veronica quickly realized that he and his friends had rented the Petersons' house on the corner and that they were the hippies Miss Betsy and Miss Sadie had been talking about.

"Well, I still say we go. We were invited, he was nice, and I think it'll be fun," Veronica insisted after ten minutes of back-and-forth.

"No surprise there," I said dryly, tired of the subject.

"Oh, come on, Zelda," Veronica said. "You'll meet new people, so stop being such a wet blanket."

"I'm not being a wet blanket," I said, mildly insulted. "I'm trying not to get arrested. I have no intention of having a police record. That does not go with a law degree."

"Arrested? What are you talking about?" Daphne asked.

"You heard what those neighbors across the street said: drugs. It might get raided by the cops."

"Oh, please. Those two call baby aspirin 'drugs.'"

"Well, I still vote no."

"I vote yes." She looked at Daniel.

"Hey, leave me out of this. I pass."

"Daphne, what do you think?"

We both turned to look at her. "Why am I always the tie breaker?" she asked.

Veronica and I looked at each other and shrugged simultaneously. Veronica and I were regularly at extremes and Daphne was the voice in the middle. But before either of us could answer, we heard voices as the front door opened. We walked out to the living room and saw Trudy and the two men from earlier.

We exchanged pleasantries. Meanwhile, Kimo hadn't taken his eyes off Daphne the whole time.

"You're just in time," Veronica said. "Dinner's ready."

"You cooked," Trudy said, surprised.

"Actually, Daphne cooked. Zelda and I helped in setting the table. She's a far better cook than either of us."

"That's right," I acknowledged.

"Well, thank you very much, Daphne," Harold said.

"We'll be ready in a few minutes," Trudy added.

Trudy, Harold, and Kimo went to freshen up while we put the food on the table. We ate on the screened-in porch, where the big table was set up. I couldn't be certain, but it seemed Daniel subtly moved Veronica out of the way to sit next to me. Surprisingly, I didn't mind. It was still hot outside, but there was a breeze that kept us comfortable.

Kimo sat next to Daphne, and I believed the whole table could feel their chemistry. As the conversation flowed around them, they seemed to be in their own world.

"It's going to be wonderful having you girls around. With all that luggage, I presume you're staying the rest of the week," Trudy said.

"Oh no, we're not staying," Daphne said. "We're driving back to school on Sunday."

"Well, I'm glad you have this young man for protection," said Trudy. "I know you all read the black newspapers, not that whitewashed news we see on television? Colored people, men and women, boys and girls, are being killed, particularly in the South. This family has shielded you from such things, Veronica, but this world will eat you alive if you're not careful. White people think black people are a threat to them. They don't even consider how we feel in their presence all the time, given America's violent history at their hands. We don't know who is friend or foe."

Veronica rolled her eyes and looked at me. My eyes widened, but I didn't say anything.

"Do you have any idea what uncivilized hell you're driving into?" Uncle Harold chimed in.

"It's not like we've never been down south before. We have. This is our fourth year in college in Atlanta. We've never had any problems before."

"That's because you've always taken the train down," Trudy said.

"Dr. Martin Luther King Jr. was just killed in the South. It didn't matter that he was a prominent spokesman, a leader, a minister, and Nobel Prize winner. He was still killed."

"We're not Dr. King."

"Medgar Evers—shot and killed in his driveway in front of his wife and children. Harry and Harriette Moore—home blown up on their twenty-fifth wedding anniversary. The Orangeburg Massacre—three students shot and killed by the local police."

"We're not demonstrating or doing anything else with civil rights."

"That's just it. Young blacks never think it could be them. It doesn't matter who you are or what you're not doing. If whites can brutally murder a fourteen-year-old boy or blow up a church with four young girls inside, there's nothing hatred won't do."

"I don't want to live my life in fear just because I'm black."

Trudy and Harold looked at Veronica. I could see that neither of them was moved.

8

I YIELDED. VERONICA AND I HEADED TO THE PARTY A little before nine o'clock. Daniel, now lagging behind us, decided to come along. The sun had set. The air, smelling of salt and roses, was heavy and thick, like rain hung on the horizon. The narrow streets were eerily empty, and a heavy muffled roar hummed in the distance. "What's that noise?" I asked.

"The ocean."

"That loud?"

"Yep. You get used to it after a while."

"So, what do you think about Kimo asking Daphne to go for a walk on the beach?" I whispered to Veronica.

"She likes him and she never takes to anybody that quickly," Veronica said.

I nodded. "I think he might be good for her."

"Me too. I hope so. She could use some happiness."

We heard the music long before we came to the big house on the corner, surrounded by lopsided hedges and wide trees. As we got closer, my heart started beating faster. I should have stayed at the bungalow.

"This is a bad idea," I whispered. Veronica didn't respond.

Three young white guys were standing outside smoking. They didn't say anything as we walked past; they didn't even look our way. They just kept talking and smoking.

"Are you sure about this?"

"Oh, don't be such a chicken," she scolded. "Come on."

The door was wide open. As soon as we walked in, Harry started clapping, and his other friend from the beach, who had been standing on his head for some reason, joined in. "There they are," he exclaimed loudly.

Harry started calling us heroes. Soon others began applauding as well. And there were so many others. Everywhere. Others. People started patting me on the back, trying to hug me, and thanking me for what we did. Veronica was eating up the attention.

She curtsied and bowed, smiling, waving, and giggling. I stood there shell-shocked. The bombardment of admiration was unsettling. Being at the center of white people's attention made me uneasy.

I could hear my father's voice. *Get out*, he would have said. *Get out of here now.*

I took a step back. Daniel placed his hand on my waist as if to assure me he was there. Veronica grabbed hold of my hand. I tried to loosen her grip, but she held tightly and turned to me, smiling. "It's okay. We'll be fine. If nothing else, it'll be far out."

"No," I said to her, "come on. We have to leave before something happens."

"Nothing's gonna happen. Zelda, cool it. Mingle. You might just have a good time and learn something."

Harry came up with open arms and hugged me. He did not have on a shirt but wore a psychedelic-colored Nehru jacket with a peace sign medallion around his neck, tight skinny white pants, and bare feet. I cringed awkwardly. He reeked of alcohol, cigarettes, and an abundance of musk aftershave. He didn't seem to notice my recoil. When he hugged Veronica, she giggled and hugged him right back with more enthusiasm than the circumstances called for.

There was a guy wearing a huge purple hat with lime-colored ostrich feathers sticking out of the top, while another wore black-and-white polka-dot pants, shirt, jacket, hat, and shoes. Someone shoved a glass of something amber into my hand. "Here you go, babe. You're out of sight."

"Thanks," I said as he walked away. I tipped my nose into the glass and grimaced. It had a strong smell. I figured I'd carry it around the rest of the night, to blend in.

I looked over at Veronica, across the room. The music was loud, and she was dancing. Harry was with her and doing some kind of jiggling, wiggling movements. Veronica started doing the same insane thing: jiggle, jump, and jiggle. Soon others stood and began doing the silly dance.

Veronica always blended in. I admired that about her. We had met on a train headed to Georgia. I saw her sitting alone, laughing at something she was reading in a magazine. I found out later it was an article about her parents. The article had called them "America's New Black Family." I had sat down across the aisle from her. She turned to me and smiled. Her first words were "Can you believe this bullshit?" I had liked her right away. She was smart, crazy sarcastic, way more cynical than me, and she was funny.

Someone fell down next to me and then lay on the floor, laughing hysterically. I moved out of the way. I walked around smiling and nodding as I kept an eye on Veronica, who was still laughing and dancing with Harry on the other side of the large living room. I stood by the wall listening to the rock and roll that played. A girl walked by and added more liquor to my glass and then handed me a half-filled bottle of Johnnie Walker Red.

"No thank you," I said louder than I expected. She grinned and kept going. I walked into another room. It was dark with dim lights in the corners, and a purple haze emanated from a couple of psychedelic lava lamps, offering a mystic voodoo vibe. I sat the bottle down on a table when two black guys walked past me, nodded, and kept going. I was going to speak, but they moved too fast. Then someone called out.

"Hey, hero."

A brother was sitting in the corner on a mass of pillows, strumming the guitar lying across his lap. His Afro was sliced through with a purple paisley scarf. He wore a black halfway-buttoned shirt and a white fringed leather jacket.

Like everyone else there, he was a mishmash of colors and prints, but for some reason it worked on him. He licked his full lips, then frowned, looking mean and hateful. But then just as quickly he smiled, and his perfect white teeth seemed to brighten the room. "Yeah, I'm talking to you, hero."

"That's heroine," I corrected.

He took a long drag of a marijuana cigarette, then half coughed and chuckled while looking me up and down. "Yeah, somehow I doubt that. Sit," he instructed simply.

Ordinarily I would ignore a command, especially from a man and a total stranger, but I sat down. His presence alone made me feel less anxious.

He looked sly, like he was in on a joke and no one else knew what was going on. Or maybe he was just high. He took another puff of his joint, then offered it to me. "No thanks," I said.

He shrugged and nodded. "Good for you. You stay clean. This shit will mess you up."

I couldn't think of a response, so I just nodded. "You play?" I asked, motioning to the guitar on his lap.

He chuckled and nodded slowly, his eyes half closed. "Yeah, I play. Do you?"

"No, just asking," I said. There was a pack of cigarettes on the table. I knew it was that kind of party, so I grabbed one and lit it. I had smoked on occasion, and at the moment I felt like I needed it. I wanted desperately to look cool. I took a deep drag and blew the smoke straight out. I leaned back and tried to look at ease.

He closed his eyes and played a couple of chords. The guitar screeched loud and long as his fingers quickly danced across the strings as if they were on fire. Everybody in the room started applauding, and others in the living room cheered and shouted.

"You like that?" he asked, locking his eyes with mine.

"Yeah, that was pretty good," I said.

"Thanks. It's something I been working on. So what's a cute little foxy lady like you doing in a scene like this?"

"I was invited."

"You were invited, huh. So what's your hustle?"

"My hustle?"

"Your gig, your job. What do you do?"

"Oh, I'm in college. I'm going to be a civil rights attorney."

"Oh yeah, really? That's cool. I can dig it."

"What about you?" I asked, trying to sound equally hip. "What's your hustle?"

He chuckled, then played a few notes on his guitar.

His bloodshot eyes bore into mine. It was intense. I felt like he knew me even before I had sat down or before I had gotten up this morning.

He played a few more chords softly. "You look scared, but these cats are cool. You gotta let that shit go or you gonna be scared of the wrong cats all your life."

"My dad was killed five years ago by white cops. What if I can't let it go?" I didn't know where the words had come from, but I think I was trying to impress him—somehow.

"Then you gotta find a way to reconcile. Evil is evil, don't matter what you look like. Can't do much about cats like that. But I see you. I have a feeling you'll be okay. You'll see your way through all that."

I nodded as if he was some mystical guru with all the knowledge and answers of the universe at his fingertips. Just when I was finding my mojo, Daniel approached us. He wore a black beret, like the ones the Black Panthers were wearing. My guitar-playing guru instructed him to sit beside me.

They talked while I played at smoking my cigarette. I even took a sip of the amber liquid in my glass. It was god-awful, but I pretended it was okay.

The guru started strumming on his guitar again. His sound was deep and thick and rich like something you could scoop up and eat with a spoon. He started drawing attention from the others so he put the guitar down.

Someone mentioned the war. Guru joined in the conversation. Everybody talked and gave their opinion. I mostly listened. He was out there. He rambled from subject to subject, not really focusing in one thing. Then, out of the blue, he kissed me goodbye, grabbed his guitar, and walked out.

"He's an amazing talent. His music is aesthetically significant."

I shrugged indifferently.

"What, you don't like his music?" Daniel asked, bemused.

"No, not really."

"No?" Daniel questioned. "Why not?"

I grimaced. "I like Motown music."

"Oh, you're one of those," he said, then snickered.

I immediately took offense. "What do you mean, 'one of those'?" I asked.

He smiled and chuckled.

"I don't appreciate you laughing at me," I said, then stood to leave.

"Hey, relax." He grabbed my arm to stop me. I yanked away. "Whoa. I'm sorry, okay? I wasn't laughing at you." I glared at him. "I'm sorry. It's just that I'm not a big fan of the syrupy sweet love-machine music. I like real music. Motown isn't. It's too commercial for me."

"What do you know?" I said. "You don't even know your place." After the words left my lips, I wasn't even sure what they meant.

"Where's my place?" he asked.

"Certainly not here," I said, trying to compensate for my dumb remark.

"I'm here because you're here," he countered. "I've wanted to meet you for a very long time."

Whoa! Was that a pass? I quickly moved beyond the moment, even though he was trying to find my eyes. "Motown is real music to a lot of people. It tells the story of our people and that there's a better world out there for us. It helps us when we have nothing else, and it gets us through hard times. Some people need Motown music."

"Like you, I assume," he assessed.

I looked at him but didn't say anything right away. He had belittled my music and it seemed he was belittling me. "Yeah, like me."

"I'm sorry," he said, then placed his hand on mine.

I slid my hand away.

"You know, you don't have to walk around with that huge chip on your shoulder. Not everyone is your enemy."

"You don't know me. So what you say about me, my music or my life, doesn't really matter."

He nodded. "You're right. So why don't we call a truce?"

At that moment someone nearly fell on top of me, but Daniel blocked him. The party had gotten louder and wilder. A lot of the people were drunk and falling around acting stupid.

"Come on. Let's find Veronica."

I didn't really want to go with him, but I did anyway. I nodded and followed him to the front of the house. I saw Veronica straightaway. She was sitting on the steps by the front door talking with some girls. Harry was lying on the floor talking up at them.

"Hey, there you are. I was just about to . . ." she began.

All of the sudden Harry jumped up and started doing his jiggle, jump, and wiggle dance. Soon the whole room was doing it. We figured that was as good a time to leave as any.

As soon as we got outside, Veronica asked, "So, Daniel, we are on our way on Sunday—why should we let you come with us?"

He folded his arms across his chest. "Aside from the fact that my father's friend asked me to take care of you ladies, I'm also on my way to school. I will be at Morehouse, right across the road from you."

"Really?" she said, her voice rising three octaves.

"Miss Motown, what do you think?" he asked. "May I accompany you to Atlanta?"

Veronica looked at me. I glared at him. His snide remark didn't faze me. I shrugged. "It's up to you. I don't care."

"See? It's cool," Veronica said.

Daniel looked directly in my eyes and smiled. His eyes were warm and inviting. "I dig your 'fro," he said.

9

SATURDAY WAS CALM AND RELAXING AND THE FIRST TIME I felt truly at ease all summer. In the afternoon, we went back to the beach. Kimo went with us. He and Daphne played at the water's edge. Veronica and I stayed on the blanket playing cards, and Daniel sat with us reading his book.

After a while we had chicken and waffles at a small black-owned restaurant near the bungalow and then later Kimo drove us to Wildwood. We strolled the boardwalk, played some of the amusement-park games, and went on a few rides. It was obvious that he and Daphne were getting along well. It was early evening when we got back to Cape May. Veronica's aunt, uncle, and Kimo went to a meeting at the hospital, and the four of us stayed in.

Sunday morning we dressed in traveling clothes and prepared to leave. Daniel was wearing a short-sleeved shirt and blue jeans, which accentuated his strong build. He had broad shoulders and long, slightly bowed legs. His skin was like sweet caramel, rich, soft, and smooth. I couldn't deny that he was attractive—if you liked that type.

He had black hair cut real close, not a perm or the Afro most guys sported. His face was strong with sharp angles, and his lips were full and thick. But it was his soul-piercing eyes that cut into me like a switchblade.

"Good morning, Motown," he whispered, his voice deep and raspy as his eyes focused solely on me. I stood there numb and breathless.

Harold took Daniel's suitcase and fit it perfectly into the trunk, leaving plenty of space in the back seat. Daniel got in. I hesitated a split second, then got in and sat beside him.

Trudy gave Veronica a small green book and told her to be careful and pay attention and to use the book if she needed. "We will," she promised.

"Okay, Daniel, rule number one," Veronica said as she glanced in the rearview mirror, "I'm driving and we're in charge of the radio." She turned it on for emphasis.

"Fine with me," he said. "I don't mind sitting in the back seat with Miss Motown. I prefer jazz."

"Who do you like?" Veronica asked.

"Miles Davis, Hugh Masekela, Ramsey Lewis, Nina Simone, Sergio Mendes, Young-Holt Unlimited, and a few more."

Veronica smiled. "I love Miles and Ramsey, and 'Soulful Strut' is one of my favorites," Veronica readily agreed. "And Nina Simone is simply boss."

I liked them all as well, but I didn't say anything.

"Okay, so what's rule number two?" Daniel asked.

"We'll let you know," I said.

Daniel chuckled, then pulled out a transistor radio and put a crystal earpiece into his ear. He winked at me, then closed his eyes and laid his head back. A sly smile pulled at his lips.

"Soooo," Veronica said, smiling over at Daphne.

Daphne looked puzzled. She turned and looked at me and then at Veronica. "Soooo what?" she asked, faking innocence.

"You know what. Kimo," I said from the rear.

"So what happened between you two the other night?"

Daphne shrugged. "Nothing happened. We talked and walked on the beach."

"Did you kiss him?" Veronica asked.

Daphne looked back at Daniel. His eyes were still closed and his head was still tilted back. She grinned and nodded her head excitedly, then squealed. "He's so wonderful." She sighed. "Our conversations were therapeutic. I told him stuff I have only told the two of you. He listened to me."

"Ooooooo," Veronica and I said.

"Shhh," Daphne said, glancing at Daniel again.

"So do you like him?" Veronica asked. Daphne didn't reply. "Come on. Tell us. Do you like him?"

"Yeah, I do. He's nice and kind and thoughtful."

"And he's a doctor," I said.

"He wants me to visit him in Cape May this Thanksgiving."

"Well, isn't that a good thing? Don't you want to?"

"Yes, but I don't deserve someone like him."

"Don't ever say that about yourself. You are a strong woman. Keep your faith in God, and don't lose your faith in yourself now," Veronica said.

"It's just that it feels like I've been holding my breath all my life waiting for something good to happen."

"I feel that way too."

"Me too."

"Well, maybe this road trip is that something good we've all been waiting for."

"Now, wouldn't that be wonderful," Daphne said.

I smiled and glanced over at Daniel. He hadn't moved or said a word, but I knew he wasn't asleep. I wondered if he was waiting for something good too.

The rest of the drive I stared out at cars passing by and highway signs pointing to places I had no interest in ever going. I noticed that Daniel had a book with him. It was a copy of Eldridge Cleaver's book *Soul on Ice*. It looked like mine, worn and well read.

Traffic was light so travel was quick and easy. I saw more black faces on the road this time. When we got to Baltimore we turned on WSID, and when we neared Washington, DC, we listened to Petey Greene, a disc jockey on WOL.

"I met him once," Daniel said. "Nice guy."

"Yeah, me too," Veronica said.

"You've met everybody. I still can't believe you met Dr. King. What was he like?"

I saw Veronica smiling in profile. "Calm," she said, then nodded. "Yeah, that's the word I'd use for him. He was serene and at peace. I was fifteen, and my parents took me to the March on Washington. With all the craziness around him, he was so amazingly focused. His gaze was intense and purposeful, and his voice was strong and comforting. I remember I thought at the time that you could believe what he was saying, even if he had just read the telephone book."

"To be there, that must have been an incredible moment," Daphne said.

"It was. The people, the crowds, the speakers, everybody seemed united in one voice. It wasn't just black people there, but it felt like it. And the power of being in the presence of all my people, all the same pain, all the same struggle. A shared spirit. It was overwhelming."

"I was there too," I said. "My uncle and aunt took me. We were far away from the stage, but his words reached us with force. I hoped that one day we would all live in his new world, where everyone was equal and there was peace. It felt like it could truly happen.

"My uncle told me that 1963 was going to be a pivotal year that rocked the world and shaped a generation. And that Dr. King's speech was going to be a historically defining moment, and in years to come I would tell my children and grandchildren that I was there and I witnessed that amazing message.

"My father was supposed to stand with him on that stage at Lincoln's feet. But hearing Dr. King made me hopeful, and that's when I decided to follow in my father's footsteps and become a civil rights attorney."

"I watched on television," Daphne began. "I was staying at my grandmother's house, my mother's mom. She didn't want me there. I was too much of a reminder. You see, my grandmother worked as a domestic, and her employer, a white man, had raped her. My mother was the living proof, and so was I.

"But sitting and watching Dr. King on that tiny black-and-white television set with my grandmother seemed to bring us together. I remember she reached out and hugged me. She told me that I was not my mother and that I had to make different choices and to always remember who I was and where I came from. And no matter what happened in the past and what will happen in the future, I was always a child of God and that he would never leave or forsake me. All I had to do was believe. That made me feel so good."

"What about you?" I asked Daniel as the car went silent again for a few moments. "Where were you in 1963?"

"Germany. My dad was in the military, an officer. We moved around a lot. My father had a ham radio and we all listened in to the speeches. Some of the other officers warned my father not to, but we did, and some others came to listen as well. I was young, but I knew it was special. I could see it on the faces of the men and women sitting there. I remember hearing Mahalia Jackson singing 'How We Got Over,' and then listening to Dr. King's words. He was inspiring. I'll never forget that moment."

"I don't think anyone will. Everybody will remember exactly where they were on Wednesday, August 28th, 1963."

"I still can't believe he's dead."

"I know. Me either."

"Even when we were standing in Sisters Chapel on Spelman campus and looking down at his body a few months ago, it just didn't seem real that he was lying there."

"I remember standing in that long line outside and everybody was so quiet. No one talked."

"I think everybody was in shock."

I reached over and grabbed the book Trudy had given Veronica, *The Negro Motorist Green Book*. They had stopped publishing these two years ago, and this was an older copy. I flipped through the book, reading listings on a few of the pages. "Wow, this is really wild."

"What is?" Daphne asked.

"The listings in this book. It's like black people couldn't go anywhere in this country and be safe."

"It's better nowadays," Daphne interjected. "Segregation is over. There are laws to protect us."

"You know laws don't mean anything," Veronica chimed in unexpectedly. "It's just a false sense of security."

"So what's in the book?" Daphne asked, turning to me.

"There are listings for hotels, service stations, and restaurants, but also surprisingly for taxicabs, barbershops, beauty parlors, and nightclubs." I started reading off some the places I found in the book.

"Well, I guess it's comforting to see there are so many safe places for black people to travel," Daphne said.

"Yeah, but it's disheartening to know a book like this is needed to ensure our safety."

"One day everything will be different," Daphne said.

"You really believe that?" I asked.

"Yeah, I do," she said as Veronica exited the highway and drove through the streets of Washington, DC. Some of the streets were blocked off, so we detoured.

"I wonder what's going on," Daphne said.

"It looks like another protest march," I said.

It was Sunday afternoon, another hot day, and a lot of people were out in the streets trying to get relief from the sweltering heat. We detoured again and had to find our way back, driving through Northwest neighborhoods that seemed to have been demolished by a bomb. We drove down Fourteenth, then U Street to Seventh Street. "Geez, look at this. What the hell happened?" Veronica asked.

"The riots in April after Dr. King was killed," I said. "A lot of the city's neighborhoods still haven't recovered."

At the side of the road there were shells of cars burnt and overturned. Street after street of vacant buildings had been gutted by fire, interiors caved in and floors covered with charred beams and twisted metal. Broken glass and debris littered the pavement. "It looks like a war happened here."

"It was a war," I said, "and we all lost."

"All this is going to change things, isn't it?" Daphne said.

"Yeah, it will change. But I don't think it will be for the better. At least not for us," Daniel said. I nodded.

"We destroyed our own neighborhoods. This didn't honor Dr. King's memory."

We found our way back to where we needed to go. My aunt and uncle lived midway between Adams Morgan and Dupont Circle. They had a large three-story house similar to my family's house in Harlem. There was even a small park that reminded me of Mount Morris Park. We got to their house and parked in the first spot we found, halfway down the street.

Veronica shut off the engine. "Remind me to get some gas before we leave DC, okay? We're almost on empty."

"Okay," Daphne and I said.

We got out of the car and started walking. A few houses away I saw a man dressed in all black with black shades leaving my uncle's house.

"Who's that?" Veronica asked.

I shrugged. "I don't know. Come on." We got to the front door. It was already slightly ajar. "Why's the door open?" I muttered as I pushed it open.

"Wait, me first," Daniel said, quickly pushing past me. I was going to say something, but he was too fast. We followed until we got inside, then I pushed around him.

10

"HELLO?" I CALLED OUT.

There was no response. I called out again as we walked through the foyer to the living room. A young woman I didn't know approached. "Who are you? What are you doing in here?" she asked.

For a long moment I was too stunned to answer. I looked around behind her, seeing the television on with no sound and two men, both dressed in black, sitting on the sofa. They were looking up at us with agitated expressions, as if we had walked in and interrupted something incredibly important.

I looked in the dining room. There was a display of guns and bullets on the table along with a newspaper. As I walked over, the woman blocked my way.

"Hey, I asked you a question," she said. "Who are you and what are you doing here?"

The two men in the living room stood up.

Suddenly I could feel the closeness of Daniel behind me.

"Who are you and why are you in this house?" I asked.

"Who wants to know?" she asked.

I pushed around her and quickly read the newspaper article headline: "Local Attorney, Beaten, Accuses Police of Brutality." I didn't have to read the rest of the article. My heart lurched. I straightaway knew it was my uncle. He was in the newspapers a lot, defending against police brutality, unfair housing, and unfair employment practices. Arthur Livingston, a brilliant attorney, was my father's younger brother. He had taken me in when I couldn't stand to be with my mother and her new husband anymore.

"Uncle Arthur," I muttered.

I started to panic, looking around for my aunt and uncle. The door to my uncle's office was closed, so I headed to the kitchen to find my aunt.

"Hey, what do you think you're doing?"

"I'm looking for Arthur Livingston or Dorothy, his wife."

"Who?" she said.

"She means Art," a man called out from the living room.

"What do you want him for?" the woman asked.

I looked at her like she had lost her mind. "Why are you in his house? What's going on?"

"You and your friends get lost sightseeing?" she said, looking us up and down again. "Y'all need to get the fuck out of here. You don't belong in this scene. So get out!"

"Who the hell are you cussing at?" Veronica said, stepping forward. Daniel took her arm to hold her back.

"You don't understand. I need to find my—"

"No, you don't understand," she said. "I told you to get out." She stepped up to me real close.

"You need to back up," Daniel told her roughly.

A man stepped up to Daniel and they started arguing.

"All right, all right, that's enough," one of the two men said, stepping between Daniel and the other guy. "We don't need to be fighting among ourselves. What do y'all want with Art?"

I looked at him and refused to speak. The room was deathly silent. Everybody was staring at us.

"Hey, I'm talking to you. What do you want here?"

"Back up," Daniel shouted, stepping up again.

"Look at them. They ain't down with the program. They probably with them fascist pigs," the woman said. "Probably squealers here to spy on us. Get out before we put your asses out."

"You shut up," Veronica shouted.

"Enough! What do you want?" the big man said again.

The door to my uncle's office opened. "What's all this yelling out here?" He looked around and then saw me. "Zelda?"

"Zelda?" Aunt Dorothy pushed around him. "Zelda, *Tu es ici enfin. Ta mère a appelé tout le week-end.*" She hurried over and wrapped her arms around me and squeezed tight. She greeted Veronica and Daphne, and I introduced her to Daniel.

"What's going on out here?" Arthur asked.

"I didn't know who she was, so I told her to leave, but she wouldn't."

My aunt turned to the young woman. "Who the hell are you to put anybody out of my house?" No one said a word to defend her. "You think 'cause you wear all this black and you down with the cause that you belong here? Let me tell you something, honey child, my niece has sacrificed more for this cause than your ignorant ass will ever know. And let me tell you something else . . ."

My aunt went off, using cuss words combined in ways I had never heard before. Then she ended in a righteous blaze of fury, sounding like a minister in a pulpit, scripture references and all. "You know what? You get out! All of you, get the hell out of this damn house now!"

"But what about the protest? We're supposed to—"

"Did you not hear what I just said to you? Get out!" Her voice was ferocious, like a lioness protecting her cubs. I had never seen this side of her.

Some of the men looked to my uncle Arthur. He pointed to the door. "I'll be there directly." As they were leaving, the woman glared and rolled her eyes.

"And get the shit off my dining room table. What's wrong with you? You got no manners?" One of the men quickly gathered the guns and ammo and shoved them in a black cloth sack. "And if you want to blame somebody for getting your asses kicked out, blame this chick. You come to my house next time, you better be respectful and act like you got some sense."

We went into the kitchen and found a couple of men sitting at the table. They looked up as we entered. "I'm sorry, Mrs. Livingston," one of the men said. "They're just upset about everything that happened last night."

"Upset my ass. You tell that woman I said, 'Don't ever darken my doorstep again.'"

"Yes, ma'am. Again, we're sorry. I'm sorry. That's not what we're about. Respect. We don't need to tear each other down."

"You damn right," she said.

The men shook my uncle's hand. They thanked my aunt, and my uncle walked them out.

My aunt was still complaining about the guns on her lace tablecloth and the cigarette smoke in her living room while she made us bologna and cheese sandwiches.

"Since when did Uncle Arthur start working with the Black Panther Party?" I asked.

"He's helping them with the legal aspects of their breakfast programs, health clinics, and other issues. He represented a few of the members last week, and a few others stopped by for more advice. They know having the Livingston name means something in the city."

My uncle returned, and I hugged him. "Are you okay?" I asked quietly about the bandage on his head.

He nodded. "Yeah, it looks worse than it is. And the optics work in our favor for the newspaper articles."

"What happened?"

"He was beat by the damn police," my aunt responded. "They accused him of inciting a riot and tried to arrest him. People came out and went wild. The police blamed your uncle and hauled him off to jail. Apparently he was beat while resisting arrest and damn near shot when trying to escape, which of course never happened. But that didn't matter."

"My God," Daphne muttered.

"I'm fine. I'm fine," Arthur said.

"Are you okay?" Veronica asked my aunt Dorothy.

"Yes, just stressed, and I know my blood pressure is through the roof. But never mind all that. You all sit down and eat."

Obediently, Daphne, Veronica, Daniel, and I sat down and started eating the sandwiches. We weren't hungry, but we didn't want to go against my aunt right now.

"When did you get hurt?" I asked.

"Friday," Arthur said. "I announced my candidacy and—"

"You did! That's wonderful, Uncle Arthur. I'm so proud of you," I exclaimed, hugging him. Then I turned. "Ladies and Daniel, I'd like to introduce the future Washington, DC, councilman Arthur Livingston." Everybody applauded and cheered.

"Don't forget your mother called," Dorothy said to me. "She wants you to call her back. She said you left Friday. What took you so long to get here?"

"That's my fault, Mrs. Livingston," Veronica said quickly. "We stopped at the beach to visit my family."

Dorothy nodded. "Just call your mother back."

"I'm really not—"

"No sass. Call her. Use the phone in the living room."

My aunt Dorothy had a way of commanding a room. She was not a very large woman, but when she spoke everyone listened. She was smart, loving, and generous. She'd do anything for anybody, but getting on her bad side was never a good idea.

I got up begrudgingly and headed to the living room.

"Zelda," my aunt called out, following me into the living room. I saw that Veronica, Daphne, and Daniel had stayed in the kitchen with my uncle Arthur. I looked at Aunt Dorothy and tears began to flow.

"She didn't remember Friday." I spoke in French, knowing no one else would understand us even if they overhead. "It's like he never existed."

"Don't fault your mother," Dorothy replied, also in French.

"Why not? It's her fault, all of it," I yelled. "If they hadn't argued that night, we would have all stayed in the house and never gone to the movies. She was always arguing with him. I don't understand."

Dorothy sighed. "That's because you don't want to," she said. "You never did."

"What?"

"Take him down from that pedestal, Zelda. It's time."

I looked her directly in the eyes.

"Your father was no saint, and that's what you've made him out to be. He was a man—fascinating, yes, brilliant, yes, but at times imperfect. He had affairs, a lot of them."

"No. That's not true."

"Yes, it is," she insisted. "When have I ever lied to you?" Our eyes held. She waited expectantly.

"Never."

"So fault your mother for being possessive with the man she truly loved and for being selfish and wanting him all for herself. But it's time you know that she went through her trials with your father. He had a wandering eye, and women loved him. They loved him too damn much."

"No. I can't believe this."

"A white woman accused him of being the father of her child. That's what they argued about. The woman said she was going to make it public. He decided to give her money to disappear."

"No, that didn't happen."

"Yes, it did."

"No. Not my father. He was a good man. He was—"

"Zelda, stop it. Grow up. Life isn't black and white. It just isn't. Yes, your father was a good man, but he was also flawed. He was human. We all are flawed, one no better and no worse than the other. Call her. Make this right. Do it now." She started to walk away.

"Wait. Is that what got him killed?"

She shook her head. "I don't think so."

"Was there a baby?"

"No, the woman lied. She just wanted money."

"Mom knew and she didn't tell me?"

"She was trying to protect his memory and you. Call her."

She walked away. I turned and looked down at the phone. I picked up the receiver and dialed my home in New York. My mother answered on the second ring. "Hi, it's me," I said, gathering my composure as I reverted back to speaking English.

"Zelda, Lawd chile, I was worried sick. Are you okay? I've been calling your aunt and uncle since Friday. Where have you been?"

"I'm fine," I said but was a little upset.

She exhaled. "Zelda," she began. I could hear the tremble in her voice. "You shouldn't have left like that."

"I didn't have much choice, did I?"

"I'm sorry, sweetheart. We should never speak like that to one another. You're all I've got left."

I didn't answer.

"Zelda, can you hear me?"

"Yes, I hear you."

"You're my daughter. From the second you were conceived and every day after. I love you. Don't you know that?"

"No, Mom, I don't know that," I said truthfully.

"Well, don't ever believe otherwise. This is your home. Do you want me to take the train and meet you in DC?"

"No. We'll be fine. I'm fine."

I turned toward the back of the house. Everyone was in the kitchen, but Daniel had come into the dining room. He sat at the table with the newspaper in his hands, but I knew he wasn't reading it. He looked at me. His eyes were intense, and his expression was uneasy. I turned away. "Mom, this is long distance. I have to go."

"Wait," she said softly. "Did Darnell's friend's son meet up with you ladies?"

"Yeah, he's here," I said softly, smiling to myself.

"Good. I'll try not to worry then. He'll take good care of you. He's a good man, an honest man. Call me when you can."

"I will."

I pressed the button on the phone to end the call, but I held on to the receiver. When I released the button, I stood there and listened to the whining *buzz* of the disconnected line. I realized that I had wanted to tell my mother that I loved her, too, but I had never said that to her before and she had never said it to me before this moment. It seemed like there was no room for those words in our families. It would mean that we cared, and it was tough to do that when from the very beginning of our time here in America, people of color could be stolen and sold out of our lives on a slave master's whim. I finally hung up.

"She's your biggest supporter."

I turned, finding Daniel standing behind me.

"How would you know?" I asked.

"Because you're all she ever talks about. She'd go on and on about how smart you are, and your accomplishments, and how proud she is of you. Funny, the more she talked, the more I wanted to hear."

"I don't know what my mother said to you about me, Daniel, but you don't know me. You may think you do, but you don't."

"I know that you're funny, smart, beautiful, and passionate about what you believe. I know that I liked you even before we met and I know that I want to get to know you better." He stepped closer. "Zelda—"

My name hung in the scant air between us. That's when I first saw it there in his eyes, a spark that I can only describe as intense passion. It was raw and urgent and nearly stole my breath away. I quickly averted my gaze. I wasn't ready to hear what I knew he wanted to say to me. "Daniel, I can't. Not now. We should get back to the others."

He nodded and walked away.

I didn't move. I looked down and noticed a flyer on the end table beside the telephone.

It was about the protest rally we had passed on our way to the house. It listed my uncle as a speaker. I took it to the kitchen. "Aren't you supposed to be there, Uncle Arthur?"

He checked his watch. "Yeah, I'd better get going."

"You be careful, you hear me?" Aunt Dorothy said and kissed him. I smiled. Their relationship had always been affectionate no matter who was there and what was going on. Thank God they always found time to say "I love you."

"Aunt Dorothy, you're not going?"

"No, child. My marching days are over."

"Can we go?" I asked, looking at Veronica and Daphne. They shrugged and nodded. "Yeah, can we?" they asked.

Aunt Dorothy frowned at us, sighed, and shook her head. I just knew she was going to say no. "You all just be careful and stay close to Arthur and Daniel, you hear me?"

"Yes, we will."

Aunt Dorothy turned to me. "Zelda, *écoute. Ça peut devenir fou à ces rassemblements, alors fais attention et sois en sécurité.*"

"*Oui, nous promettons. Nous serons en sécurité. À plus tard.*"

We all piled into my uncle's car. Daniel, who sat up front, was a sports nut just like my uncle, and they talked about sports and Daniel's plans to be an engineer and laughed the whole time as the three of us sat in the back. Veronica nudged me and smiled. "It's so cool that you and your aunt speak French. What did she say?"

"She told me that the rally could get crazy and to be safe. I told her we would."

It didn't take long to get to the protest rally. We walked into a room full of people cheering and applauding my uncle the moment we entered. A few of the men dressed in black who had been at the house earlier were there too. They ushered us through the crowd, making sure to hold others back as we passed. My uncle stepped up onto the stage, and the crowd of people went crazy.

He motioned for Daniel, Veronica, Daphne, and me to step up behind him. We seated ourselves on some folding chairs on the makeshift stage and listened to his speech. I watched as the people stood in silence, enthralled by his words. He stressed education, employment, and voter participation while asserting the immediate end to police brutality and black-on-black crime.

There were several hundred people as far back as I could see. They were all listening in awe. I saw the woman I had argued with at the house. She was sitting off to the side, at the voter registration table. She looked at me up onstage. I nodded to her.

"Zelda, Veronica, look." Daphne nudged me.

"Yeah, I see it," Veronica said.

There was a commotion building all the way in the back. My uncle had a concerned look on his face. Police officers were surrounding the crowd. Some of the attendees began to yell and push, and a scuffle broke out. My uncle stopped speaking and stood with his hands raised.

Some in the crowd closer to the stage raised their hands as well. It took about a half minute for people in the crowd to notice he had stopped talking. They ceased. Soon the entire crowd held their hands up in silence.

"This is *not* what we're here to do today," my uncle said in a firm voice. The last remnants of the ruckus subsided, and others around it were making the troublemakers stop and pay attention. He softened his tone, and the crowd grew even quieter still. "No one gets that power over us. We will not give anyone cause to beat us. We are better than this."

Someone yelled, "That's right. You tell 'em."

"We come from better than this," he added.

"Amen, brother. Preach on."

Another person screamed, "Someone killed Dr. King."

"Yes, he did," my uncle said sadly.

"Yeah, they shot him down like a dog," a different person shouted.

My uncle nodded sadly as a small commotion began again.

"Shit," I muttered. All I could think was *A riot is coming.*

"And what are we going to do?" he asked the crowd.

"Kill the pigs!"

"Yeah, kill the pigs!"

"No." He shook his head and moved the microphone away slightly. It quieted the crowd. "No. Let me tell you a story," he began. "Five years ago my older brother, Owen Livingston, a civil rights attorney in New York City, was pulled from his car right in front of his house. Four police officers detained him as my niece at fifteen years old could only stand and watch."

A lump the size of the Rock of Gibraltar jammed in my throat. I sat stunned, barely breathing. Veronica and Daphne grabbed each of my hands and squeezed tight. The crowd was completely hushed as he told them how my father was handcuffed, beaten, and killed.

"Kill the muthafuckin' pigs!"

Many of the cops were in ready position. And the ones stationed at the stage gripped their batons in their hands. One was even anxiously slapping his baton against the palm of his hand.

"*No!*" My uncle shouted. "It's not the pigs we need to attack. It's the system that protects them and the systemic apathy that we perpetrate day in and day out. We need to change this broken system by stepping up and voting them out and taking responsibility for our actions and inactions. Cut the legs off their power, the corrupt judges who send us to jail disproportionately and do nothing to the real criminals, the blinded police chief who only sees blue power and greed, the muted mayor who only speaks out to put money in his own pocket, and the deafened councilmen who pretend not to hear our cries of abuse and brutality. My brothers and sisters, it's time for something new.

"All of you fat cats out there, you listen to me and listen good. Your time is up. Your days are numbered. It's a new day. This is our time, the people's time. And you can't keep all of us down. The poor, the brutalized, the disenfranchised, we stand all in accord. It doesn't matter, your race or your religion or whatever else you are. We'll stand together. And we're going to the voting box."

By this time the cries of exultation and endorsement were deafening. There were women shouting "Amen" like they were sitting in church. The police just stood there, as people rushed to the voter registration table, which was packed three or four rows deep. People were listening to my uncle.

"Cut the legs off," he continued. "Vote them out. Then we'll take this power all the way to the White House. Go to the voting box and watch them fall. Step up. Get out and vote. Get out and vote them out!

"Let me tell you, I have a future judge, a future teacher, a future businesswoman, and a future engineer right here with me on this stage." He motioned for us to stand. We did. "My niece and her friends attend college. They want to change this world and make the future brighter for my children and your children. So I tell you now, keep your children in school, give them a future, and get out there and vote!"

Cheers rang out at a blistering volume.

"This is not the end. This is only the beginning. Are you with me?"

As my uncle finished his speech, the crowd became ecstatic and started chanting his name. We all joined in.

11

WE PLANNED TO LEAVE DC EARLY MONDAY MORNING, BUT we didn't make it out until almost two. Uncle Arthur had reminded us of the notorious harassment of black motorists and speed traps on Virginia's Interstate 85. Instead of getting on I-85 in Petersburg, we decided to take an alternate route until we got to North Carolina. Traffic on Interstate 95 south was impossible. We got stuck behind two different accidents and had to detour around them, leading us onto Route 1. It was crowded, but not too bad. I stared off at the scenic beauty.

We were officially in the South. The blood of our ancestors had seeped into the red clay. The bones of men, women, and children long forgotten had been crushed and buried beneath the trees, the roads, and the homes.

Living in the city, I sometimes forgot how picturesque the rural South could be. The trees, lush and full, were a mass of vibrant green, and the rolling countryside appeared to go on forever, untouched by expansion and civilization. The placid serenity of the drive was ideal.

"Tell me about your father," Daniel said. "Your uncle mentioned him on the podium at his rally."

"His name was Owen Livingston. He was murdered."

"I'm sorry."

"Last Friday was five years, but most times it feels like it was just yesterday. My father was a civil rights attorney in New York City. A few months before he was assassinated he won a huge police brutality civil rights case. It was a major lawsuit, what they call a career-making case. They said he would never win, but against all odds, he won. People were comparing him to Thurgood Marshall, and politicians came calling.

"But some people, the police mostly, weren't happy about it. The case cost the city millions of dollars, and it shined a light on police discrimination practices that had been going on for decades. The newspapers covered the case on their front pages almost every day. People on the street recognized him, and he was approached about running for public office. But he didn't want that. He always said his calling was to work for the people, all the people.

"The day he was killed he took me to the movies. My mother didn't want to go. She never did. So going to the movies was our father-daughter time together. We went at least once a month ever since I can remember. I wish I had known then that time was going to be our last time together.

"He had been working so hard on the case and on his business. We had missed the last few months of movies, but I understood. He was doing important work. So for him to take this time for us was so special to me. We laughed and sang during the movie," I said, smiling and remembering a particular part we had liked a lot. "Then as soon as the movie was over and we went outside, the police were waiting for us.

"They said he'd been causing trouble in the theater. That was ridiculous. He protested. They started yelling at him and threatening to take him in. All of a sudden there was a crowd around us. Some of the people recognized my father, and both black and white, they started to protest too, so the police backed off. But they followed us home, and another police car showed up. They said he was driving drunk. He wasn't. My father didn't drink. But they were going to arrest him anyway. They handcuffed him behind his back, then he made me go into the house. I said no, but he insisted and made me. So I did. I looked out the window in the front parlor and watched what they did to him.

"They started yelling and beating him on his head and all over his body. He was balled up on the ground in front of the car with his hands behind his back, and they just kept beating, punching, and kicking him over and over again. Then one of the cops yelled, 'He's going for his gun,' but he didn't even own one. He was on the ground barely moving. One of the cops pulled out his gun and shot him. The other cops shot him too. He had twenty-three bullet wounds in his body, six in his head. He died in the street like a dog, and they just stood there looking at him."

The words had tumbled out of my mouth like they had been waiting an eternity to be set free. Vicious. Brutal. Repugnant. Hateful. True. They lashed out in every direction, retaliating for a wrong so vile and despicable that it had stopped all feeling in my heart. There was no love to give or receive. There was just the reality of never moving forward since both time and the feeling of love had stopped for me that day.

I hadn't talked about that afternoon in years. Yet it was the nightmare of brutality I relived every day of my life. Tears streamed down my face as I still saw the image of my father in the street covered with blood.

"Why? Why would they do that to him? Why would they kill him like that? I remember screaming. I ran outside and tried to put my father's shattered head back together. Blood, brains, bone, dripped through my fingers. I held on to what was left of his lips and tried to remember how he had kissed my forehead just a few minutes earlier.

"They kept trying to pull me off him, but I wouldn't let them. I had to protect him. I couldn't let them hurt him again. I looked up at each of them. Their faces were ineradicably engraved on my soul. They didn't smile. They didn't say or do anything. They just stood there with their mouths open like they had no idea what had just happened."

I stopped talking.

"He sounds like he was a remarkable man."

"Yes, he was an amazing man, blemishes and all."

"What happened with the police? Did they—"

"There was a report, which got buried for no justifiable reason. There was a public outcry and a massive funeral with politicians vowing answers and swift justice and, most of all, change. Dr. King marched on Washington, and then there was nothing. I heard later one was killed in a shoot-out in the line of duty, and the other three resigned shortly thereafter. One of them committed suicide with a bullet to the head. It was too good for them."

"What about the other two?"

"I want them to live long and know that my father's work didn't end with his death. It only made people more determined for justice. And it made me even more committed to step into his footsteps and continue his work."

"I know your father would have been so proud of you."

"I haven't done anything yet," I said.

"You will. I know you will."

"Look. What's going on over there?" Veronica asked.

We saw white men dressed as guards with rifles and black men chained together. Some were bare-chested. Others were dressed in sweat-soaked striped shirts and pants so filthy we could scarcely discern the colors. Hair matted, lips parched, faces scarred and bruised. They were hauling massive rocks and digging a long trench using pickaxes, shovels, and sledgehammers.

One of the guards on a horse was looking our way. Daphne turned and looked as we passed them. "No, don't turn around," I said. She whipped around quickly. We all faced forward and kept driving.

Then a whistle blew loud, long, and hard.

Veronica checked the rearview mirror. "Oh my God," she shrieked. "They're chasing us, two men on horseback. What do I do? What do I do?"

"Stop the car," Daphne said.

"No! Keep driving," I shouted. "Go faster."

"Stop the car," Daniel instructed. Veronica pulled over to the side of the road.

I forced myself to look forward. They rode up alongside the car, riding fierce. One stopped his horse in front of the car, and the other circled us with his rifle pointed down into the car. The horses panted heavily; I could swear I saw fumes bellowing from their widened nostrils.

"Git out!" the gunman raged. "Git out!"

The one in front yelled, then reared his horse up as if to stomp down on us.

Shaking and trembling, we all got out of the car. No one spoke or looked up at the guards.

"Where you going, boy?" he said. "You think I don't know that's you? Cut your hair, change your clothes all you like, your nigga ass is still going back to Lorton Prison wid an added ten years for 'scaping."

Daphne whipped around. "What? No!" she screamed tearfully. "He's with us. He didn't escape any prison. He's driving to school with us. Please no, don't do this."

"Shut your mouth, gal!" the one in front yelled.

"Leave her be," the other spoke up. "What's a white girl doing with these coloreds? You need to be wid your own."

"I'm sorry, sir," Daphne pleaded. Her voice was soft and contrite. "It's just that this is Daniel and he's with us, helping us get back to school in Atlanta. He's our driver, but he needed a break. Please don't do this. Don't take him."

The guard closest to Daphne moved to where Daniel stood. "Look at me, boy. Let me see your identification. Take your wallet out slowly."

Daniel gave his wallet to the man. He flipped through, then tossed it to the other guard. "Look at me," he instructed. Then after what seemed like forever, he spoke again. "It ain't him. You told me it was him," the first guard said to the second. "Come on. Let's go."

"So what? He could have faked all dis shit."

"It ain't him," the first one yelled.

"He's black. That's what matters. Dey all look alike. It could be him. What's the difference as long as we bring us another darkie back?"

"It's the wrong man," the guard said gruffly. "Come on. You fucked up. That escapee is long gone by now."

"Bullshit! I say we bring his ass back."

"Let's move!"

"What and we just leave him go? Hell's no."

"Come on with your foolishness. We gotta get back," the first guard said, pulling his reins and backing away. The other rode his horse by us so slowly and so closely, I could see and smell the sweat matting the horse's mane. We all leaned away. Any closer and we would have been smashed between the horse and the side of the car.

One of the men tossed something over his shoulder, then they galloped away. I walked over and picked up Daniel's wallet. I saw that a military ID card was lying on the ground. It belonged to Daniel. I turned as he approached. "Thanks," he said, taking the wallet and card from me.

"Are you okay?" I asked.

"Hell no, I'm not okay," he said, scowling and looking back to the men on horseback. "Sons of bitches stole my money."

"All of it?"

"Three dollars," he said.

"Three dollars—that's all the money you have?" I asked.

"No, of course not. That's the money I keep in my wallet. This isn't the first time I handed my wallet over and got nothing back."

I looked over and saw Veronica and Daphne holding each other.

"Come on. Let's get our asses out of here before they come back and take my butt to jail for loitering and you all for crying."

We scrambled into the car and sped off.

"Crap. I forgot to get gas," Veronica said.

Daphne and I leaned over and peeked at the gauge. The pointer was hovering near empty. "Shit."

"Okay, we just have to stop somewhere."

"Maybe we should check the *Green Book*."

"Yeah, good idea. Where are we exactly?"

"Umm, Dumfries, Virginia," Daphne said.

I flipped through to find the section in Virginia and quickly read as Daphne checked the map we had gotten from my uncle Arthur. "Richmond, Charlottesville, Fredericksburg," I read out loud.

"No. No. No. They're all too far away."

"Lynchburg?"

"Hell no," Veronica said.

"No thank you," Daniel added.

"Well, that's it. There's no mention of anyplace remotely close to where we are now," I said.

"It looks like Fredericksburg is the closest."

"How many miles?" Veronica asked.

"I don't know exactly. Maybe twenty or twenty-five, perhaps more."

"We're not going to make it. We need to stop someplace near here and take our chances."

"Okay." We all looked around. "Over there," Daphne pointed. It was a gas station with a small eatery attached. "It looks okay. What do you think?"

Veronica steered into the next lane, turned into the gas station, and parked at a pump. No one came out. "Maybe we have to go inside."

"I'll go," Daniel said. "You stay here. If anything—"

"No. We all go," I said, interrupting him.

"That's right. Safety in numbers."

"Come on. We do this together."

We entered the eatery cautiously. For a moment, we stood just inside the door surveying the room. A woman was at the counter with her young son and daughter, and four older men were sitting in a corner booth laughing and talking. There was a black man wearing a white T-shirt and peeking through an open window shelf between the kitchen and the dining area. He shifted a bell to the side to get a better look at us. The customers quieted, noticing us in the doorway. Time stopped. No one said a word. They all just stared.

"What them niggas doing here, Ma?" the little boy said.

The four men cracked up laughing. The little boy joined in.

A young white girl, who was popping gum, wearing a red-and-white checkered shirt and a pair of blue jeans with an apron tied around her waist, walked over to us. "Don't listen to that riffraff," she said, bending down, looking out the window. "Well, damn. Is that y'all's car out there, the red one?"

"Yes. It is," Veronica said.

"Wow, that's nice. I bet it drives as fast as hot lightning. That's boss."

"I don't drive that fast, but, yes, I'm sure it would."

"So what y'all need, gas?"

"Yes, a fill it up, please." Veronica said.

"Yeah, sure," she said, then yelled over her shoulder. "Reggie, tell Cooper to get his ass outside. He got some customers need some gas. They want a fill up." Then she looked at us and smiled. "Y'all want the oil checked too?"

"Yes, that would be nice."

"Tell him to check the oil and wash the windows."

"Thanks," we said and turned to leave.

"Hey, wait. Y'all don't want nothing to eat? The food here is real good. Reggie's a damn fine cook. He knows all those fancy recipes. He used to cook at a big restaurant in New York City."

I looked at the counter and then at the four men who hadn't taken their eyes off us since we walked in. "No thank you. We'll wait outside," I said.

"And did I tell y'all Reggie makes the best apple pie and sweet bread cake in the county? People come from clear over in Haymarket and Manassas just to get some of his cake. His mamma told him the recipe, and he won't tell nobody, not even me." She yelled the last part over her shoulder so the man in the kitchen could hear her. He laughed.

"Well, if that's the case, we should get a slice," Daphne said.

"We'll take four slices of cake," Daniel said.

"Sure thing," the waitress said, smiling. But we didn't move an inch. "What, y'all ain't gonna eat in the car, are you?"

"We don't want to stay too long."

"Don't be silly. Y'all sit on down over there by the window, and I'll get you some menus just in case you're hungry and change your mind. Go on, have a seat."

We moved slowly, still looking at the little boy sitting at the counter with his mother and sister. He took the straw out of his milk and blew spittle at us. His mother quickly gathered her purse and grabbed the kids and hurried out.

The young waitress walked to the counter and started cussing. "That cheap heifer ain't even leave me a penny for a tip. Bitch."

The man in the kitchen started laughing again. "Serves you right for being nice to her dumb kids."

Daphne and I slid into the booth. Veronica and Daniel took the end seats with Daniel sitting beside me. The waitress walked back over to us with four laminated menus. "My name's Tammy. The cheeseburgers and fries are real good here. You should try them."

I looked at her and couldn't seem to figure out what she was doing. She was sassy and bubbly, and her generous smile was infectious. I guessed she could be just that nice and welcoming, but she was white, and that just blew my mind. I didn't trust niceness. "Thank you," I said.

She walked away. Noticing the men were still staring at us, she yelled. "What are y'all looking at? Turn around and mind your own business."

"This is so weird," I whispered.

"To say the least."

"So what do we do, eat?"

"Yeah, okay, let's order. We can always take it to go if there's trouble," Daniel said. We all three nodded in agreement.

Tammy came over with four glasses of water and took our order. She smiled, popped her gum, and headed back to the kitchen.

"Think the cook's gonna spit in our food?" Daphne asked.

"I hope not," Veronica said.

"No, I saw him. He's black. He seems okay."

The four men in the corner started talking loudly about Major League Baseball splitting up into divisions. "I blame them damn niggas," one of them said loud enough for us to hear. "They're tearing this country apart."

Daphne looked up. "Daphne," I cautioned, "don't look at them. That's what they want us to do."

"We should just go," Veronica said.

"Yeah, as soon as he finishes with the car," I said, seeing the young man with the hood up checking the oil as he filled the car with gas.

"Where y'all headed?" Tammy returned, asking loudly, which seemed to be her only way of talking. "To college, right?" she said, grinning from ear to ear. "Anywhere near Tuskegee?"

We looked at her surprised. What did she know about Tuskegee University?

"No," I said politely, "Spelman and Morehouse. Both in Atlanta, Georgia. Tuskegee is in Alabama."

"Oh, okay. I gotta remember that."

She leaned against the end of the booth and asked other questions about college life. After a while we laughed and talked with ease. Then the men in their booth got loud again. "If y'all don't shut your mouths, I'm gonna spit in your food the next time you come in here. And you'd better believe I'll do it too."

The cook rang a bell and sat four plates on the shelf window between the kitchen and the dining area. "I'll be right back with your food."

"Don't spit in it," Veronica joked.

Tammy laughed. "Nah, I only spit in white bigots' food when they sit in their damn booth all day long bitching and complaining about everything and don't leave me a damn tip for putting up with their dumb asses," she said, getting progressively louder and louder with each word.

Seconds later Tammy returned with our food. Daphne said grace, and we started eating. Tammy grabbed a chair, sat down beside the booth, and shared her dreams of attending college.

Out of the corner of my eye, I saw a patrol car pull up out front. The food lodged in my throat. An officer got out of the car and entered the restaurant. He looked at the four men and nodded, then yelled a greeting to Reggie the cook. Reggie came out, and they talked, looking over at us.

"We need to go," I said.

Veronica and Daphne slid over on the seat, moving to stand.

"Why are y'all leaving? You're not finished eating yet," Tammy said.

The cop walked over to where we were and removed his hat and dark sunglasses. "That's a real nice car you got yourselves there, folks."

"Thank you, sir," Veronica said standing.

"We're just leaving now," Daniel said standing also.

"Tammy, you get these folks some cake yet?"

"No, not yet, Daddy."

"Well, get up from there and get them four big slices of cake on me."

"I sure will."

"Thank you, sir, but—"

"No thank you," he said.

We looked at each other in confusion. "Y'all sit down and finish your meal." Daphne and I slid back as Veronica and Daniel sat down. The officer sat down where Tammy had been sitting. "You going south?" he asked. We nodded. "How far down south?"

"To Georgia, sir. To college."

"Good for you. Been trying to get my son and daughter to get back to school—"

"They already talked to me about college," Tammy yelled out.

The cop laughed. "That girl, she's something else. But she's a blessing. And I thank you for that."

"Sir," Daniel said, "why are you thanking us?"

He shook his head. "I was in World War Two. Them colored boys with the 332nd and the 477th saved my ass over there. You colored people are all right with me. If it weren't for them boys, I wouldn't have gotten back here and my two kids wouldn't have been born. A lot of fine fighters died with their stupid prejudice, but not me. Them colored fighters saved the day many a time. And I'll be forever grateful. So thank you. And you thank them colored boys down there too."

"Yes, sir, we sure will," Daniel said dutifully.

The sheriff stood and headed back into the kitchen, and after we finished eating, we went to the counter to pay. On our way, the four men said something derogatory about us. "Y'all shut the shit up," the sheriff said.

We asked for our check. "Oh, my daddy already took care of that, and he said to make sure you have cake for the road."

"Thank you."

She smiled. "I know you don't know the men who saved my daddy's life back in World War Two, but thank you for pretending. He's grateful, and it makes him feel good."

Since the check was already paid, we left her a big tip. Tammy was thrilled. "Hey, Reggie, you see what they left us? We got ourselves a big fat tip. Y'all come back when you're in the area. You're always welcome here. Always," she shouted. "Y'all boys see this?" she said to the four white men in the back. "This is what a tip looks like."

We paid for the gas and drove off. Two minutes down the road, Daniel said, "It's a shame they don't print *The Negro Motorist Green Book* anymore. That place would have been the perfect addition."

12

WE WERE BREEZING THROUGH VIRGINIA AS DAPHNE, with map in hand, read out the cities and small towns we passed through. When we got to Richmond, we debated if we should stop at either Virginia Union University in Richmond or Virginia State University in Petersburg. We wound up not stopping at either. We didn't stop at Norfolk State University or Hampton University either. We were soon to enter North Carolina and decided to stop since everybody needed to go to the bathroom. But trying to find a decent restroom was a problem. Every place we stopped, we were told that the bathrooms weren't working. But we knew what was really going on.

Yes, the Civil Rights Act had desegregated the South. We were now allowed to drink from all water fountains, sit anywhere we pleased to eat, and use any and all available bathrooms. So saying that the bathrooms were out of order when a black person asked to use them was the last recourse of the desperate racist. There was never an available bathroom except when a white person asked.

"What about that one?" I asked.

"Eww, no," both Daphne and Veronica said.

We drove a bit farther and came to a nice clean gas station. We pulled in and saw that the bathroom had a lock on the door. I went inside the gas station. There was a man behind a counter and two others sitting at one side of the room playing checkers. A dog was in the corner tied up and growling.

"Good afternoon, gentlemen," I said nicely. They glared at me, but no one responded. "I think we took a wrong turn. We're trying to get back to the highway. And we need to use the restroom." Still no reply. "Excuse me, may we have the key to the restroom?"

"The bathroom ain't working, gal. Now, git on outta here afore I sic my dog on you."

I nodded. "Do you know where I can find other accommodations?" I said contentiously.

"I'm fixin' to call the law. Now, you heard me. Git!"

I left.

"Hey," one of the men playing checkers came outside after me and yelled, "Hey, what y'all coloreds doing with a fancy car like that? Y'all steal it?"

"No," I said over my shoulder.

"You sassing me?"

The other man who had been playing checkers came

outside. "Dey stole dat dere car. Niggas always steal. Y'all know that. Dey's probably some white man and his family lying in a ditch on the side of da road wid his head bashed in. Call the sheriff."

"We didn't steal anything. It's my friend's car. We just needed directions and a bathroom."

The man behind the counter came out with the barking dog. He yelled, "I told y'alls to git outta here."

I hurried to the car and got inside. "Get in," I shouted. Daphne quickly slid into the back seat with me, and Daniel sat in the front passenger seat. "Come on, let's go."

"What's wrong? What happened?" he asked, looking at me.

"We have to get out of here. They're crazy," I said.

"Let me just . . ." Daniel began, but before he could finish his sentence Veronica drove off fast. The man released the dog, and it ran after the car until he whistled for it.

"What happened back there?" Daniel asked.

"He threatened to call the sheriff if we didn't leave."

"Assholes," Veronica yelled.

We drove farther down the road. "We should get back on the highway. I don't like passing through these little towns anymore."

"Yeah, me either."

"Fine. Let's find a restroom and get back on I-95."

Daphne opened the map, and we started checking the listings against the *Green Book.* We followed her directions and came across a dilapidated gas station. We saw men inside a small building. We didn't say anything to them, and they didn't say anything to us. We actually smelled the bathroom long before we saw it all the way in the back.

There was only one dilapidated bathroom for both men and women, with the door nearly off its hinges. The old sign on the door read COLOREDS, with a rancid-looking water fountain beside it that looked like it hadn't been used in decades.

"You go first. I'll wait out here," Daniel said.

We went inside and stopped in sheer horror.

It was putrid and smelled like vomit and shit. It looked like someone purposely had thrown feces all over the walls and bathroom stalls. There were flies, maggots, and cockroaches crawling everywhere. I screamed and started jumping as a rat scurried by my foot. We ran outside holding on to each other.

"What?" Daniel yelled. "What is it?"

"Oh my God." Daphne dry heaved.

"God had nothing to do with that filth," Veronica said.

"Wait here," Daniel said, moving to go inside.

"No, let's just go and get out of here," I said while grabbing a bunch of tissues from my purse. "Here, use these the best you can and don't sit down on the seat."

"Are you kidding? Hell no. I'm not going back in there," Veronica screamed as Daphne vomited.

I didn't blame her. She was right. We held it and hurried back to the car. The men were outside laughing. We got out of there quick.

"I can't believe something like that still exists," Veronica said.

"They probably keep it looking like that just to mess with people," I added.

"Well, it worked," Daphne said.

"I'm sure there's another bathroom. We can go back and I can . . ."

"No, we're not going back there." Veronica reached over and turned on the radio.

"This is such bullshit," I shouted.

"What?" Veronica asked.

"This. That. Everything. Even this bullshit Beatles song 'All You Need Is Love.' Bullshit, bullshit, bullshit!"

No one said anything after I raged. Then Daniel chuckled. We looked at him. He shrugged. "Well, at least it's not Motown." We all chuckled, even me.

"Shouldn't we ask for directions back to 95?" Daphne asked.

"No, let's just get out of here. Use the map. I'm sure we can find our way back to the highway," I said.

"How could anyone do something like that to a bathroom?" Veronica asked.

"Because they're sick and nasty. Think of the deranged mind that actually thought to do something like that. It's revolting."

"Oh my God, oh my God, oh my God," Daphne kept saying.

"I can't believe black people actually live like this," Veronica said.

"They don't have a choice. This is all some people know," Daniel said.

"No. I refuse to believe that. There's more—they have to see that—on television, on the radio, in magazines. There's so much more, but they need to want more," I said.

"It's hard to want more when someone has their foot on your throat. You heard those men in the gas station back there. Imagine living with that day in and day out, all your life, from childhood to the grave," Daniel said.

"I guess after a while you just become what they call you, a second-class citizen."

"Times are never going change," I said.

"They have to. The future has to be better," Veronica said. "There's no going back the other way. And I can't see this nastiness lasting into the next generation or the next century."

"Oh, it will last," I assured her. "Didn't you hear that little boy sitting at the counter with his mother? They learn to hate young and are rewarded for it. You heard those old men laughing. Now that little boy thinks what he said was okay, but it's not."

"So what then? Are we as a people supposed to voluntarily return to slavery just to appease a few bigots?" Veronica said.

"No, we're supposed to pray for them," Daphne said.

"No!" I shouted. "They think we're fine as we are, in most cases ignorant of the possibilities just as long as we know our place. When is it ever going to be over? I'll tell you when. When we stand up for ourselves. When we're not taken for granted with doors slammed in our faces. We have to keep going and stop being stuck in the fear mentality, afraid to take even one step forward."

"No one can erase centuries of physical and mental slavery," Daniel said.

"No, but we can realize that racial prejudice is taught, passed down from generation to generation like slaves once were. My fear is that in times to come all this will fade into lore like it never even happened, but it did, it does. And if we don't face our past, then we as a nation will surely repeat it.

"We need to fight for our rights. We helped build the country, and we're part of it. Our blood, more than any other race's, soaks these grounds. This is our country too," I said.

Daphne started applauding. Veronica whooped and cheered. Daniel just nodded his head in agreement. "I can see you're gonna follow your uncle into politics one day," he said.

"No way. I'm going to be a civil rights attorney."

"Yeah, you can be that, and just like your uncle you can go further and make a bigger difference in politics."

"No way," I said.

"Shit."

"What?"

"Shit!" Veronica said again as she looked in the rear-view mirror. "I bet those nasty asses at that first gas station called the cops on us. There's a patrol car driving fast right behind us." She turned off the radio.

"Shit."

"Pull over," I said. "Maybe he just wants to pass."

"No," Daphne said. "Remember what happened last time."

"Yeah, but we don't have a choice this time."

We pulled over, and the patrol car pulled up right behind us.

"Okay, just stay loose. We can get through this."

A uniformed officer, tall with thick muscles and a crew cut, got out the driver seat and banged on the hood of the patrol car. The passenger door instantly swung open, and a younger, heavier man in a uniform a size too small got out. He was burly and thick, and carrying his baton. They walked toward us slowly. The heavier cop moved to the passenger door, where I was sitting. The other cop, now noticeably much older, moved toward Veronica in the driver's seat.

"I wasn't doing anything wrong," Veronica said softly.

"I know," Daniel said.

"I don't think that really matters," I muttered. We didn't say anything else as they approached. We looked straight ahead and kept our hands visible.

"What y'all think y'all doing speeding down the road like dat? See, I'm the sheriff and dis is my deputy, and we don't like speeding in dis county."

"I'm sorry, sir," Veronica said. "We won't do it again."

The heavier man leaned down and got right near my face and snarled. "You bet your ass y'all ain't doing it again," he said with an exaggerated Southern drawl.

The older man said nothing as he walked around the front of the car, nodding and smiling. Then he kicked the front tires and continued to the back of the car. I glanced in the rearview mirror as he rubbed his hand along the convertible top and smiled. "You ain't from around here? Where you gals coming from?"

"New York," we all said at once.

"And you, boy, where you from?"

"I'm from Philadelphia."

"New York City and Philadelphia, huh. Big city coloreds. Well, New York City and Philadelphia, y'all is in Virginia now, and I don't like people coming to my town tearing up my roads. Y'all understand dat? Gimme all your IDs and your car registration."

We handed them over. Veronica gave him her car registration. "We're very sorry, sir," she said again, even though she had been careful not to exceed the speed limit. But he paid more attention to the car than to us. Then he read through the ID cards.

"Daniel, what's this last name? Never mind. That's you?"

"Yes, sir."

"Zelda Livingston."

"Yes, that's me," I said.

"Zelda, what kind of god-awful name is dat? Must be one of dem African jungle monkey names," he said, chuckling. The deputy stood beside me, laughing.

I saw the muscle in Daniel's jaw tighten. I hoped he wouldn't say anything to defend me and make matters worse.

"Veronica Keller Cook. Which one's dat? You?" He pointed to Daphne, sitting in the back seat.

"No, sir, that's me," Veronica said, raising her finger. "I'm—"

"Don't need no more out of you, just your names."

"And that would make you Daphne Brooks. Okay, Daphne Brooks, what's a white woman doing riding in the back seat of a colored's car?"

"We're going to college," she said.

"What college? Where at?"

I answered.

The sheriff looked at me harshly. "Am I talking to you? No, I don't think I am. I'm talking to this pretty young lady over yere. Now, you shut your colored mouth or I'm gonna shut it for you. You understand dat?"

I quickly nodded. I didn't want to get us in any more trouble.

"Now, what college and where?" he repeated.

"We attend Spelman College in Atlanta, Georgia, and Daniel goes to Morehouse College."

He looked at his deputy. "You heard of dem?" he asked.

"Yeah, fancy, uppity schools that accept everybody, don't matter what color you are."

"Figures."

"I bet that was the best you could do," he said directly to Daphne. She didn't reply. "Dat's a damn shame." He paused a few seconds to look at the car again. "All right, whose car is dis?"

"Mine," Veronica said.

He looked at her driver's license again. "Veronica Keller Cook. Dat you?" She nodded. "And dis your car?" She nodded again. "Where you git it? You steal dis car?"

"No, sir. My father gave it to me for a graduation gift."

"So y'alls one of dose rich coloreds from up there in New York City. Good, 'cause your fine is gonna be a whopper."

The deputy started laughing hard. Then the sheriff laughed, too, taking another look at the car. "This a convertible, right?"

"Yes," Veronica said.

"What year is dis?"

"It's a 1968."

"Nice, very nice. Looks like y'all gonna be needin' gas. Got a brand spanking new convertible, and y'all just driving it around like y'all own the world. Well, we'll see about dat."

The sheriff reached into the car and removed the key from the ignition. He tossed it in the air, caught it, then smiled. "A 1968 and do I likes that color red." He walked around the front of the car and motioned for his deputy to follow him. The deputy nodded the whole time they talked. They went back to the patrol car, continuing their discussion. The deputy came back to us, slapping the baton against his hand.

"Y'all get out of the car and get in the patrol car." We looked at him. "Come on, now. I don't have all day. Move."

We slowly got out and walked to the patrol car. The sheriff opened the back door. Daphne, Veronica, and I got in. Daniel hesitated. The sheriff hit him on the side of his head with his baton. Then punched him in the face. The deputy stepped in and pushed Daniel into the car. He stumbled and fell to the car floor. We grabbed and held him. Daniel turned around and glared.

"That there's resisting arrest, Mr. Daniel Johnson going to Morehouse College," the sheriff yelled. "Now, y'all wanna add assaulting a deputy of the law, go on, say something back to me."

He didn't.

Daniel sat next to me and I held his hand tightly. We sat there a few minutes while the lawmen reconvened. After a short while the deputy came over and got into the patrol car. "I'm gonna take you all into town. I don't want no trouble, you understand me?" he said loudly.

As soon as he drove off he looked up in the rearview mirror and wiped the sweat from his brow.

"You all walked into a heap of trouble." He shook his head. "He's gonna keep dat der pretty red car for hisself. After you all is locked up, the car will be his. Listen to me, and I'm a-get you all out of here. But you keep your mouths shut and get out of town, and don't stop till you all get to Georgia."

We were silent. We didn't know if we could trust him.

He drove us to a small town. The people there stared and pointed. He took us into the tiny sheriff's office and told us to sit down. We sat.

"I don't know how I'm gonna do it yet, but I swear, I'm a-gonna get y'all out of here 'fore sunset."

We stared at him blankly.

"Sir," I said, "do you have a bathroom we can use?"

He grinned deviously. "No, but use dis one. It's the sheriff's personal bathroom. He don't let nobody use it 'sep him." He stood and opened a door. "But hurry up 'fore he gits back, and leave it the way you found it."

It was neat and clean with soap at the sink and towels. In the waiting area, the deputy gave Daniel two aspirin and some water.

A short while later, we saw Veronica's red car pull up in front of the sheriff's office. The top was down. The cop was driving it and smiling like it was his already. He got out of the car and spoke to a man passing by. They admired the car together before the sheriff came inside.

He sat on the edge of a desk and looked at us. He said our names again. "I don't have to tell y'all that y'alls coloreds are in a world of trouble. Speeding, half drunk, fighting, resisting arrest, acting all wild like y'all ain't got no couth. Now, I'll try and git y'all a break 'n' go easy." He pulled our IDs from his shirt pocket along with Veronica's driver's registration and a notebook. The deputy grabbed a pack of Lucky Strike cigarettes off the desk and handed them to him while he took our stuff out of the sheriff's hand, examining our identification.

The sheriff lit a cigarette and continued talking about how we were breaking the law and the judge we would have to stand before in the morning. "Y'all got other peoples coming down yere, friends, family, or such?"

"No, sir, we're just driving to school," Daniel said.

"Yeah, to some fancy colored colleges." He took the car keys out of his pocket and tossed them to the deputy. "Y'all sure y'all ain't come down yere like dem voter registration people come down yere a while back fittin' ta stir up trouble?"

"No, sir. We're not."

"'Cause we ain't 'bout no trouble with our coloreds down yere. Dey some good quiet folks. And we gonna keeps it dat

way. Y'all understand me? 'N' dey can cook too." He smiled
and laughed with a raspy cough. "See, I ain't prejudice. I
know some of dem colored folks. Ain't that right, Jimmy?"

"Sure is right."

"Now, you coloreds mind your manners and y'all be
out of yere real soon. There's a bus leaving town in 'bout
half hour."

"A bus?" Daniel said.

"Dat's right. See, I gotta keep dat dere car outside to
do a thorough check on it. Make sure it ain't got no fines
and warrants and such. Don't worry. I'll take good care of
it, like it's my very own." He paused and looked at us hard.
"Now, y'all ain't got no problem wit dat, do you?"

"No, sir," we said all together.

The sheriff faked a smile. "All right den." He looked at the
deputy and nodded. "You call dis in and make sure dat car
ain't stolen. I don't want no trouble wit dat car, ya hear me?"

"Will do," the deputy said. "Sheriff, I'm fixing to get me
a Coca-Cola from Mr. Barker's place. You want a chicken
dinner?"

"Yeah, dat'd be real good. 'N' a large ginger ale. My
guts are killing me," he said, rubbing his stomach.

"Yes, sir. Think I'll pick a platter up for me too. I'll
be right back. I'll lock the front door. Dey ain't going nowhere, are you?" the deputy asked gruffly.

"No, sir," we said.

"Good." The sheriff walked to the bathroom. "I gotta
pee like a racehorse. Hope y'alls coloreds ain't gotta pee or
nothin' 'cause y'all is shit out a luck." He motioned to the

bathroom we had just used and smiled smugly. "That dere's mine, a white man's bathroom. Don't nobody be using it 'sep me, but we got us a tree out back if you gotta go."

The deputy was laughing at the sheriff's joke like it was the funniest thing in the world. We looked at each other 'cause we wanted to laugh too.

As soon as the sheriff closed the bathroom door, the deputy turned his attention to us. "Drive down the street to the gas station, den make a right and keep going until y'all see a big red silo. Make a left after the silo. A mile from dere, y'all see a sign to head on back to I-95."

"Thank you," we whispered.

"Y'all want a slice of apple pie, Sheriff?" he called out loudly.

"Yeah," the sheriff grunted noisily.

The deputy pushed the IDs and car keys close to us. "When I leave, go."

We kept an eye on the bathroom door. As soon as the deputy left and closed the front door we stood up. Daphne didn't. "What are you doing? Get up," I whispered.

She shook her head, panicked. "We can't. What if he's lying? Trying to trick us?"

"What if he's not?"

"We're gonna get caught," Daphne said fearfully.

Veronica tiptoed to the front door and peeked out. "Daphne, stop it. Come on," she said in loud whisper.

Daniel moved to the closed bathroom door. "You all go. I'll stop him from following you."

"What if he comes out and shoots you?" I asked.

"Then at least you'll be safe. Now go. I'll hold him back," Daniel said, looking right at me. "Go."

"No," Veronica and I whispered. We looked at Daphne.

"We all go together," I said.

Then we heard water running in the sink. Daphne jumped up. We hurried out the door. Outside, there were people walking around on the sidewalks. We got in the car and Veronica started the engine.

"Drive like nothing's wrong," I whispered to her.

She nodded with trepidation as we followed the directions the deputy had given us. Once I saw the I-95 sign, I felt relief. The sun faded as we put the sundown town in our rearview mirror.

"I hope the deputy is gonna be okay," Daphne said. "I know that sheriff is going to be mad as hell when he sees us and the car gone."

"Well, too bad for that stupid, flatulent-ass sheriff. This is my car."

I repeatedly turned around, and Veronica kept glancing in the rearview mirror. My heart was still beating hard as we turned onto the highway. Cars sped by us.

"Hey, slow down, why don't ya." Daniel chuckled.

Veronica, already driving slowly, took him seriously and slightly lifted her foot off the pedal. She pointed to the dashboard. "Looks like the sheriff put gas in his *new* car."

I smirked.

13

ONCE IN NORTH CAROLINA, WE STAYED ON THE MAIN highway as long as we could. Eventually, we had to get off Interstate 95 to cross over to Interstate 85, the road that would take us directly into Atlanta, by way of Raleigh and Charlotte.

The summer sky was dimming and the beautiful sunset had hurried its pace into the darkness of twilight. The trees on the horizon stood against a backdrop ablaze with stunning reds, yellows, and purples. Individual trees began to turn into stoic columns en masse.

"Hey, we're almost there," Daphne said with optimism as she turned to look at me. She put on a smile that didn't quite reach her eyes. "I don't know if I can take any more craziness."

"Me either," I said, then looked at Daniel. He had his head back, and his eyes were closed. There was a bruised lump on the side of his head, and his eye and cheek were swollen.

Veronica didn't say anything. She drove slowly with deliberate ease. A driver in a car behind us blew his horn, swerved around us, then yelled at us to get off the road. Unaffected, Veronica continued to drive at her same slow pace. She yawned and sat up closer to the steering wheel. She was staring intently at the road ahead as if she would miss something at any minute.

"Veronica, are you okay?" I asked.

"Oh wow, would you look at that sky," Daphne interrupted. "Isn't it just glorious?"

"Yeah, it is," I said but focused on Veronica. "Veronica, are you okay?" I asked once more.

Veronica shook her head. "No. My heart is racing and I feel nervous. I don't know what's wrong." She began to pant and put her hand to her chest.

"We're okay," Daphne said. "There's no one behind us."

"No. That's not it. It's getting dark out here, and I've never driven at night before. I can barely see the road right now."

"I have money," Daphne said. "We can stop at a motel."

"No," Veronica said. "I don't want to stop anymore. I just want to be at Spelman."

"Look, there's a rest stop. Let's just take a break."

We pulled over at the rest stop. The small parking lot was half full with a couple of travel trailers, a truck, and a few other cars. We went to the anyone-can-go bath-room. We refreshed ourselves with four Coca-Colas from a vending machine. As we sauntered back to the car, we saw other drivers asleep in their vehicles. When we got back to ours, we put the top up, munched on some Bugles, and rested.

A loud knock on the window startled us out of our slumber. A blinding bright light flashed in our eyes.

"Roll the window down," said the state trooper. With apprehension Veronica did as told.

"What's going on in there?" he asked. We stared blankly. "This is a rest stop, not a motel. You need to get moving or I'll take you in for vagrancy."

Barely awake, we hurriedly got ourselves together as the trooper stood there and waited for us to drive off. Driving out of the lot, we could see others in their cars still asleep. Needless to say, none of them were black.

It was the early morning hours and pitch-black outside. No moon, no stars, just complete blackness.

Even with her glasses on, Daphne, now behind the wheel, had trouble staying in her lane. "Have you ever driven at night before?" I asked.

"No. Have you?"

"Yes, I drove my aunt from Washington to Philadel-phia last year. Her mother was rushed to the hospital and we had to get there fast. Uncle Arthur was out of town and she was too nervous to drive, so I drove us."

"You drove to Philadelphia from DC at night," Daphne said.

"Yes. On the way, she told me that before she met my uncle she loved to drive at night. Her father would drive to Howard and pick her up, and she'd drive them back home to Philadelphia. Then one night some men drove them off the road and left them pinned beneath the flipped car. They were trapped for hours. She watched her father die that night. She never drove at night again."

"That's horrible."

"I drove us to Philadelphia and got us there safely. So why don't I drive and you take over in a few hours, okay?"

"No, let me," Daniel said. "I'll drive."

"What about your swollen eye?" I asked.

"I can see fine. Let me drive."

We pulled over and switched seats. "Do you want the top down?" he asked.

"Nah, leave it be," I said, picking up *Soul on Ice*, the book Daniel had brought.

"The memoirs of Eldridge Cleaver. You know it was written while he was in Folsom State Prison. Have you read it?"

"Yes."

"What did you think of it?" he asked.

"I thought it was profound and troubling."

"I get profound, but troubling, how so?"

"The confessions of serial rape bothered me."

"Ah, but he is repentant," he defended.

"Yes, but that doesn't change the scar those women feel every day. Just saying, 'Oops, I was wrong, I'm sorry,' doesn't change the fact that it happened, and the women have to deal with it over and over again every day of their lives," I said, thinking about Daphne and her pain. We went silent for a few moments. "What did you think of it?" I asked.

"It's a compelling observation on the vibe and struggle of black Americans today. I get what you're saying, but understand that this is also a confession of redemption. I think the essays will serve a purpose in future years."

"As a cautionary reminder?" I asked.

"Perhaps."

"Do you think change will ever come?" I asked.

"I don't know. It's easier for people to close their eyes and ignore what's going on right in front of them than to deal with injustice. That's the simple truth."

"Change is coming, slowly, microscopically slowly, but it is coming. It has to."

"I envy you," he said softly.

"Me? Why?" I asked him.

"You know your future. I used to know mine too. I always wanted to be an engineer, to create and build things. Now I just don't know anymore."

"I saw the military ID card in your wallet."

"I keep it to remember the day."

"What day?"

"My best friend, Calvin, and I enlisted together. He planned to become an engineer like me. We were going to open a business together. He was killed over there."

"I'm sorry. He sounds like Veronica's cousin, Anthony. He was killed in Vietnam, too."

"We'd been friends all our lives. I watched him get blown to pieces and I couldn't save him."

"That war is not our war. We don't know those people over there. Why should we want to kill them? Because some men in Washington told us to, even when their sons are exempt from ever going? It's wrong and it's unfair," I said.

"My father once told me that integrity matters. He was an army officer, and he was over there. He was the most courageous man I know."

"What's it like over there?" I asked.

"Raw. Dirty. Loud. Bloody. Horrifying. I watched friends die all around me—blown up or shredded by bullets. One minute we'd be joking around, the next they'd be lying at my feet with no limbs, moaning, crying, or just mangled beyond recognition. It's nine thousand miles away, but it's still a nightmare that I relive every day of my life. Calvin was killed right in front of me. I'll never get that out of my head."

We fell silent. There were very few cars on the road. The darkness of trees and sky were interrupted sporadically by the occasional billboard and town signage, declaring its prominence and avowing "the best of the best" of whatever the town grew. But mostly we passed large crop fields that smelled of manure and rural areas with open expanses of darkened farmland.

"Are you asleep?"

"No," I said, "I'm awake."

"I'm glad we have this time together."

"Me too."

"It's kind of peaceful and unnerving at the same time." I shivered.

Daniel moved his arm around my shoulder and hugged me close. I laid my head on his chest. This was a closeness I hadn't felt in a long time. I liked it. And the realization that I liked him was even more comforting.

Near Greenville I saw a billboard for South Carolina State University. I remembered the name. Aunt Dorothy had told me about the tragedy that happened there. It was called the Orangeburg Massacre. In February, just a few months ago, at a campus bowling alley three college protesters were killed by state troopers. That had terrified me and still did.

We had less than thirty miles before we would reach the Georgia state border when I noticed some smoke coming from under the hood of the car.

"The car's smoking," I said.

Veronica woke up. "What? What happened?" she said anxiously. "Look at the signpost. We're almost there."

"Smells like it's overheated," Daniel said and pulled over beside a lit billboard.

We all got out and Daniel popped the hood. As soon as he did, steam came pouring from the radiator.

"What's that awful odor?" Daphne asked.

"The radiator fluid is leaking and it's burning."

"Can you fix it?" I asked.

"Yes, but the engine is too hot right now and I don't have the tools."

"Can we make it to Georgia?" Daphne asked.

"I think so," Daniel said.

"Can we make it to Atlanta?" Veronica asked.

Daniel shook his head. "I doubt it. Get in."

"We're never going to make it to Atlanta with the car smoking like this."

"Where's the *Green Book*?"

Veronica quickly found Mr. Sam's Auto Garage just a few miles into Georgia.

"Can we make it there?"

Daniel nodded. "Yeah, but we'll need to keep the engine cooled down along the way."

I looked at the dark road ahead. We were so close and still so far.

14

IT TOOK SOME TIME, BUT WE HAD FINALLY ARRIVED IN Georgia. As soon as we got out of the car, a black man in his mid-thirties, tall, thin as a rail, and with a head full of overprocessed hair and nappy roots strolled over to us. He smiled, showing two gold teeth. "Morning, all," he said pleasantly, his beady eyes shifting between staring at Daphne and admiring the car. Back and forth, back and forth. "Nice car. Fill her up?"

"No, there's something wrong under the hood."

He looked at the car again and nodded. "Don't worry. We can help y'all out. Hey, Gunner, call Mr. Sam," he yelled. "My name's Winston," he said, smiling at Daphne.

An older black man with the same slicked-back hair, but in black and gray, came out. He was heavy and stout and ambled like it was a chore for him to cross the small lot. He was wearing blue overalls and a dirty white cap. He smiled, oddly displaying perfect white teeth. "Morning, folks. The name's Mr. Sam," he greeted us. He looked at us good. "You okay?" he asked. We nodded. "You okay, son?"

"We ran into some trouble a ways back, but we're fine now, sir. Can I trouble you for an aspirin?" Daniel asked.

"Yeah, sure. Gunner," he called out over his shoulder. He nodded, looking at the car. "Wee-oo, whatcha got yere? That's a mighty fine car." He wiped his hands on a rag, then stuffed it in his back pocket. "Looks like a 1966 Ford Fairlane."

"It's a '68 Fairlane," Veronica corrected him.

"Yep, that's what I said. Guess she giving you trouble?"

He reached under and popped the hood up. Thick white smoke bellowed out with a foul burning odor of antifreeze fluid loss. "Yep, smells like she's overheated." He shook his head. "You gotta take care of this lady. Treat her right. She won't ask for much. But you gots ta give her what she needs. Else she'll kick you to the curb quick, and in a hurry."

I half expected him to kiss the caps and caress the wires. But he just shook his head and sucked his teeth loudly.

"Yep, I can see right off you needs a new radiator hose. But I need to get up under her to make sure you ain't cracked the radiator proper. Ya see it's made out of rubber. It ain't all that uncommon for dem to crack or leak, 'specially if you been driving steady for a while. Where you coming from?"

"New York."

"Yep, that'll do it. So what happened is the engine didn't get the coolant it needed and overheated. Your engine 'bout to burn itself out. Good thing you came in when you did. It's probably been happening since you left the North. And any longer and it would have damaged the engine, and den you got yourself some real big mess."

"Can you fix it?" Veronica asked.

"'Spect I could. Don't think I have that hose yere, but I can fetch one from the big shop. I gotta get an order from dere later today. So I'll just add the hose to the order."

"Where is y'all headed?" the younger mechanic asked.

"To Atlanta," Daniel said. "To college."

"Well now, good for you. It does my heart good to see our young men and women getting dey education and making a way for theyselves. Makes us rightly proud."

"My girlfriend—well, I guess she's my fiancée now— she goes to Spelman," Winston chimed in. "Y'all might know her. Her name's Mazie."

"Mazie Campbell?" Veronica asked, stunned.

"Yeah, dat's her. I figured y'all did. Everyone does."

"She's our soror," Daphne added.

"She's your what?" Winston asked.

"She's one of our sorority sisters," I clarified.

"So I bet y'all look up to her, am I right? Yeah, she's something else, my Mazie. She's a beauty queen and just as pretty as a movie star."

"Well now, looks like I got a handle on dis. You all just leave it to me. I'll git you back on to road in no time." Mr. Sam closed the hood, interrupting our conversation.

"Thank you," Veronica said. "About the cost, how much—"

"We'll worry about that later," Mr. Sam said.

"How long do you think it'll take?" Daniel asked him.

He took a deep breath and blew it out, shaking his head. He took his cap off and then scratched his head. "First off, I gotta really look under dat hood and make sure dat's all that's wrong wid her. If'n it's just the hose, I'll get you back on the road in a few hours, give or take. Otherwise, we'll just have to see. I'll let you know what I find."

Veronica gave him the car key.

"If you all are hungry, there's a nice little place round the corner and down the end of the block." He pointed. "Come with me, young man. I'll get you that aspirin."

"I'll meet you there," Daniel said and followed Mr. Sam into the garage.

We headed in the direction Mr. Sam had pointed.

"Well, I hope the food is decent in here. I'm starved."

We walked into Hattie's Diner. The small place was bustling. It was basic and homey with the usual ceiling fans and a speckled linoleum floor. It was clean and airy with windows at each table along the perimeter. There was a long counter with stools across the front. People were sitting and eating, both blacks and whites.

Just then two tall men with huge Afros came in and stood behind us. They were talking and laughing as one of them slipped coins into a cigarette machine. A woman behind the counter looked over and yelled, "Jeffrey, Earl, you can go on have a seat at the counter." Then she looked at us. "You can have a seat anywheres."

We found a table in the back and sat down.

A waitress, older, with big chunky rubber-soled shoes, came over with three glasses of water and silverware. She had black cat-eye glasses hanging from a chain around her neck, and a black hair net covered her big bouffant. Her uniform was tan with a name tag that read LOUISE.

"Good Lawd, we are so busy this morning, I ain't had a moment to myself," she complained. "You girls are in for a treat. We have the creamiest grits in the county and the best steak and eggs. It's the morning special. Coffee?" she asked.

"Yes, please, and there's four of us," I said.

"Veronica, I have money," I said. She looked at me questioningly. "For the car, I mean. I'll call my uncle and have him wire enough to have the car fixed."

Before Veronica could reply, the waitress returned with four cups of coffee. "You know what you want?" she asked. We ordered the morning special, steak, eggs, pancakes, and sausages with a side of famous grits. We ordered the same for Daniel.

"I can help too," Daphne added, turning to Veronica.

"No, that's okay, but thanks. My father is going to pay for it," Veronica said, smiling, "as soon as I tell him I took the car."

"He doesn't know you have it?" I asked, stunned.

"Not exactly," she said.

"Veronica Cook, are you insane?" I lowered my voice to a whisper. "This means the car is technically stolen."

"It's not stolen. It's my car. They just don't know I have it yet," she said. "It's my graduation gift and I've been driving it all summer. They didn't want me driving it out of the city alone. But I have you guys, so I'm not alone."

"What about your aunt and uncle—they know?"

"That's right. Surely by now they must have told your parents you have the car," Daphne chimed in.

"So what if they have? We're in Georgia. My parents are not going to come and get it, are they? Besides, I have leverage."

"Leverage," I repeat. "What kind of leverage?"

"The best in the world. My father needs me right now."

I shook my head. This was 100 percent pure Veronica— scheming. With the innocent smile of an angel, she could promise you the world was flat, the sky was green, and the earth circled the moon. And you'd believe every word she said.

"What do you mean he needs you?" I asked her finally.

She chuckled. "My father is a financial manipulator. He's a master puppeteer who uses aggressive dominance and intimating tactics to get what he wants. He's very good at it, and as his daughter, I've learned a thing or two from him."

"Like what?"

"Like the reason they set up the engagement so quickly is so my father can borrow money for his business from my fiancé's father, who just so happens to own a bank and is one of the richest black men in the country."

"So what does your fiancé's father get out of it?"

"Pedigree."

"What?"

"He's going along with it because he grew up poor and my family's linage is long and distinguished. Think about the connections he'll make in building the business being associated with my family."

I shook my head and sipped my coffee. Given everything that was going on in the world, her issues did not move me.

Daniel walked in and sat down just as the waitress came with our meals. Daphne said grace and we started eating.

"So, Daniel, what do you think about marriage?" Veronica asked, grinning.

Daniel looked directly at me even though I hadn't asked the question. "If I'm blessed to find that one special woman who fulfills all my needs and the thought of her not being in my life is physically painful, then, yes, I'd marry her in a heartbeat."

In all sincerity, his eyes never wavered from mine. Then he smiled at me and my insides turned to mush. I eased my coffee cup to my lips and took another sip.

After a long, leisurely breakfast we headed back to the garage. The earlier, brilliant sunshine had given way to clouds. We approached Mr. Sam, who had the hood up working on another car and was studying a part that looked like the inside of a television set. "I ordered your part. But I 'spect it'll get here mayhaps tomorrow morning."

"Tomorrow morning," I repeated.

"So we're stuck here for the night."

"Best I can do. Just don't have dat part," Mr. Sam said. "I could rig you up something to get you to Atlanta and you could get her all fixed up there."

"Good idea," Daniel said. "Use a larger hose, cut it down, and clamp it."

"No. It's my car and I want the right part."

"We need to find someplace to sleep tonight."

"Phone book's in the office," Mr. Sam said.

"Thank you for your help, sir," Daniel responded.

15

I COULDN'T BELIEVE MY EYES WHEN I SAW MAZIE CAMP-bell sitting in the small office at the garage, powdering her nose as she looked at herself in a compact mirror. Once a local beauty queen, Mazie was pretty with a clear honey-toned complexion and a bright, dazzling smile. She had large brown doe-like eyes with long, curly eyelashes and perfectly pursed lips, making it look like she was constantly pouting. She wasn't slim and she wasn't heavy. She was somewhere in the middle, shapely with narrow hips and long legs.

Mazie had never been my cup of tea. She adored Veronica and Daphne and had tried to put a wedge between us on more than one occasion. I once overheard her question Veronica and Daphne as to why they allowed me to hang around with them. They told her that I didn't hang around with them, but rather, they hung around with me. After that, she did just about everything to become part of our little group—but she never quite fitted in.

"Ugh, Mazie," I groaned as we headed to the office.

"Oh, hush, Zelda. Mazie's fun," Veronica said.

"She's a flirt who lives for attention," I said. "She's spoiled, and she's naïve if she thinks that kind of attention from men is okay. It's not. Look at the trouble she caused for Professor Jacobs and his family. She deliberately and openly flirted with the man, and nearly ruined his reputation and career, not to mention his family."

"She didn't mean anything by it. It was just harmless flirting. Nothing bad happened. Not really," Veronica said.

"I heard Professor Jacobs got a better job and his wife is expecting another baby," Daphne said.

"That's right," Veronica concurred. "See? All's well."

"I think she's just insecure. She wants people to like her, that's all," Daphne said.

A year behind us at Spelman, Mazie spent most of her time tumbling from one calamity to another, all brought on by her flirty, thoughtless behavior. But someone was always there to get her out of her predicaments. Veronica adored her, and at school they would get into all kinds of trouble.

Mazie was dressed in a floral crop top and in what must have been the shortest shorts on record. She hurried over as soon as Veronica and Daphne caught her attention. As usual, she made a spectacle of herself adjusting her crop top over her large breasts.

"I can't believe y'all are here," she squealed. "I'm so happy to see you. When did y'all git here? Is anyone else here with you? Your timing couldn't be any more perfect. Today is my birthday, and y'all got to come to my party, later tonight at the barn! It's gonna be a blast."

No one had a chance to say anything, let alone answer the questions she kept shooting out.

Abruptly, she grabbed and hugged Daphne like a hungry bear. "It's so good to see you. I've missed you so much." She then did the same with Veronica.

A second later she hugged me—and my skin began to crawl. I could not get out of her embrace quickly enough. Daniel, standing behind me, placed his hand on the small of my back. Mazie noticed the gesture. She smiled like he was a plate of biscuits and gravy. "Well now, who is dis?" she asked in an exaggerated Southern drawl.

"Daniel Johnson," he said firmly.

"Daniel's a Morehouse man escorting us to Atlanta," Daphne said.

Mazie introduced herself breathlessly, grinning. "What happened to your face? Are you a bad boy rebel like James Dean?"

I noticed Winston coming toward us, but he was stalled by one of the customers.

"This is so exciting. I can't believe y'all are really here," she declared, gliding her arm around Daniel. He casually took a step away.

"We stopped because the car started smoking," Daphne said.

Mazie turned around and saw Winston. He waved. She waved back. "Oh, you don't have to worry about your car. Mr. Sam and my fiancé, Winston, will have it as good as new in no time.

"Is that it? I love it. Red is my favorite color. I want Winston to buy me a red car too. He's going to be a big star, you know. And he promised to buy me a mink coat, a Cadillac, and tons of jewelry. You see, he's much more than just a grease monkey. He's in a singing group too. They perform all around the county. They're real popular. And there's a record producer working with dem to make an album. Can you believe it?"

"Wow, that's exciting," Daphne gushed.

"It is. He's going to be a big star, just like Sam Cooke. I just know it. You wait and see. By next year this time we'll be traveling all over the world and attending all kinds of concerts and movie premieres and such." She turned and waved again. He waved back. "So y'all coming to my birthday party tonight, right?"

"Of course we are," Veronica said, "but first we have to find a place to stay."

"My mamma owns a guesthouse just outside of town. Since the party is going to be late, y'all can stay with us. It'll be absolutely, positively perfect," she rejoiced. "Don't worry about the bags. I'll have Winston put them in his car. He'll drive us to my mamma's place. Winston!" Mazie called out. He came over immediately, wiping his hands on a rag.

We piled into Winston's old tan-and-black four-door Studebaker Lark station wagon.

Winston took the scenic route, giving us a tour of the town, with Mazie as our nonstop-talking host.

I was surprised the town was as big as it was. The main street was lined with all kinds of shops, stores, and restaurants. There was a laundromat and liquor store right in between a barbershop and beauty shop. A funeral home was on the corner, another restaurant on the opposite corner, and a bakery and a butcher shop.

We passed a huge lumber company nearby along with a large factory making train and airplane parts. Mazie explained that most of the locals worked in the two plants. The others had worked at a textile factory until it had closed a couple of years earlier.

Winston spent way too much time keeping his eyes on Mazie and not enough on the road. He swerved several times as we reached the more upscale residential section of town. The houses, perfectly symmetrical and overly extravagant, reminded me of the photos I'd seen of slave plantations. One in particular, with looming pillars, large windows, and a full balcony along the front and sides, caught my attention. It had a painted white-brick front, black shutters, a sloping front path, and a Confederate flag.

The whole area consisted mainly of Southern antebellum architecture—big, grand, and glorious. Even the smaller homes appeared stately. I saw a woman in a floral dress and big straw hat standing on the front porch of one of the homes, her eyes tracking us as we drove by.

"So how did you two meet?" Daphne asked Mazie.

Mazie cooed adoringly and scooted closer to Winston. He threw his arm around her shoulders. "It was love at first sight. I was at the barn one Tuesday night with a friend, and Winston and his group was performing. He was amazing."

"I couldn't take my eyes off her the whole time. She was so beautiful," he said, winking at her. "Still is."

"Now, don't y'all get jealous back there," Mazie teased. "Dis one's all mine."

"When are you two getting married?" I asked.

"Soon," he replied, only half smiling this time.

"He won't set a date," Mazie said, frowning. "But don't worry. Soon as his wife agrees to a divorce y'all be my bridesmaids."

Winston didn't say anything. Mazie turned and winked at Daniel, but he acted like he didn't see her.

We turned the corner at a furniture store. Farther down the street there was a car lot, a sheriff's office, and the town hall, with a small white steepled church at the end of the block.

After we crossed over train tracks, everything drastically changed. It was like we had driven into another world. The streets, if you could call them that, were mainly dusty dirt roads. The houses were closer to the road, no expansive lawns out front. There were a lot more people sitting around, under the shade of trees and on crates along the roadside, their expressions listless. Grass was either near dead or overgrown, cars were up on blocks, and the homes looked unkempt and disregarded. The neighborhood appeared to outdo the poorest neighborhoods in DC and Harlem.

"It's called Lila Mae Butler's Guesthouse," Mazie said, breaking the silence in the car.

"Who's Lila Mae Butler?" Daphne asked.

"Lila Mae was my grandma. She was a bit crazy and senile 'fore she died. My mamma, she's a widow, she took over running the guesthouse when grandma got real bad off. People come dere all the time and stay. Mr. Jackson— y'all meet him later—never left. He's old and has lived dere almost since the beginning."

"Your mamma ain't no widow. Your daddy left to get a pack of cigarettes when you was five years old. He ain't never come back," Winston said, then chuckled.

Mazie stopped and looked at Winston. "My daddy died and my mamma's a widow," she stated insistently. Then she turned back to us. "The house has been in my family for ages. My grandma told me that when she was twenty, her lover"— she paused and whispered—"he was white. He bought the land and built it for her. It was a big-deal scandal back then. Anyway, he died and she got to keep the house."

"Do the people here have jobs?" I asked, looking around.

She sighed after I interrupted. "Most got laid off when the textile factory closed down a few years back."

"Did they only employ blacks?" Daniel asked.

She giggled. "Course not."

"So why didn't they get jobs in the lumberyard or the factory as I assume others did?"

"Dere aren't enough jobs to go round to everybody."

"So the blacks were sacrificed so others could work?"

"Sacrificed? Damn, Zelda, you make it sound like dey was put on some Mayan altar and beheaded," Mazie said.

"What Zelda is saying is that it seems unfair that just the black people around here appear to be unemployed," Daniel clarified.

"Daniel," Mazie huffed, obviously annoyed by his comment, "don't tell me you're one of those too."

"One of what?" Veronica asked.

"If you're asking if I'm one of those concerned about my people, then, yes, I am," Daniel said, looking at me. I smiled and nodded my appreciation. "You're educated. I'm surprised you aren't concerned."

"I am, I am, but . . ." Mazie said, stammering and huffing as she most often did when she was frustrated. "I swear, Zelda, look what you did. You got Daniel on your side. You always touting that Black Power stuff. Does it ever occur to you dat dey like how dey live? Right, Veronica?" she said, soliciting support.

"How can anybody like this?" Veronica asked.

"'Cause I know dem and y'all don't, and dis is what dey like," she said, looking directly at me.

"Three years of college and you consider that a well-reasoned argument?" I said calmly.

"You don't live here, so you don't know. Everybody round here is just fine, so just cool it. Northerners always think they got it better than us in the South. But it ain't no difference, except y'all have concrete under your feet and we have red clay. Our racism is out in the open, where y'all's is niced up."

After that tirade, no one said a word.

A few minutes later Winston pulled into a narrow street and parked in front of a big corner house.

"We're here." Mazie beamed. "Isn't it beautiful?"

The neighborhood was nice and quiet. The house was big, three stories and stately. The bricks were painted bright yellow, set off by white shutters, and the landscape was pristine. It looked like it should be on the other side of town. Winston and Daniel got our bags out of the trunk.

A woman was standing in the doorway smiling. "Hey, baby," she said, opening the screen door wider and stepping out onto the porch. "And who do you got yere?" she asked with a Southern twang much more pronounced than Mazie's slight drawl.

"Hi, Mamma. These are some of my friends from Spelman. They're staying with us."

My jaw dropped. *Mamma?* She must have had Mazie when she was four years old. She didn't look her age at all. She looked just like Mazie, with the same twinkle in her eyes and deep dimples in each cheek.

She was slightly more petite and shapely, had dark brown hair pulled into a tight bun at the nape of her neck, and was wearing dark blue shoes and a modest floral-print short-sleeved dress with a white lace collar. With just lipstick, her skin was positively, perfectly flawless.

Mazie hurried up the steps to hold the screen door open for us to enter as her mother greeted us individually.

"Veronica, so nice to finally meet you. Mazie just goes on and on and on about you and y'all's family. I feel like

I already know you. And y'all must be Daphne. Why, you are just as beautiful as my Mazie said you are."

Then her showy Southern smile faded slightly as she turned to me. "And you must be Zelda, the revolutionary," she said. "My goodness, what on earth have we got yere?" she asked, staring up at my hair.

"It's called an Afro," I informed her politely.

"Yes, of course. But it's so big and . . . uh . . . uh . . . big."

Instead of taking offense, I gave her my brightest smile. "Yes, it is, thank you."

"And powerful," Daniel added.

Mazie rushed over to him and intertwined her arm with his. "Mamma, this Daniel. He goes to Morehouse College," she announced with a familiarity I didn't appreciate. Daniel winked at me and I felt a little better.

"Well now, a college man. Dere ain't a lot of college men round yere. I always say that Mazie needs to get herself a college man. And you are handsome to boot. Are you married or engaged?" she asked boldly.

"Neither."

"You have a girlfriend?" Mazie asked.

He glanced at me and smiled. I looked away. "Where can I put the suitcases, ma'am?" he asked.

"Oh my goodness, dey must be heavy. Y'all can put the girls' cases at the top of the stairs. Daniel, take your bags all the way up to the third floor. That's where the young men stay."

Daniel and Winston took the bags into the house, then Winston hurried back to the car and left after giving Mazie a quick kiss goodbye.

We walked into the foyer, and there was an old-fashioned French-style writing desk with an elegantly scripted WELCOME sign sitting on top. The parlor was small and cozy with a big black wood stove in the corner, a sofa, two wing chairs, and a marble-top coffee table with neatly stacked copies of newspapers and magazines.

"How long will y'all be with us?"

"They're just staying the night, for my birthday party."

Mazie led us up a narrow staircase to a wide hallway. Before directing us to our accommodations, she showed us a second staircase down the hall that led to the outside.

She put her finger to her lips and whispered, "I used to sneak boys up to my bedroom all the time. They come up the fire escape, in through the window down at the end of the hallway." She giggled. "My mother doesn't know."

We went inside our room and looked around. It was large and old-fashioned but nice. There were four single beds in the room. I collapsed onto one of the beds. It felt like heaven. Veronica and Daphne sat down, talking as I lay there, and Mazie went into town with her mother.

16

I TOOK A NAP AND WOKE UP A FEW HOURS LATER TO THE smell of a cake baking in an oven. It smelled amazing. I put on my shoes and went downstairs. Veronica was headed to the front door. "Where's Daphne?" I asked.

"Talking to Mazie and her mother. I'm going outside. I need some air."

I joined her. As we passed through the screen door, we found an old man sitting on the front porch outside with a pipe in his hand and a newspaper in his lap. He looked up wearing thick glasses, like the bottoms of soda bottles. He smiled at us, greeting us with a wide, toothy grin. "Good day, young ladies," he said.

We nodded and smiled. "Good afternoon, sir."

He was wearing a dark suit and a freshly pressed white dress shirt with a big blue bow tie and suspenders pulling at his pants. His shoes were shiny, like he had just polished them.

"Ya smells dat? Yes sirree, 'spect that cake will be ready shortly. Smells good, don't it? I'm partial to a slice of pecan cake or cornbread cake myself, but that lemon pound cake in the oven got my mouth a-watering. Been all over these United States, but I ain't never had no lemon pound cake like baked right yere in this house. I lived in Alabama in the thirties, a place called Belle's. Dat's when I drank whiskey and such. I thought she had the best tasting cakes ever, but I was wrong. Must be the water round here." He shook his head, seeming to ponder the remark. "Yep, must be the water."

He took a deep puff from his pipe and blew it out slowly. He tapped the ash and embers into an ashtray, then bit down on the well-worn stem. He reminded me of my grandfather, with his deep, raspy, preacher voice and pipe smoking.

He motioned with the pipe. "Cherry tobacco, the only kind I smoke. Picked it up from my paps. Though his pipe wasn't fancy lak dis one. It was whittled by his own hands out of a real corncob. He chuckled. "Pocketknife, a tree branch, and an old dried-up corncob. I watched him make it. The name's Jonathan Jackson."

After we introduced ourselves as Spelman students, he smiled and chuckled heartily. "Well now, I'll be a monkey's uncle. Ain't that just something? My wife's name was Zelda. She had eyes dat sparkled and a smile dat lit up the night sky. She was the most beautiful woman in the world, inside and out. We got ourselves wed June 9th, 1898. It was a bright and sunny Thursday afternoon. I was twenty-six years old and she was my angel, heaven on earth, just for me. God, I loved that woman, every bit of her. Don't get me wrong, she was a handful, my Zelda. 'Spect she'd say the same o' me. Marriage ain't easy. Lawd knows dat's the truth."

"I don't want to get married, ever," Veronica said plainly.

"Then don't," I said. "Your father can't make you."

"Ain't nothing wrong with marriage," Mr. Jackson said firmly.

"It's not a marriage for love; it's a business deal," I told him.

"Ain't nothing wrong with dat. Many a good marriage start out arranged. You youngins thinkin' you knows, but you don't knows nothing. Dez been arranged marriages since the world been round. Some good, some bad—don't matter none in the end. Marriage is hard, going in, you each got your own ways. Don't matter if'n it's arranged or not. You gets to know dat person, and he gets to know you. In the end y'all see what's what. My Zelda and me, wez arranged by her daddy, and I loved dat woman till the day the good Lord came and got her," he said, wiping his eyes with a big white handkerchief.

"We had one fine son, Adam. He fought in World War One. He came home and marched down Fifth Avenue in New York City as a member of the Harlem Hellfighters in 1919. We watched him parade dat night, den buried him four weeks later. Got hisself beat in the head with an iron pipe. Ner'd find who done it. He gots all the way through the war and gets hisself killed on the front steps.

"I'm here now. Finally found a nice, quiet spot on God's green earth to settle down before they bury my bones in the dirt and I join my Zelda. My only job now is to sit here and wait for Mr. Death. He's taking his sweet old time."

The screen door squeaked open and Daniel came outside. "Hey," he said.

"Daniel, what you knows 'bout dis Zelda gal yere?"

Daniel smiled. I rolled my eyes. "She's okay. A little bit stubborn and bossy, and she likes Motown music, but she's okay."

"I ain't ner heard nothing bad 'bout a young lady named Zelda. You gots a boyfriend, Zelda?"

"No, sir," I said.

"Well, Daniel, dere you have it. She's just right."

Daniel smiled and looked at me. "Sounds good to me."

I looked at him to reply, but the words caught in my mouth. I changed the subject. "You've seen a lot of history."

"History, Lawd yes. I seen my fair share of goings-on. Some good. Some bad. Most will just sit a spell and be judged by folks way smarter dan me. I seens good men gets demselves killed and bad men wage war. I seens when we had no rights and now civil rights. I seens the beginning of radio, television, movies, buildings climbing to the heavens, the start of cars, the reign of trains, planes, and now we're heading into space. Yes, sirree, I seens dem all."

He tapped his pipe again and put it in his pocket.

"It's a good fine day, and I sees the future when I look at the three of yous. Getting your education. Can't nobody take dat from you, never. Dat's something you hold on to all you life. 'Member that. Small-minded people kicking up strife don't stands for long. I seens change and I seens men fight it. Den one day dere ain't no more fight left in dem. Change is yere and it be a-comin' fast."

Daniel and I looked at each other.

"Wee-oo!" Mr. Jackson tipped his head up and smiled. "Dat lemon pound cake just about perfect. I 'spect I better gets myself inside and take a look-see."

He reached down and picked up a long, thin cane beside his foot. "You young people stay out here in da cool afternoon. I'ma sit a spell and watch my television shows."

"Think I'll come with you, Mr. Jackson," Veronica said.

He looked at Daniel and me and smiled. "Good idea."

"He's sweet," I said, leaning back on the railing, alone with Daniel. "What are you smiling at?" I asked.

He didn't answer. His smile broadened and my stomach did a somersault. "You, Miss Motown. I'm smiling at you. I like you," he confessed, softly.

"You do?"

"Yeah." He nodded. "I do. And I think I want to see more of you when we get to Atlanta. If that's okay with you."

"Hmm. I don't know about that. See, Mr. I Only Like Real Music, I like guys who are fans of syrupy sweet love-machine music," I said. "And since you're not, well . . ."

He laughed. "Okay, well, you know, maybe Motown isn't all that bad after all."

"Maybe?" I teased. "Sorry. See ya later." I stood to leave.

"Wait, wait," Daniel said and quickly grabbed my waist and pulled me close. I laughed and tried to squirm away from him, but he held me tight. "I take it back," he protested. "I take it back."

"No, don't," I said, laughing. "You like what you like."

"I like you, and I'm not taking that back," he promised and started kissing me with loud, playful smooches.

I laughed and squealed until finally surrendering. "Okay, okay, okay, I believe you," I said, yielding.

We stood together in each other's arms, our eyes locked. The desire in his eyes reflected my own desire for him. My heart pounded as I ran my tongue over my lips. I wanted him to kiss me for real. He lowered his head and I tilted my head up to meet him. The kiss was short and sweet. I pulled back and looked into his eyes, seeing that he wanted more. He wrapped his strong arms around me and I melded to his body. We kissed again. This time it was different.

Our tongues intertwined in a passionate dance of burning hunger. He ravished my mouth, leaving me in urgent arousal. We clung to each other as passion swelled around us. I heard a deep guttural groan and knew we had gone too far. We parted breathless with my heart racing. We stood there on the porch holding each other.

After a while we heard talking and I stepped away. Daphne and Mazie came outside. Veronica followed. "Mazie's taking us into town," Daphne said. "Come on."

I didn't particularly want to go, but staying here with Daniel was too tempting, so I left with them. Daniel stayed.

We went into just about every store in the town. Daphne and Veronica bought slacks and tops and I bought a scarf. Mazie, who had gone shopping earlier, bought shorts. When we got back to the house, we watched game shows and soap operas on the television the rest of the afternoon while Mazie's mother cooked. By the time supper was done, we were more than ready.

We walked into the dining room, where we found a table full of food. There was also sliced ham on a buffet table, along with deviled eggs, corn pudding, and green beans. The fried chicken was about the best I'd ever tasted, and so were the potato salad, macaroni and cheese, and turnip greens. The corn bread had actual corn in it, and the candied yams were mouthwatering. There were also black-eyed peas, chitterlings, and red beans and rice. Even the ice-cold lemonade was delicious.

Mr. Jackson had thirds, then wiped his greasy mouth with a big red napkin and patted his stomach. "Well now, I'd say the only thing missing from dis table is fried okra and a couple of pigs' feet covered with vinegar and hot sauce."

Daniel, Mazie, and her mother—quite proud of the birthday spread—agreed. On the other hand, Veronica, Daphne, and I made faces and balked at the thought.

"Y'all Northern gals don't know what real good food is," Mr. Jackson said. "Ain't I right, Daniel?" We laughed as he started naming other foods we'd never even consider eating. Tongue. Gizzards. Rocky Mountain oysters. Then he stood, kissed Mazie's forehead, and wished her a happy birthday.

Mazie's mother got up and headed into the kitchen. "Dat's not all," she said, bringing out a lemon pound cake with white icing. "Surprise!" she said and we began singing the birthday song.

After we finished eating cake and ice cream, we helped clean up the kitchen while talking about the evening's plans. The phone rang and Mazie jumped to answer. "That was Mr. Sam. The car's ready. The part came early," she said. "Gunner is gonna bring it here when he gets off work. We can either go to the barn with him or you can drive your car," she said directly to Veronica.

"I'll drive. We can make sure the car is working fine before we hit the road tomorrow."

"Come on. Let's start getting ready."

17

I PUT ON MY SHORTS AND A HALTER TOP WITH LONG straps that wrapped around my neck into a bow in the back and twice around my body to accentuate my slender waist. Veronica had on a one-piece strapless jumpsuit, and Daphne had on a simple V-neck shift dress, with short, puffy cap sleeves and a scalloped hem, and low-heeled sandals.

"What's taking her so long?" Daphne asked as she flopped down on her bed and fidgeted with the crocheted afghan.

Mazie was still in her room getting ready. We heard her mother bouncing to and fro like a spinning top in a wooden box. She ran up and down the hall between her bedroom and Mazie's room six or seven times.

"What is she doing?" Veronica whispered.

"Training for the Olympics maybe," I joked.

"Hey, come on. Let's go," Mazie invited finally.

Mazie was posed in the hallway with her mother taking Polaroid pictures. My jaw dropped open. I couldn't believe my eyes. Mazie, in a long blond wig, was wearing a skimpy white crochet mini shift dress that was nearly see-through. Beneath, I could see she was wearing black panties and a black bra. By all standards, her outfit was positively scandalous.

"Ta-da. Well, what do you think?" she asked proudly. She spun around, and the back was just as see-through and barely covered her buttocks. "My mother made it for me. It's very lightweight, and it's one of a kind." She posed again, waiting for compliments. "I look pretty, don't I?"

"You look beautiful, Mazie. Prettier than any girl there," her mother said.

"Let's go," Daphne said.

"Yes! I don't want to be too late," Mazie said.

Daniel was waiting for us on the porch. He was talking with Mr. Jackson, who was sitting sipping lemonade with a pipe in his hand and the newspaper on his lap. Daniel grinned at me. I thought my heart would stop beating right then and there. Unshaven, in a dark navy shirt and slacks, he looked handsome, dangerously handsome. Better than Sidney Poitier, Ivan Dixon, and Harry Belafonte all put together handsome.

"You look beautiful," he said. I could swear I blushed for the first time in my life. "You all do," he said to the other girls without taking his eyes off me.

"Y'all girls be careful out dere tonight," said Mr. Jackson. "Dere's a lot of fast boys with heat in their britches and no good sense. Don't let 'em talk you up on a hummer, ya here? Daniel, you keep a eye on 'em."

"Yes, sir."

"Where's Winston? I thought he was coming with us," Daphne asked.

"No. He's gonna meet us there," Mazie said. "He needs to rehearse and do microphone checks. That's what all professional entertainers do before they perform."

"Have fun," her mother called out, waving to us as we headed out.

"Let's put the roof down," Mazie announced, approaching the car.

The sun was low in the sky, and the last remnant of evening was about to tuck away for the night. Yet it was still sweltering hot.

"It feels like it's going to rain," I said.

"No, it doesn't," Mazie insisted. "Come on, please?"

Her whining, childish pleading quickly got the best of Veronica. "Fine," she gave in. She and Daniel pulled the top down and secured it.

Mazie plopped her butt in the front passenger seat next to Veronica. Daphne, Daniel, and I sat in back. As soon as we drove off, another car pulled up and took our spot. I saw an older white man get out of the car, walk up the porch steps, and go into the house. "Hey, who's that?" Veronica asked.

Mazie turned around and looked. "Oh, that's my mother's boyfriend. He has lots of money," she said, sounding overly impressed. "Does this radio work? Let's hear some music."

Mazie clicked the radio on and turned the dial until she found a station she liked. The song, a Motown favorite, put us in the perfect mood for the night ahead. Even Daniel was singing along.

Veronica followed Mazie's directions, although she got us lost twice.

"You have been to this place before, right?" I asked.

"Of course I have," Mazie said, sounding annoyed. "But somebody always drives me. I don't pay attention to how to get there. Why would I?"

I wanted to tell her why, but I didn't.

We drove around an old church, passed a row of billboards for Waller Car Sales and a small school with a green school bus. There was a short series of telephone poles along the road that we moved past quickly since it looked as if they'd fall at any moment.

"It's up dere on the other side of this covered bridge and then round the bend to the left."

What she called a bridge was a mass of rotten wood with a barely standing overhead covering. It creaked and moaned as we crossed over. I feared we'd drop into the stream and rocks below at any second.

We arrived at our destination right before the sun set, giving us just enough light to be seen by those standing around outside. There were dozens and dozens of cars already parked and two more cars behind us. One with head-lights so close I could hear the four passengers in the back seat laughing. Cars were everywhere, parked haphazardly beneath trees, in mud, and on what must have once been a field of grass. The remote farmhouse and barn were sur-rounded by woods and what probably had been an orchard at one time.

"All this here used to be farmland, but the owner died and then his son died. And then this just sort of became the place to hang out."

"A nightclub?" I asked.

"Yes." Mazie turned and stared at me. "It may not be as fancy as the ones in Washington, DC, or New York, but dat doesn't matter 'cause we still have fun here."

"Do we just park anywhere?" Veronica asked, pulling over.

"No! No! Don't stop here. Get closer," Mazie instructed.

"There's no place to park closer," Veronica said, "and I don't want to get jammed in by other cars."

"Don't worry. Your precious car is going to be just fine. Look. There's Gunner," she said, pointing happily. He was motioning for us to come forward.

He waved us toward an open space alongside a barn. Veronica pulled up and turned the engine off. By this time Mazie was kneeling up on the seat, waving at people stand-ing around outside, wanting them to notice her in the car.

Mazie dashed off, leaving us, heading right to the big opening at the front of the barn. Daphne, Daniel, and I stayed to help Veronica put the top up. Mazie hurried back.

"What are you doing?" she insisted. "No, leave it down. It looks better down."

Veronica was frowning. "This is my car, and I'm not going to have the inside rained on. I'm putting my car roof up."

Mazie turned on her heels and stomped away. We continued as Gunner came over and helped Daniel finish. "So you and Mazie are friends?" I asked him.

"Yep, known her all my life. I was her boyfriend once."

"That was before she met Winston, right?" I said, half joking.

"I introduced 'em. Didn't know he'd steal my girl away, but dat's water under the bridge. We're all friends now."

"It's Tuesday night. Why are there so many people here?" I asked him.

"Oh, it's always crowded on Tuesday night. Dey have dinners for sale in the back on Tuesdays and Fridays, so dere's always people here to get something to eat. Plus, Winston is performing and everybody wanna see him."

"What's this nightclub called?" Veronica asked.

"Nightclub? Oh, you mean the barn," he said. "To tell you the truth, it ain't got no name, never did. We all call it the barn, and everyone knows what we're talking 'bout. It's been yere forever. It caught fire twice, but it's still standing."

"Who owns it?" I asked, wondering about the property.

He chuckled. "Nobody and everybody. The town's been fighting over this land for decades. It started about sixty years ago. Some Northern white folks wanted to buy this property to build a golf course and start moving all the blacks out.

Old Mr. Jenkins wouldn't sell his land. He was killed a few months later. Dey say it was the night riders dat did it. They didn't know he had a will. The land went to his son.

"Then his boy was killed 'fore he could sell or take hold, so the town claimed it 'cause a back taxes. But the people made a fuss, and dat started the legal battle dat some say is still going on. Now every year the taxes get paid somehow. So the town has no claim to the land. And since none of them fine folk on the other side of town wants to come over yere, we claim it as ours."

"Can the people build something on the land, like a school or something like that?"

"Nah, the town ain't give us no permits."

"So this land just sits."

He nodded. "Pretty much."

"Hey, what's taking so long? Come on," Mazie insisted as she came back to get us. "Let's go inside."

As we walked up to the front opening, a group of young women turned and stared at us—well, they mostly stared at Mazie. She was making a spectacle of herself, laughing and talking loudly about college life and how much fun we had. The girls glared at her as if she were the devil incarnate.

As we got closer, I half expected they'd come over and start pounding on her. When we walked past I heard malicious grumbles as their nasty glares turned vocal.

"Look who's yere, Miss Beauty Queen."

"She's got some nerve showing her face yere again after she flirted with my boyfriend last week."

18

THE HEAT IMMEDIATELY DESCENDED LIKE A PLASTIC BAG
over my face when we entered the barn. I felt like I was
suffocating. But it was the stench that hit me hard. It was a
nasty menagerie of barnyard excrement, putrid muck, fried
food, and body odor. Seconds later my eyes started burning, from our smoke-filled surroundings.

Barely through the entrance, we stopped and waited for
Daniel and Gunner.

There was a cover charge, and before we could reach
into our purses, Daniel paid for all of us. Mazie took his
arm, batted her eyelashes, and kissed his cheek in gratitude.
Gunner walked away.

"What's up with Gunner?" Daphne questioned. "He
seems a bit miffed."

Mazie replied, "He's jealous. He says he's over me and that we're all just friends, but he's really not. He's cute and all, but he doesn't have no future. I want a boyfriend who's going someplace." She looked up at Daniel and smiled sweetly. "Like Daniel here, right?"

"You mean like Winston, your fiancé," I corrected.

"Or maybe Daniel," Mazie said again as if she were joking, but we all knew she really wasn't.

She beamed her beauty-queen smile, and I cut my eyes at her.

Daniel untwined her arm from his and wiped her bright red lipstick from his cheek. "But not this Daniel," he said. "I make it a rule never to date another man's fiancée."

While the others grinned, I smiled and looked around. The barn was crowded—mostly blacks dressed in their "Apollo Theater on Friday night" finest, with a smattering of white faces here and there. The inside of the barn was just as decrepit as the outside. With peeling paint, termite-infested wood, and a rusting tin roof dripping bright orange water. The noise level was deafening. Everybody was shouting over everybody else, making it difficult to hear anything. Plus loud music was playing.

There was a crooked hayloft above us. The rickety overhang was the remains of partitioned stalls and overhead framed crossbeams, which looked as if they might give way at any moment. Underneath, the people laughed and joked and ribbed each other in the dim room. I saw a woman with her back against the wall. Her skirt was hiked up, and a man in front of her had his pants dropped to his ankles and was pushing into her. Her legs were wrapped around his waist. Her red lips were parted and her head was thrown back as she held tight to his white shirt. They were in plain sight and no one seemed to care. I looked away quickly, right into Daniel's dark brown eyes.

Daphne broke our connection. "Are you hungry?" she asked jokingly, pointing.

I turned and saw a board hoisted up behind a makeshift bar, which was made of stacks of cinder blocks and a plywood top. A selection of drinks and food platters containing fried chicken, fried porgies and trout, cornbread, barbecued pork, chitterlings, turnip greens, dirty rice, and potato salad. On the bar were jars of pickled pigs' feet and hard-boiled eggs, as well as small whiskey glasses and wax-coated cups.

People with bloodshot eyes staggered around bumping into each other, yelling, screaming, pushing, and shoving. There was a scuffle going on in the corner by the bar.

"Hey, over here," Gunner called out to us. We went over to a long rectangular table with six chairs near the crudely improvised stage. "What do you want to drink?" Gunner asked.

"Nothing. I'm fine," I said.

"I pass," Veronica said.

"Me too," Daphne added.

"Oh, come on. It's my birthday. Y'all have to drink," Mazie said, overly pouty. "Get something. Dey have gin, whiskey, beer, corn liquor, all kinds of stuff."

"Dey also have homemade peach wine," Gunner suggested.

Daphne grimaced and looked at me. I shrugged. "Okay, I'll have a beer," I said. Both Daphne and Veronica asked for beers as well.

"Not me. I want whiskey," Mazie said.

"Whiskey? Mazie, are you sure about that?" I asked.

"Sure I'm sure. I've had it before. Besides, it's my birthday and I'm celebrating," she insisted, slapping her hand on the table for emphasis.

Gunner and Daniel went to get our drinks. They came back a short time later and set the beverages down in front of us. Gunner pulled a pint of whiskey and two small glasses from his shirt pocket. He poured whiskey for himself and Mazie and then held his glass up. "Okay, here's to Tuesday nights at the barn."

"No," Mazie contended quickly. "To my birthday." Mazie drank the whiskey down in one straight gulp, then shivered and shook and made a horrendous face. She started coughing and gasping as she slammed the glass down. "More," she said, laughing.

"Are you sure?" Daniel asked.

"You're not my boyfriend. I want more," she repeated.

Gunner filled her glass again. She drank it down just like the first and did the shuddering, coughing thing again.

"More."

"Maybe you should slow down," Gunner warned.

"No way. It's my birthday and I'm gonna have me some fun. More."

He looked at us, shrugged, and poured her another

one. This one she didn't drink straight down. She took a small sip with the same reaction.

"How 'bout I get us all some water," Daniel said.

"I'll show you where the water hose is," Gunner said.

As soon as they walked away, Mazie picked up her glass and downed the drink. "That's so nasty," she said, pouring herself another from the bottle Gunner had left on the table.

"Then stop drinking it," Veronica said soundly.

"Maybe I'll date Gunner again," Mazie said.

All our jaws dropped.

"Winston's cheating on me. He's always cheating on me," Mazie said matter-of-factly. "He told me that it was over with those other girls, but he lied. He's still sleeping with dem."

I shook my head. "What makes you think he's cheating?"

"'Cause she told me and she's here tonight."

"So what? I'm sure there are a lot of girls who like him. He's got a good singing voice. Maybe she just came to hear him sing."

"No, she came for Winston. I heard her say so," she said, taking a sip of the whiskey. "But that's okay. She can have him. I'll make him jealous and sleep with someone else."

"Mazie, you can't—" Daphne said.

"You should talk to him," I said.

"No. I don't care anymore," she continued. "If he can cheat, den so can I. I'm a find me somebody better than him, like Daniel." She picked up the glass and swallowed the rest of the drink straight down.

"Mazie, let's go back home. We can celebrate there," I said, hoping she'd listen to sense.

Before anyone could seriously consider my suggestion, two men came up and asked for a dance. Mazie got up and pulled Veronica with her onto the dance floor.

"Oh dear Lord, look at her out there." Mazie was flirting with both men. She was shaking her breasts and wiggling her butt, rubbing up against them. Then she kissed one and then the other. The men smiled from ear to ear as she danced between them.

"There was a long line outside at the water hose," Daniel said, placing three cups of brownish water on the table.

"Where'd Mazie go?" Gunner asked, smiling. But before we could answer, he located her on the dance floor. His smile disappeared and he walked away.

Daniel sat down next to me. "What's wrong with Gunner?"

"Mazie," I said.

Just then two white guys came over and stood at our table. "Well, well, now, who do we have here?" one of them said. "These two lovely young things belong to you, boy?"

"We're not things and we don't belong to anyone," I said. He was tall and muscular with a flat face, a once-broken nose, and barely focusing eyes that were bloodshot and too close together.

He looked down at me with a menacing grin. "I see we have a smart-mouth here. Do you know what I like to do with smart-mouths?" He leaned in close and I could smell the stink of whiskey on his breath.

"Back off, boys," Daniel warned with a mean scowl.

"Ohh, the black boy ain't sharing his booty," he said and chuckled loudly. "I'm just joking around. Can't you take a joke?"

"No, we can't."

"You know, I don't like your attitude, boy."

"And I don't like yours, boy," Daniel said.

"Cool it," the other man said quickly to Daniel. "He's okay. We're celebrating, that's all. Ladies, my name's Rob and this here's my best friend Billy."

We nodded silently but didn't give our names.

"We just quit the war. We're headed to Canada," Rob said proudly.

"Shut up, Rob, you dumbass. Keep your mouth shut. Y'all gals want to dance with us?" Billy said. We both declined.

Just then Veronica came back and sat beside Daphne. She was giddy, until she took a sip of her beer and made a repulsed face. "That's disgusting," she said.

"Whoa, now I like these odds," Billy responded. "I'll take all three of them with me. Come on, dance with me, gal."

"No thanks," Veronica said, fanning herself with a napkin. "It's way too hot out there on that dance floor."

"Don't worry about the heat. It's good for you. Come on, stand up and dance with me," Billy seemed to order her. He reached for her hand, and she quickly moved it away. He glared at her fiercely. "What? You think you too damn good to dance with me? I said, get up and dance with me, now."

Daniel jumped up. "She doesn't want to dance. So move on," he warned firmly.

"Is that an order, boy?" Billy said, redirecting his attention to Daniel. His words slurred and dripped with malice. He started laughing. "You shut the fuck up," he said, pointing his finger at Daniel, then staggering into the table, nearly knocking it over.

"Come on, man. Cool it. Let's go," Rob insisted. "Sorry. He's drunk. I'll take him out to cool off."

Daniel glared at them.

Rob grabbed Billy's arm. "Come on, man, let's beat it," he said, pulling him away from our table. "You need some fresh air. Come on."

Daniel sat back down. "You okay?"

"What a jackass," Veronica said.

"Amen to that," Daphne agreed.

It wasn't just the shifty eyes and slicked-back greasy hair, it was everything about him that had made my skin crawl. He had an air of entitlement, like a fox in a henhouse.

"Hey, I'm sorry about that. Are you okay?" Daniel asked, touching my arm. I nodded and took a sip of my beer. It was hot and watery.

I glanced up and saw Mazie sashaying back over to us. She looked right at Daniel. "Hey, I'm back," she said sweetly, standing in front of Daniel. Her chest in his face.

He eased away from her and returned his attention to me. "I can get you another beer if you want. Can't promise it's gonna be any better than that one."

"No, that's okay," I said. "I'm not going to drink it anyway."

"Hey, remember me?" Mazie asked Daniel.

We both looked at her. She grabbed her beer, which Gunner had left, and took a long swallow.

"Mazie, that's enough drinking," Daphne said.

"You're not my mother," she said before tilting the glass to her mouth.

I turned to Daphne and Veronica. "She's drunk. Maybe we should get her home."

"She won't go. She saw Winston kissing some girl."

Mazie pushed her butt between me and Daniel, then turned her back to me. Daniel moved away and she moved right with him. She grinned. "Do you want to dance?"

"No thanks," he said. "Actually I was talking to Zelda."

She turned around and looked at me, seemingly puzzled. "Why? I'm a beauty queen and I'm way prettier than she is. You can ask anybody."

"Mazie, shut your stupid mouth!" Veronica yelled.

"I don't want to talk to you, and for the record, I think Zelda is very beautiful," Daniel said, then leaned forward and looked at me.

I looked away quickly, too embarrassed to hold his eye with mine.

"Zelda, are you okay?" he asked.

I nodded.

Mazie continued to bat her eyes and flirt with Daniel. But he ignored her, which made her even more determined. And each time he tried to strike up a conversation with me, she got madder and madder.

"What is wrong with you? I'm sitting right here. Look at me," she demanded. "It's my birthday," she shouted. "Say happy birthday to me."

"Happy birthday," Daniel said.

"Kiss me?" she insisted.

"No."

"Why not?" She pouted and started rubbing his leg.

He pushed her hand away. "Don't do that," he said firmly.

"I want to kiss you," Mazie protested. She pouted her lips. "I bet if Zelda asked you to kiss her you'd do it. Wouldn't you?"

My heart thudded.

"Yes. Absolutely. In a heartbeat. And what makes you think we haven't already?"

"Fine." She stood up. "You can have her, den. I didn't want to kiss you and I didn't want to dance with you."

"I'll dance with you, baby."

We looked up and saw that Rob and Billy were back.

Mazie took Billy's hand just as he walked up, and they went to the dance floor. Everything about it looked wrong.

Two other guys came over and asked Veronica and Daphne to dance.

"Did you want to dance?" Daniel asked, taking my hand.

"No. Thank you," I said, nervously pulling away.

"You've seemed edgy all evening. Is it because of the kiss?" he asked. I didn't respond. "Because if it is, and all this is moving too fast, we can—"

"No. It's not the kiss. Not really. It's everything—you, me, all of this. I guess I'm overwhelmed. I don't know what to think anymore, or what to expect next. It feels like I'm haphazardly tumbling from situation to situation."

He nodded. "I can see how you'd feel that way. It's been chaotic."

"To say the least." We smiled. "Thanks for understanding."

"I do like you," he said. "A lot."

I touched his hand. "Me too."

Everybody started clapping and cheering as they moved toward the stage. Winston's group came out dressed in shiny suits, looking like the Temptations minus one. They started singing. His a cappella rendition of Sam Cooke's "Twistin' the Night Away" was flawless. His voice was smooth and as sweet as honey, and he sounded just like him.

I could see Mazie jumping around like a fool. Billy right there by her side. He had his hand on her ass.

Daniel reached around my waist and pulled me closer. He wove his fingers through my hair and held the nape of my neck. He inched closer as if he was going to kiss me. "Your skin is soft like your lips."

I opened my mouth to respond and he kissed me. I wrapped my arms around his neck and enjoyed the taste of his lips with mine. He pressed his tongue between my lips and I opened wide for him. He kissed me in such a way that made my whole body want him. Deeper and deeper we kissed. Just as I was about to break the kiss, he leaned back. We were both breathless, staring at each other.

Suddenly, the noise in the barn elevated. I couldn't hear him and he was right in front of me. "Come on," he shouted. He stood up and took my hand. "Let's go talk someplace quieter." We were just about to leave when I heard someone screaming. I turned around and saw a fight.

"Zelda, come on. Let's get out of here," Daniel yelled.

I shook my head. "It's Mazie screaming."

"What?" he yelled.

"I think it's Mazie," I said, pointing.

He ran toward the commotion, and I followed close behind him. Someone shoved him, and I shoved them right back. Then I saw Winston in his shiny suit fighting Billy. Rob was fighting a couple of other men in shiny suits. Mazie was screaming and jumping on Winston's back.

Daphne grabbed my arm. "We need to get Mazie." I struggled with my girls through the crowd, leaving behind the vision of Daniel trying to break the fighting men apart. A couple of other guys were trying to help him.

"I hate you! I hate you!" Mazie screamed at Winston when everyone was finally separated. Then she fell down drunk.

"Good Lord, we have to get her out of here," Veronica said.

There were women laughing and making fun of Mazie. We rushed over and tried to grab her, but she fought us off. Gunner came out of nowhere and grabbed her. He hoisted her up over his shoulder and hauled her, like a sack of wheat, out of the barn. We followed. I called to Daniel, who came running out. I saw a huge mass of confusion behind him in the barn. There was fighting, pushing, screaming—a battlefield of madness.

19

IT WAS PITCH-BLACK OUTSIDE, AND THE AIR WAS THICK
with moisture as the sound of thunder rumbled in the far
distance. We hurried to our car but discovered that it had
been blocked in. We weren't going anywhere any time
soon. "Shit."

"Here, Daniel, you have to drive," Veronica said, press-
ing the key into his hand. He nodded wordlessly. We all got
into the car. I sat up front beside Daniel while Veronica and
Daphne were trying to take care of Mazie in the back. She
was mad, drunk, and crying hysterically. We could barely
understand her. She wailed louder and muttered about
keeping her ring.

Daniel nudged the car forward and backward several
times until he had enough room to free us. "Mazie, you're
going to have to calm down," I shouted, looking around at

the chaotically parked cars. "How the hell do we get out of this mess?"

"Mazie, you have to tell us how to get back to your mother's house."

"I hate him. He kissed her," Mazie sobbed. "I saw him."

The thunder rumbled closer, and a flash of lightning lit the inside of the car. Mazie mumbled again and continued crying. Then after a while she sniffed loudly and looked at us. "Why are men so cruel? They say they love you, but they lie. Right beside the stage I saw him with her," she said through tearful sobs that quickly turned to bawling, wailing heaves of distress. "His old girlfriend before me. She dumped him and I made him a star. Now she wants him back. He-He-He . . ." she stuttered.

Veronica put her two cents in. "She's right. They lie. My father lies to me all the time."

They went back and forth for a short time, until Mazie passed out.

"I can't believe how dark it is out here. Do you even know where you're going?" Veronica asked Daniel.

"No, but I'm following the car in front of me until hopefully I see something familiar."

He kept driving. I saw billboards for Waller Car Sales and I remembered them from our drive over. "There should be a white church up ahead here," I said. A few seconds later, we saw the white church. The car in front of us turned to the left. Daniel stopped.

"Do we keep following them?" Daphne asked.

"No, I think we turn down there," I said, pointing right.

"Are you sure?" both Daniel and Veronica asked.

"No, but I think so."

"Mazie, wake up," Veronica said, shaking her. Mazie moaned but didn't verbally respond. "Shit."

Daniel turned right. Ten minutes later we were driving through the center of town and saw the place where we had eaten breakfast. "Okay, I think this road should lead us back to the other side of the tracks."

Daniel kept going and turned where I remembered Winston had turned earlier. We crossed over railroad tracks and kept going. He turned down another street, and I saw the small park and on the other side a big yellow house. "We're here," he said.

Daniel parked near the front of the house. The car we'd seen pull up earlier was gone. It took a few minutes, but we finally woke Mazie up and got her out of the car. "I'm gonna be sick," she slurred, staggering up the porch steps. Her mother met us as we opened the screen door. She was dressed as if she was going out.

"You're back early," she said. "Well, at least you beat the storm." Examining Mazie's condition, she asked, "What the hell happened? What did y'all do to her?" she screamed. "Move, move, give me my baby," she yelled, pushing us out of the way and cradling Mazie as if she were a child. Mazie threw up all over her as soon as we released her. "What did y'all do to her?" her mother screamed again.

"We didn't do anything. She got drunk."

"Y'all are lying! She doesn't drink. Y'all gave my baby drugs, didn't you?" her mother yelled at us. "What is wrong with you? Mazie is a good girl. She doesn't drink or smoke or do drugs. Now y'all tell me the truth. What did y'all give her?"

"Nothing. She got herself drunk."

"You were supposed to protect her," she said, pointing to Daniel. "What kind of man are you?"

"He tried to help her," I defended.

"Don't you lie to me."

We looked at each other, stunned. Mazie threw up again, this time all over the living room floor.

"We're not lying. You can ask just about everybody at the barn. They'll tell you."

"As if I would believe that pack of low-life scum. They've always been jealous of Mazie, of us. Y'all were supposed to be her friends and take care of her."

"Ma'am, we tried to help her," Daniel said.

"I just bet you did," she said sarcastically, then turned to Mazie. "Baby, what happened? Who did this to you?"

Mazie barely opened her eyes. She shook her head. "I don't remember. I feel sick."

"You're sick. Sick! All of you, to do this to someone who saved your asses from sleeping on the street. We gave you food and a place to lay your heads tonight. I won't throw you out, although God knows I should. But I'm a Christian woman. So y'all just get out of my sight. I don't want to see you. Go, get out of my sight!"

We went upstairs to our room and Daniel to his. As soon as we closed the door we rolled our eyes. "What the hell happened at the barn that started this chaos?" I asked.

"Mazie was dancing with that white guy and she got really suggestive."

"And so did he," Veronica added.

Daphne nodded. "Yes, and so did he. And so when Winston saw her he went ballistic and came down from the stage."

"Oh, but he didn't just come down. He literally dove off the stage and flew onto them," Veronica said. "If I'm lying, I'm dying."

"He was just like Superman," Daphne added.

We laughed, making sure to keep our voices low to prevent Mazie's mother from hearing us.

"It all happened so fast. All of the sudden that white guy picked Mazie up and they were almost doing it right there in the middle of the dance floor right in front of Winston singing onstage. He stopped singing and yelled, 'What the fuck!' He flew down from the stage right on top of the white guy. Then the other white guy tried to pull Winston off, and that's when everybody else onstage jumped in," Veronica said.

I couldn't believe what I was hearing. I just kept shaking my head.

Through the door, we heard Mazie's mother take her to her bedroom. A few minutes later we heard her fussing as she walked back downstairs. The front door slammed, then moments later the screen door opened and closed.

"Sounds like she went out," Daphne said.

Veronica yawned. "Well, that's it, I'm done. Let's get some sleep so we can get out of this crazy-ass town first thing in the morning. I've had it with this place."

Veronica and Daphne changed into their nightclothes. I didn't.

"Aren't you going to bed?" Veronica asked.

"I'm too charged up to sleep. I'm gonna step outside and get some air," I said.

"Do you want us to go with you?"

"No, you two get some sleep. I'll be fine."

I grabbed my shawl and went downstairs. There was a dim light on in the living room. The front door was open, and the screen door was unlatched. I stepped outside onto the porch. It was quiet except for the sound of crickets.

I was out there for several minutes when I saw a figure in the park across the street. He was in shadow, but I recognized him as he moved closer to the streetlamp. It was Daniel. He still looked dashing and dangerous.

I began to walk toward him, slowly at first, as if I was going to change my mind at any minute. He started walking toward me too. We both moved faster until we met in the middle of the street. My heart was racing. He touched my face and kissed me tenderly.

"I was thinking about you."

I nodded. "I was thinking about you too."

He took my hand and kissed it while looking deeply into my eyes. Unnervingly, there was a flash of light and a heavy rumble of thunder. We looked up, and as if a spigot had suddenly been turned on, it began to rain just enough to let us know the storm was arriving.

Daniel took my hand, and we ran back to the guest-house. By the time we reached the porch, wet and breath-less, we were laughing hysterically.

"Zelda, I'll never ask you to do anything you don't want to do," he said. "So if you don't want me to . . ." He stopped and let the sentence rest there. I heard the aching hesitation in his voice. I didn't say anything for a few sec-onds. "Come on, I'll walk you to your room."

"No," I finally said, "I want to go to your room."

I looked down at my trembling hand and tried to steady it as I reached out to him. His hand was gentle and strong. "I'm ready."

20

WE WENT UP THE STAIRS TO HIS ROOM ON THE THIRD floor. It was smaller than the one we girls shared. The lighting set a warm ambiance, illuminating from a small lamp. From across the room, Daniel looked at me all shy like he was a boy on his first date. I felt an electricity pulling us together.

All of the sudden I felt emboldened. "So, Daniel, do you come here often?" I joked. I loved his laugh. It was from the gut, and it made me smile and feel good inside, like everything was going to be okay no matter what.

"This is a nice room," I said, walking over to him like it was the most natural thing in the world. "What would you like to do tonight?"

He took my hand and placed it on his chest. I could feel his heart pounding wildly. "This is what you do to me."

I laid my other hand on his chest and spread my fingers wide, feeling the solid strength beneath his shirt. My insides quivered.

"Are you a virgin?" he asked in almost a whisper.

I shook my head no. I was not ashamed and I knew exactly what I was doing. With my mother going on and on about saving myself until marriage, and since I wasn't sure I'd ever get married, I had wanted to experience it. It was no big deal. I didn't see what all the fuss was about. I did it with a guy I'd met at Howard University when I came home on spring break in my freshman year. It was during a frat party, and we did it in his dorm room. I saw him once, we did it once, and that was it. I never saw him again and didn't particularly want to. Not that the experience was bad. It was that he was unremarkable.

"Do you want a drink?"

"Um, yeah, sure."

He opened his suitcase and pulled out a flask. "This belonged to my father," he said proudly. "A general gave it to him after my father saved his life." He grabbed two glasses from the bathroom and poured liquid into each. "What is that?" I asked.

"It's called schnapps, peach schnapps."

"Schnapps. I've never heard of it before."

He handed me a glass. I put my nose to the rim and inhaled. "Mmm, it smells like sweet peaches," I said, smiling.

"It is kind of. I think you'll like it."

Our glasses clinked and we each took a sip. He looked at me cautiously. At first there was nothing, just warmth in my mouth. Then I sensed heat, and it seemed to simmer down my throat, but not in a bad way. Afterward I tasted the sweetness of peaches left behind. "Mmm."

I took a bigger sip and then ran the tip of my tongue across my lips. He slid the glass from my hand and set it on the dresser along with his. He leaned down slowly and we kissed. Six, seven, eight, nine times, one right after another our lips danced together playfully. We kissed over and over and over again. Smiling. Kissing. Laughing.

Then, as if catapulting me to the heavens, he cupped my face and the kiss deepened just like it had in the barn earlier. He pressed his tongue between my lips, and I greeted him with equal fervor. In urgency and need, feasting as if on the brink of starvation, we devoured each other. We kissed like our lives depended on it. I reached up and wrapped my arms around his neck and pulled him close. And just like the first time, he set my body on fire with the wet, hot heat of passion.

Backed against the dresser, I felt his arm, strong and firm, holding me tight. His other hand caressed my arm and traveled down, touching beneath my halter top to barely stroke my nipple. My stomach shuddered. I felt the hard thickness between his legs pressed against me, and the luscious wetness between my legs surrendered.

A silent tremor ran through my body as I heard a deep, throaty groan rumble through him. His hand traveled to my waist, hip, and thigh. Then lower, he lifted the hem of my shorts and he grabbed my butt, squeezing tight. I broke the kiss and flung my head back. I heard my own panting moans as I squirmed against him. I wanted more. I needed more. My body reeled as passion and hunger surged.

He ran his fingers through my hair, gently scratching my scalp. I staggered back. The sensation was arousing beyond measure. Then he pulled my hair and kissed my neck, my throat, and my shoulders. My thoughts whirled in a hot, sultry haze of mindless rapture.

I surrendered and the moment took me.

He stepped back at arm's length and stared, unblinking. The look in his eyes stilled me. "I want to make love to you tonight, but we don't have to do this if you're not ready. I just want to be with you. We can talk or just sit here and look at each other."

I looked at him. "I want to make love to you too."

"Turn around," he whispered, his voice husky.

I turned. My heart pounded as he placed his hands on my shoulders and then leaned down and kissed my neck again. I tipped my head to the side and felt the roughness of his unshaved chin. He placed my hands on the rim of the dresser. He untied the bow around my waist and then the bow at the nape of my neck. He pulled the zipper down, and my shorts dropped to the floor. Slowly he knelt to remove my panties. Then I felt his hands all over my naked body. He was tender and firm, caressing playfully, purposefully. The arousal inside me swelled. He nipped at my butt and kissed my waist. He removed his clothes, and seconds later he leaned in close. I gasped. I felt his skin on my skin and his massive protrusion pressed against me.

"You're so beautiful," he murmured.

He wrapped his hands around my waist and moved them up to my breasts. He caressed and cupped them, then held still as he kissed my shoulder. "I wanted to do this, to touch you like this, at the party in Cape May, in the diner this morning, and in that barn tonight. And every other time in between."

I was giddy with desire. "Then touch me," I muttered. He squeezed my breasts, and his thumbs teased my nipples. My body trembled. I moaned and pushed back from the dresser. He dipped his hand between my legs, nudging them apart. I took a step out. He began to stroke me there. Soft and tender, the torturous torment was exquisite pain. I felt that amazing something building up inside my body as my legs trembled and my body tensed.

"Please, can I touch you more?" he begged.

"Yes. Yes," I barely murmured. "More."

"I want to pleasure you all night long," he whispered, his breath tickling my ear. I shuddered and nodded.

I began moving, rocking my hips as he touched and teased me down there. The more he stroked, the tighter I felt my insides winding. He encircled my waist with his arm and started bumping his erection against my butt faster and faster. My legs shook uncontrollably. I felt an explosion coming from within. Seconds later I threw my head back and cried out as a feeling I had never felt overpowered me. My body twitched and writhed frantically.

He took my hips and turned me around. Then he bent down and licked my nipples, one right after the other. He followed up by taking one breast into his mouth and sucking while he teased me there again. I looked down and saw his mouth on my body and grabbed hold of him. I scratched his scalp like he had done to me. He looked up and smiled. I leaned down to kiss his incredible lips. He stood and tried to dip his hand between my legs again. But I pushed him away.

He looked at me, surprised. Ignoring his confusion, I chuckled and sashayed over to the bed and sat down. I admired his naked body. His hard penis was long and thick and stood straight up at me. I scooted back on the bed and crooked my finger for him to come join me. I watched, mesmerized, as he came to me.

I raked my teeth over my bottom lip as I watched him part my legs. Slowly he crawled over me and started kissing my naked body everywhere. The roughness of his beard was even more tantalizing and exaggerated. It scratched and tickled my skin. I leaned up on my elbows, watching him doing all kinds of things, kissing and licking me everywhere, in places I had never even imagined being touched.

I closed my eyes. I moaned and tried to close my legs, but he was there between them, kissing me, licking me. I reached down and grabbed his penis and held firm, then rubbed up and down his shaft. He made a guttural sound that made me bolder still. I started massaging him, feeling wetness trickle out. He leaned back and looked at me. He grabbed his penis from my hand and pushed it deep into me. I gasped. I felt the staggering pain of his sudden entry. I screamed out and moaned.

"Yes, don't stop." I wrapped my legs around his waist as he kept pushing into me, quicker and deeper, over and over again. Every thrust pushed me closer and closer to the edge again. I dug my nails into his back, holding on for dear life. My body shivered and quaked. I moved my hips against him, and we collided and joined as one. A violent rage was coming and I couldn't stop it. I exploded a second time and then a third.

He held me tighter and I felt him quicken the pace. His hips pushed, pounded, thrust. Then he tensed and shivered as his breathing got heavier. He groaned louder and deeply, then called my name like it would forever be the last name on his lips. He convulsed in spasm after spasm. His body jerked. My body tingled, and I felt like I was floating.

I wanted to speak, but I didn't trust my own voice. I lay there with him on top of me and relished the moment. Just as I got comfortable with him there, he rolled over and wrapped his arm around my body and held me close. I lay on my side, using his arm as a pillow.

Moments later, still breathless with passion, we kissed and touched and caressed and surrendered to the smoldering fire still simmering deep inside us. He touched my neck and ran his hand down to my breasts. He playfully tweaked my nipples and smiled as I gasped. I watched as he licked his lips. I knew he wanted more of me.

I sat up and straddled his hips, then looked down as his eyes pierced right through me. I kissed him sweetly, and he raised me up so that my nipples hovered over his face.

I watched, enthralled, and I arched my back as he tasted me. His tongue was gentle with long, luscious, exaggerated strokes sending me down that path to desire once more. Then he took my breast into his mouth and suckled, causing unimaginable delight. My body soared.

Without realizing it, I rested my hand on his chest. I felt the swell of strong, toned muscles flex beneath my fingers. I touched the tight firmness of his stomach and teased the tiny hairs just below. I touched his penis, still slightly stiff, and heard him moan his pleasure. Emboldened, I impaled myself. I rode him with fervor and delight until he was no longer slightly stiff.

Sexually spent and decadently sated, we lay side by side facing each other. His eyes stared at me, and his oh so tender lips nibbled my shoulder, then my neck. I reached up and felt the scruff of tiny hairs on his face.

"I read an article in the newspaper that we're gonna have a man walk on the moon next year."

I chuckled. "Where in the world did that come from?"

"I just thought of it. So what do you think about that?"

"I think it's going to be amazing to watch," I said. "I hope it happens."

"Oh, I think it's going to happen. Technology is advancing by leaps and bounds. That means people are going to have to learn to change and keep up. In a few months we're supposed to take off from the Kennedy Space Center, fly to the moon, orbit it, and then come back to Earth."

"I'd love to watch them take off. Blasting out into the unknown."

"Do you ever think about the future?" he asked.

"The future? You mean flying cars, Dick Tracy telephone wristwatches, and spaceships like that TV show *Star Trek*, where people are green with pointy ears?"

He smiled. "Well, maybe not that far in the future. I mean like in five or ten years, or even twenty years from now."

"Well, hopefully the war will be over by then. I can't see it going into the next decade."

I looked into his eyes. Suddenly I wasn't so sure.

"The day Calvin was killed I was out on operations. We were supposed to secure a small village. Intel said it was deserted. It wasn't. I stepped on a booby trap. For some reason it didn't detonate. I should have been killed right then, but I wasn't. Suddenly there was an attack, and the routine turned into hell. We were taking on enemy fire from all directions. I was hit in the shoulder and side. But others were slaughtered. We were rushed to an evac hospital near Tân An.

"Calvin was there. He shouldn't have been, but it was good to see a familiar face. He was stationed at Long Binh near Saigon. We talked for a short while, then a helicopter came in with wounded. He went to help. Moments later there was a massive explosion and firebomb. It blew me off my cot. I saw body parts scatter, men on fire, screaming, dying. The sight. The smell. The sounds. I'll never get that moment out of my head. I couldn't hear anything for weeks." He paused. "I should have saved him."

"There was nothing you could've done."

"My father had just been killed in Saigon. He was shot saving civilians. He was proud to be in the military and so was I. I was honorably discharged a few weeks later. I'm the only one left."

I didn't say anything. I understood.

"Maybe Calvin would still be alive. I should have made him stay there with me."

"No, you can't think like that. That's not how it works. It wasn't your job to protect him. You can't blame yourself for him getting killed. It wasn't your fault. It was the war."

Daniel shook his head. "We were best friends, brothers. And I betrayed him. I'll never forgive myself for that."

"Of course you feel like you feel. It's only human. But it doesn't work like that. Life doesn't work like that. Your father had just been killed. You were almost killed too."

He looked at me serenely. "You know what, Miss Motown? I really like you," he said.

"I really like you too." I touched his face. "So, what about the future? Do you mean like George Orwell's book *1984*, in which Big Brother is watching over us all the time and we have no freedom?"

"I'm thinking more like the turn of the century."

"Ah, we're back to talking about flying cars, people living on Mars, robots, and computer machines the size of a fingernail running the world instead of real people."

"I don't know about all that," he said. "The year 2000 is only thirty-two years from now."

"I know, but it seems so far off, like a million years

away. I can't see myself living on Mars. Maybe I'll just go there on vacation."

"What's your major at Spelman?"

"It's a double major, political science and English. I'll be attending Howard Law School next year, and after that—"

"When we get to Atlanta, I want us to still see each other. Morehouse is right across from Spelman."

"I'd like that," I said.

"Good. You're something else, Miss Motown."

My heart swelled. "You're something else right back." He kept talking, but I didn't say a whole lot after that. I let him talk. We lay in each other's arms, and I fell asleep to the sound of his soothing voice.

21

I JUMPED UP. "DIDN'T YOU HEAR THAT? SOMEONE screamed."

We listened intently to the silence for a few moments but didn't hear anything. "Lay back," Daniel said. "It was just a bad dream."

"No. I heard it. A girl screamed and then there was a bang or a bump or something," I whispered. I didn't dare move or make a sound, fearing I'd miss hearing it again, but still there was nothing. I slid my legs out of the bed, sat up listening.

"Where are you going?"

"I'd better get back downstairs to my room."

"Stay."

"I wish, but I can't." I started getting dressed.

Daniel did too. "It's so hot. I'm gonna step outside and get some air," he said.

"Good idea."

The house was dark when we went downstairs. I opened the front door and looked outside cautiously with Daniel right behind me. There was no one around and the world was silent, except for the sound of a dog barking somewhere in the far distance. The sky was black and the stars were shining brightly, but the moon, a little less than full, was covered by dark clouds like monstrous fingers eerily creeping across its surface.

My grandmother, both religious and superstitious, called it a foreboding moon, a sign of trouble coming. She saw a moon like this the night they came for my grandfather. "Full moons drive men crazy," she used to say.

"You okay?" I jumped, startled by Daniel's affectionate touch on my back. "Hey, easy. It's just me," he said reassuringly. I nodded wordlessly and wrapped my arms around my body.

We sat down on the porch railing and he draped his arm around my shoulders and held me close. He kissed my forehead. "How do I make this night last forever?"

"You can't."

"You, my dear Zelda, are too damn practical."

"I am not," I insisted. "I'm realistic."

"Same thing, baby. This just feels right. I don't want to lose it when we get back to Atlanta," he said, nuzzling and holding me tighter.

"We won't," I said, then sighed, contented. I knew we would never see that room upstairs again and it saddened me.

He started talking, and I commented from time to time, but mostly I listened. I studied the pitch, the tone, and every inflection.

I rested my head back on his chest for a little while longer and smiled as he kept talking. Birds began chirping, and although the sky was still dark, I knew it was going to be dawn soon.

"I'd better go in before Veronica and Daphne miss me." I stood up, but Daniel remained seated. "Are you coming?" I asked.

"I'll be in after a while," he said.

As soon as I stepped inside, I heard a bloodcurdling scream. Daniel stood up. We ran up the stairs to the second floor toward the noise. It was nearly dark except for the dim light coming from inside our bedroom. Daphne and Veronica were standing in the hallway, their eyes wide with panic.

"What was that? Are you okay?" We heard another thud but couldn't tell exactly where the noise had come from.

"Maybe it was a television set?" Veronica said.

"No, not that loud. I don't think so," I whispered.

We moved down the hall closer to Mazie's room. Her door was closed. There was another loud bump and a grunt, as if somebody had crashed into a wall. And yet another terrible thud, which shook the floor. Then we heard someone running up the stairs from the first floor. It was one of the white guys we had seen at the barn. "What's he doing here?" I asked forcefully, completely stupefied.

"Who is he?" Veronica asked.

He looked confused and stunk of whiskey and foul body odor. "I'm Rob," he said.

"I don't care what your name is. Why are you here?"

"She invited us," he said. "Billy told me to drop him off and wait in the car hours ago. I guess I passed out." He rubbed his eyes.

"Who invited you?" Daniel yelled.

"I don't know her name."

"He must mean Mazie," I said.

"Son of a bitch! I'll kill you, motherfucker!"

"Shit!" Rob yelled and ran down the dark hallway. He banged on Mazie's bedroom door. "Billy, open the door. Let me in!"

"Get in your room!" Daniel yelled, shoving Daphne, Veronica, and me back into our bedroom. We heard him run down the hall toward Mazie's room.

Immediately we came right back out again.

Daniel and Rob banged on the door. "Open the door! Billy, open the damn door," Rob said.

"No! No! Leave him alone," Mazie screamed.

I saw Daniel and Rob shove the door open, then push their way inside. Daphne rushed down the hall, and Veronica and I followed. We cautiously looked inside Mazie's bedroom and found a dresser partially blocking the door. The place was a shambles. It seemed as if absolutely every piece of furniture had been either upturned or broken. Liquor bottles had been broken, and glass was all over the floor. Daniel was holding on to Winston, and Rob had Billy. They were both struggling to keep them separated. Winston and Billy were still drunk.

Winston's lips were cut and bloody, his eye was swollen, and there was a cut on his cheek where blood oozed down the side of his face, covering his shirt. Billy's face looked as if had been through a meat grinder. His nose, bleeding profusely, was probably broken, his eye was swollen shut, and the side of his face was already turning purple and blue.

"Look what dat motherfucker did to her face," Winston yelled. "I'll kick his motherfucking ass. Let go of me."

Mazie's face was a sight. One eye was puffy, her lip was cut and bleeding badly, and there was a gash on her forehead above her left eye. Her neck was red and bruised like she had been choked. She was standing by Billy's side holding on to his arm. "Get out, Winston. You cheated on me. Billy loves me. He'd never cheat."

"Get off me," Billy yelled at Mazie. Slurring his words, he shoved her away. He staggered and nearly fell. "I don't love you."

Mazie was enraged, her eyes wide. "Billy, you said you loved me. You said you wanted me."

"Do you really think I would want your dumb nigger ass?"

Mazie shrieked and flung herself at Billy with her arms straight out. Her nails dug into his face, leaving red bloody scratches down each side, from temple to jaw.

"Bitch," Billy hollered and smacked her across the face. She went down hard. Her head made a loud thud on the hardwood floor.

Veronica reached for her, and Mazie pushed her away. "Get off me. Don't touch me," she yelled.

"She's fucking crazy."

"Zelda, get her out of here," Daniel yelled.

Mazie looked at Billy. "You liar." She staggered to her feet and went after him again. This time he grabbed her by the neck and started choking her. Rob pulled him off. Winston struggled to get free, but Daniel held tight.

"Mazie, stop it," Veronica yelled, dragging her away. But as soon as Veronica got Mazie a safe distance from Billy, she went charging back at him. She grabbed a broken beer bottle from off the floor. "You son of a bitch, you lied to me."

"You stupid, crazy bitch," Billy yelled and spat on her.

I couldn't move. It was as if time stood still.

"I'll kill you." Mazie continued to charge at him.

Billy struggled away from Rob. Winston tried to get free, but Daniel held even tighter. Rob grabbed for Billy again but was shoved aside. Billy grabbed Mazie's wrist and wrestled the broken bottle away from her. "Get off me," she screamed. "I'll kill you!"

Billy tossed the bottle and punched Mazie. She fell down, crying hysterically.

"Son of a bitch!" Winston got free from Daniel and went after Billy. He tackled Billy from behind, and they both went down hard against the dresser. They repeatedly threw punches—some missed, some landed. Their faces were intense and shrouded with rage. Veronica, Daphne, and I dragged Mazie out of the room.

Mazie staggered into the hall with blood all over her clothes. She was holding her arm. It was cut and bleeding. "I hate you, all of you. Get out of my house."

"Mazie, stop it." I tried to talk sense into her. "Not every man is going to love you. Winston broke your heart, your dad broke your heart. It doesn't mean you go out and sleep with someone like Billy."

She examined herself in a mirror hanging on a nearby wall. She started bawling.

At that moment the fight crashed into the hallway as both men slammed against the wall. Two pictures crashed to the floor as the men kept punching each other. Winston grabbed Billy's head and slammed it hard on the floor. Billy punched Winston in the side. We hurriedly got out of the way. It was chaos. Everybody was yelling and screaming. Billy and Winston were really going at it. The sight of it was horrendous. They were tearing up the hallway, crashing into the walls and breaking everything in sight. Daniel and Rob still tried to pull them apart, but the fight seemed to have gotten fiercer.

"You beat her, motherfucker. I'll kill you," Winston yelled, pulling a switchblade from his jacket pocket.

"Daniel, watch out," I shouted.

Rob pulled out a gun. "Get back," he yelled. "Get back, everybody. I swear I'll shoot you where you stand. Now drop the knife."

Winston glared at Rob and reluctantly dropped the knife on the floor. He went to Mazie's side.

"Get away from me."

"Give me my mother's ring back," Winston said quietly.

She wrenched it off her finger and threw it down.

He didn't say another word. With the fight no longer in him, he picked up the ring and his knife and left. He never looked back.

Rob lowered the gun.

"What the fuck are you doing? Kill that black mother-fucking ass," Billy screamed at Rob. "Is that what you did when you was over there in Vietnam, let them Viet Cong gooks get away? You weak-ass fucker, kill that nigga. Coward! Gimme the fucking gun. I'll kill him. I'll kill all these niggas in here."

Billy rammed up against Rob to get the gun. The gun fell free and got kicked to the side in the struggle. Rob went after the gun, then Billy kicked Rob between his legs. Rob went down, and Billy jumped on top and started punching him. Daniel grabbed Billy off of Rob and punched him in the face. Blood splattered everywhere. Billy tried to hit Daniel but missed. He grabbed Daniel in a choking arm-lock, then Daniel elbowed him in the ribs. Billy went down in pain. It was like seeing Daniel for the first time. He was angry, and his fierce punches proved it. Billy was down, and Rob pulled Daniel free.

Mazie's mother, back from where she had gone earlier, came running up the stairs, screaming, "What the hell is going on? What have y'all done to my house? Get out, all of you. Get out of my house." She touched Mazie's face. "Oh my God, what have y'all done to her? Mazie, baby, somebody get a doctor. What have you done to my baby? Get out! Get out, all of you! Don't you ever come back to this house or this town again. Do you understand me? I'll sic the law on all of you. Get out!"

While her mother yelled, Mazie reached down and picked up the gun.

"Mazie, give me the gun," Daniel said calmly.

It was suddenly silent. Everyone's attention was focused on Mazie. She was wide-eyed and holding the gun. "Mazie," Daniel said slowly, taking a step toward her. "Mazie, you don't want to do this, give me the gun."

"I have to stop him from doing this again," Mazie said.

Daniel took another step.

"Mazie, listen sweetie," I said. "Just give Daniel the gun. Okay?"

Mazie pulled the hammer back and aimed the gun at Billy. Nobody moved.

"Mazie, no, you can't do this. Give me the gun," I said reaching out my hand.

Standing the closest, I slowly placed my hand on the gun with hers. She held tight. "Mazie, please, give me the gun." She looked at me and I could feel her hand loosen around the handle. I eased the gun from her hand.

Suddenly Rob dove and flung his body to get the gun away. Startled, I pulled the trigger. The violent sound of a

22

I DROPPED THE GUN ON THE FLOOR. I SMELLED URINE, charcoal, and sulfur, rancid and bitter. I tasted caustic metal in my mouth, against my teeth. My eyes watered, my ears rang. I looked at Veronica and Daphne. Their eyes were wide with shock. Daniel's were distorted in anguish and trepidation. I shook my head trying to clear away the unimaginable of what had just happened. Then I looked down.

Rob was lying there on the floor.

Everything around me was moving in slow motion. I couldn't focus. Rationally, I knew what had just happened, but I couldn't seem to wrap my head around seeing it. It was like my father all over again. This time I was holding the gun. I had pulled the trigger. I looked down at the bright red stain on the white shirt as it spread and grew bigger and bigger.

Mazie and her mother, holding each other, began screaming at the top of their lungs. I may have told them to stop, but I could not be sure.

All of a sudden Daniel was holding me. "Zelda, are you okay?" I must have answered him because the next thing I knew he was on the floor beside Rob. After rolling him over he checked for signs of life. Rob wasn't moving. There was blood everywhere. His eyes were open and he was staring straight up at the ceiling.

I shook my head, still not believing what I had done. "It was an accident," I muttered. "He jumped and the gun went off. It was an accident." I looked at Billy. His eyes were raging. He spotted the gun down at my feet. A wave of adrenaline surged through my body. I knew if he got the gun he'd kill all of us. I reached down in an instant and grabbed the gun again. I pointed it at him.

"Put it down, nigger," he threatened.

His face was blood red and contorted in a grimace so vile and hateful it made the hairs on my neck stand on end. He was drenched in sweat.

He was the cops who had killed my father, he was the men who had come for my grandfather, he was the men who had wanted to take the car from us, he was the men sitting at the lunch table across the room jeering at us. He was all of them. He was what raw hate looked like. I cocked the hammer and aimed it at him.

"You better kill me the first time, bitch."

"Zelda," Daniel said, "don't."

"No, let your nigger bitch try it. Go on. Pull the trigger. 'Cause let me clue you in, sonny. You'll be lynched, all in a row, dancing on the end of a rope." He laughed menacingly.

Daniel was fast. He punched Billy so hard on the side of his head that I actually heard it. Billy fell to the floor and didn't move again. He was out cold.

Daniel came to me with his hand out. I turned the gun away and gave it to him. "Listen to me," he said. "Go in your room and get your stuff together. Do it now."

"No," Mazie's mother yelled. "Y'all not leaving all this on us."

"Don't worry. No one's gonna leave this on you," Daniel assured her.

"But what about him and . . ."

"He's dead. No one can save him now. We need to save us."

"I'll tell them I did it. It was an accident," I said.

"They'll never believe you," Veronica said.

"Go, get your stuff together."

We girls rushed into our room. We quickly changed into our traveling clothes. I grabbed my suitcase and my tote bag and stuffed everything inside. My things, Daphne's things, Veronica's things—we would sort it out later. I stopped for a brief instant and prayed. Daphne stood at the window staring out.

"Daphne, we have to leave now," Veronica said.

She shook her head. "They're gonna kill us, aren't they."

"Listen to me. Daniel wants us to pack and leave, and that's what we're gonna do. Do you hear me? Now, come on. We're leaving now," I insisted.

We grabbed our bags. I walked out of the room first. In the hallway, Mazie was still whimpering and her mother was holding her. But where was Daniel?

"Daniel," Veronica called out.

"I'm here," he said, coming down from the third floor. He put his suitcase on the floor.

"I know I'm not taking the blame. I gave Zelda the gun. She pulled the trigger. It wasn't me," Mazie said.

"What? You did this," Veronica shouted. "This is all your fault. You were flirting with him at the barn and you brought that evil in here to make Winston jealous."

Mazie looked at Veronica, then at her mother fearfully. "No, Mamma, he followed us here. I swear. He told me so. He came in the front door and I tried to make him leave. That's when he hit me. That's when he . . . he . . ." She started crying again.

"We don't have a lot of time," Daniel said. He took my hand in his. I watched as Mazie looked down at our intertwined hands and frowned. "We need to come up with a story."

"It was self-defense," Veronica said.

"No, the gun just went off. It was an accident," I said.

"Maybe in the North, but in the South when a colored kills a white boy, it's a lynching offense," Mazie's mother said.

"She's right. Unless a colored didn't kill him," Daniel

said. We all looked down the hall to Billy, still knocked out on the floor. This is what happened tonight," Daniel began. "Mazie, you met Billy at the barn. You were nice to him. He got drunk and came over here later expecting sex. When you said no, he started beating you. You screamed. Rob was in the car out front. He heard your screams and ran up to help you. They fought in your bedroom and out here in the hall. Billy got Rob's gun and tried to shoot you. Rob jumped in front and saved you. Billy threatened to kill you. I punched him and knocked him out."

"What about us?" Veronica asked.

"You three heard the fight, panicked, and ran."

"What about me?" Mazie asked. "What do I say?"

"You don't remember anything. You fainted from the beating you took. That's all you know."

Mazie nodded. "I can say that. I got beat and I fainted."

"Good. Okay." Daniel looked at Mazie's mother. "You came into the house and—"

"No," she said softly but firmly. "I can't say that. Nobody can know I was out last night. The man I was with, nobody can know. I fell asleep on the back porch. I do dat sometimes when it's hot and rainy."

Daniel nodded. "Good," he said. "You were asleep on the back porch and you heard fighting and a gunshot."

"Yes," she said, "and I ran to my daughter as the three of them ran out. Mazie fainted."

"Good," Daniel said. "Then that's what happened. We all have to lie like our lives depend on it, because they do."

"Billy's not going to say that's what happened," Mazie said.

"Billy's drunk. He beat you. Look at your face."

We all looked at Mazie. She had a black eye, a split lip, cuts, bruises, and a swollen jaw.

"What about Winston?" Mazie asked.

"Find him and tell him he wasn't here tonight."

We nodded in agreement. His plan sounded so simple that I could almost believe it.

Mr. Jackson came out of his bedroom and into the hall.

"It's a damn shame," Mr. Jackson said as he walked over. We all looked at each other. "I heard everything. Every word. Dem boys fighting over Mazie like dat. Den the one boy said he was gonna kill her. The gun went off and somebody fell to the floor. It's a damn shame."

I smiled. I believed him.

"Mr. Jackson, for a near-blind man, you're as sharp as a tack," Daniel said.

"That I am, young fella, that I am."

"Don't touch anything. I know it hurts, but leave your face exactly like that. The police need to see it. They need to see everything."

"The police around here are—"

"I'm calling the military police, not the locals. Rob told us that they were AWOL. It's a military shooting and they'll take jurisdiction," Daniel said. "Where's your telephone book?"

"Downstairs in the living room."

Daniel nodded. "It's time to go."

"Mr. Jackson, take care of yourself," I said, hugging him.

"You too, Zelda, you too."

I grabbed Daniel's hand and held tight as we went downstairs. "Zelda, Daphne's in shock, but you make her hear me. Say it over and over again until she believes it. Do you hear me? You heard the shot and you ran. Say it."

"We heard the shot and we ran away."

"Again."

"We didn't see anything. We heard the shot and ran."

"Good. If you get stopped by the locals, stick to the story until the military police take over. They'll ask you questions and try to trick you. Don't believe them. Stick to what we said and you'll be just fine. Trust me."

"I trust you," I vowed, believing every word. He leaned in and quickly kissed me.

"Good. Now go."

Veronica grabbed the bags and pulled Daphne out the door. I turned. "Wait, you're not coming with us, are you?" I asked.

"No, Zelda, I have to stay with them. I have to make this right. I have to protect you. Billy's not going after you and your friends. I promise you that."

"No, it's like before at the sheriff's office. We all go together."

"Baby, I wish I could. But I can't. Not this time."

"Please, please come with us. Don't stay. If the local police come . . ." My voice cracked as a well of tears spilled free.

"Zelda, you can do this. I'll see you in Atlanta."

"No. I did this. I have to take responsibility for my actions."

"Not this time, baby," he said, gently stroking my face.

"Then, I'll stay here with you."

"No. I need you to be safe and that means you have to leave."

I shook my head. "I can't go without you, please, Daniel."

"You have to go on without me. Whatever happens, know that I love you."

"I love you too," I said, letting the words flow freely from my heart.

He smiled. "That's all I ever wanted to hear." He kissed me. "Go. Now."

I started walking away from him slowly. With each step I could feel my heart falling apart. Outside, dawn was hovering on the horizon. The sun was creeping up just above the line of trees across the street. It was already hot and humid. There was no one out. Veronica and Daphne were already in the car. I hurriedly put the rest of the bags in and Veronica drove off. I turned to Daniel one last time. I saw him standing in the screen doorway. He raised his hand and so did I.

"Please keep him safe," I said in prayer, not knowing if God heard me or if he even cared.

We got on I-85 and drove a long time. I didn't know exactly where we were, but I knew we would be in Atlanta soon.

Daphne was lying down in the back seat. Her eyes were open, staring blankly.

"How's Daphne?" Veronica asked.

"She's in shock," I said.

"We all are."

"I'm sorry this happened."

"Zelda, this isn't your fault, so don't you think that, you hear me?"

Lost in our own thoughts for several miles, neither one of us noticed the patrol car that had made a U-turn and was driving up behind us until the lights came on. Veronica pulled to the side of the road. We looked at each other. "We didn't see anything. We ran," we said in unison.

The cop got out of his car and walked up to us. I'm sure we looked guilty as sin. "What are you doing in this brand-new car? Did you steal it?"

I was almost relieved by his question.

"No, sir. It's my college graduation gift."

"We'll see about that." He saw Daphne stretched out on the back seat. "What's wrong with her?" He looked at Veronica and me with suspicion, like we had kidnapped her or something.

"She has a headache," I said.

So of course he banged on the car really loudly to wake her up. Daphne woke up crying. She was nearly hysterical. She looked at the cop and screamed. "Rob is dead!"

Shit! my mind screamed, but I said nothing. He stared at her, stunned by her admission. My heart thumped with such force I just knew he could hear it. "Get out!" he ordered. He pulled his gun on us. "Put your hands on your head and don't move." He walked backward to his car, keeping the gun pointed at us. He called for backup, and in an instant it seemed that two more patrol cars arrived, sirens blaring and lights flashing. We stood there with our hands in the air. Three cops jumped out of the cars with their guns drawn. They were yelling, "Don't move!" "Get your hands up!"

We looked straight ahead and stood like that for a long time. Other cars drove by, some even blew their horns and yelled derogatory comments at us, but we didn't move. We didn't say a word and they didn't ask us anything. They just stood at their cars, talking among themselves.

I glanced to the side as two more patrol cars drove up, but they looked different than the others. The cops got out of the car and they all talked. Moments later one of the cops began arguing with the others. Whatever the dissension, he was outnumbered. He got in his patrol car and left. I didn't need a crystal ball to know this was not going to be okay.

Then one of the cops came over and put handcuffs on us. "Which one of you killed that boy?"

"We didn't see anything. We ran." We all three said the exact same words at the exact same time. I knew we would take those words to our graves.

"We'll see about that. Y'all in a world of trouble now," he said, humored. "We taking you to the next county over. Y'all coloreds being arrested on first-degree murder charges in Forsyth County, Georgia. The worst place in the world for your kind."

23

THEY DROVE US TO A SMALL CITY IN GEORGIA WITH A name I'd never heard of before. Inside the two-story building there were cops everywhere. They stared at us as we walked through. I avoided eye contact. I didn't want to see or remember any of this. There was a cop holding on to each of us. The one who was holding my upper arm was squeezing it so tightly he had cut off the circulation and my arm was numb. I knew he was doing it on purpose, but I didn't say anything or try to move his hand.

They took our photographs and pinned them on bulletin boards on a wall, each outside a different door. They confiscated our purses and jewelry. We stood waiting, then we were separated and put into different rooms corresponding with the photo beside each door. The cop holding my arm took me inside and removed the handcuffs, ordering me to sit down.

"Are you going to read me my rights now?" I asked.

He walked over and leaned down to my ear. "Don't sass me. This is Forsyth County. We believe in lynch-mob justice. Dey ain't no coloreds in the county no more 'cause we up and got rid of 'em all. So y'all don't have no rights in this town. Now sit your ass down."

"I want to see a lawyer," I said.

"I told you, you ain't got no—"

"Then you can't hold me. I didn't do anything."

"So you one of those smart-mouth niggers who thinks she won't get her ass kicked. Well, you're dead wrong. I'll kick your ass, then lynch you up and tell everybody you hung yourself. Now, who you think dey gonna believe? So shut up and sit your nigger ass down," he yelled.

I sat and stayed perfectly still as he walked out. I listened. The room was bright, like a thousand light bulbs all turned on at once. It overheated the small space and caused sweat to pour down my face, between my breasts, and down my back. It was difficult to breathe, like the air has been sucked out. But still I didn't move an inch, not even to wipe the sweat away.

I waited silently, listening to my stomach growl. I had to pee, but I just sat there as time passed. My father once told me that cops do things like this. It was called sweating a perpetrator.

After a long while, two cops came into the room. They didn't say anything at first. They turned the lights down and stared at me. One of them sat down on the other side of the table in front of me and the other walked and stood behind me. I knew this tactic too. I was supposed to be scared and intimidated.

"It stinks like shit in here."

"That would be her," the one behind me answered.

They laughed. The cop sitting down looked at me with his nose turned up in disgust, then he opened a thick folder and flipped through a few papers and stopped. "Zelda Livingston."

"Yes," I said. "Am I under arrest? I didn't do anything."

"We're gonna get the truth out of you."

The cop standing behind me threw a newspaper on the table. It slid and landed right in front of me. It was upside down, but I could still read it. Someone had written a new front-page headline with a thick black marker. "Army Hero Killed by Insane Coloreds on a Killing Rampage."

The cop sitting in front of me motioned to the headline. "You see that? We already know the truth. Your two friends, Veronica Cook and Daphne Brooks, have given you up. They told us what happened. Said that you and your boyfriend pulled the trigger and killed Robert Kent. Said you're an anti-war crazy and you been arrested before for assault. You tried to rob that boy. We found his watch and wallet in your handbag." He slid a notepad across the table. "You need to write down your confession right now."

I looked at the pad. "You want me to write down what happened?"

"That's right. All of it." He pulled an ink pen out of his pocket and placed it on the pad. "Write."

I picked up the pen and started writing: *I didn't see anything. I heard a fight and a gunshot, then we ran.* I slid the pad back over to him. The cop read it, then looked up at the cop behind him. He instantly started yelling in my ear.

"Y'all killed that white boy in cold blood!"

"No, I don't know what happened. I didn't see anything."

"You lie. You and that boy did it! Say it!"

Tears streamed down my face as I shook my head. "No."

"There are other witnesses who say y'all did it."

"No. That's impossible. I didn't see what happened."

"Then tell me the truth. What happened?"

"I told you. I didn't see what happened. I heard a fight and a gunshot, and we all ran out of there."

The cop who stood behind me slammed his hand on the table. I jumped and winced away, fearful he'd hit me next. "Billy Knox is a national hero, an officer and gentleman in the United States Army. He just saved his whole platoon in Vietnam. He put his life on the line to save a dozen men. He has a spotless record. He's never been in trouble in his life. There's no way he killed anybody. You did it, didn't you?"

The cop was lying. Billy was AWOL. I shook my head. "They were fighting. I heard them. I went into the hallway and saw Billy beating Mazie. Rob tried to help her. Billy took Rob's gun and pointed it at Mazie. Rob jumped in front of her and saved her. Billy shot Rob."

"That's not what your friends are saying. They're saying you and that colored boy went crazy, grabbed a gun, and started shooting. Y'all killed him."

"No. I didn't see what happened. I ran," I repeated.

"Your daddy is gonna watch his little girl fry in the electric chair. Or maybe I'll just let them have you."

He walked over to the door and opened it.

"They killed that army hero. Bring them nigga gals out yere!"

"Get 'em out yere!"

"We gonna have us a lynching party tonight, boys."

The crowd screamed and applauded their delight.

My heart beat so rapidly. I tried to breathe, but it was getting harder and harder. My legs and my hands trembled uncontrollably.

"You hear that mob out there? They're here for you and your friends. They want us to hand y'all over to them. And you know what? I'm gonna do it too. I'm gonna stand there and watch as they tear you apart, then set your body on fire. Now tell me the truth. Y'all killed Robert Kent, didn't you?"

"No. I didn't kill anybody. I heard the fight and the gunshot and ran."

The cop slammed the door. The other cop sitting silently in front of me suddenly jumped up and flung his chair to the side. It flew across the room and slammed against the wall. Then he slammed his fist on the table in front of me. My heart jumped and I started coughing uncontrollably. I couldn't breathe.

The cop behind me locked his fingers into my natural curls with a vengeance. With a fistful of hair, he yanked hard. My head wrenched back and I could see straight up into his flaring nostrils. His eyes were blazing red and there was spit coming out of his mouth as he yelled at me. My face was covered with his spittle.

"Y'all killed Robert Kent!"

"No," I stated firmly. My father held strong until his last breath and so would I. "I don't know what happened."

"Go get that mob and bring 'em on in yere. She'll tell us the truth soon enough."

I tipped my chin up defiantly. I knew my legacy. I was determined like the men and women who had come before me. They had fought and they had survived. *I will not yield*, I said to myself. *I will not yield. I will not yield.* I repeated the words over and over again to myself. *I will not yield.*

Suddenly, a sharp pain cut through my face like the world exploded. My head spun dizzily in every direction. Everything was blurry. I tasted blood in my mouth and I coughed, choked, and swallowed bile and blood. I held the side of my face, staring at the man who had punched and knocked me to the floor. I scowled. I saw him shift his foot back to kick me. I balled up and rolled onto my side. He kicked me on my hip and thigh.

"Get up!" he screamed. "Get up!"

I tried to hold back my tears, but they came in a flood of pain and anger. *I will not yield. I will not yield.*

He grabbed my collar and yanked my shirt. The summer cotton ripped apart easily as buttons flew off. He smacked the back of my head repeatedly. He grabbed my arm and pushed me like a rag doll tossed and discarded. I stumbled into the wall and fell down.

"Sit down!" he yelled, kicking the chair toward me. It crashed against my leg. I crawled up and sat down. He stomped over, grabbed the back of the chair, and dragged it and shoved it to the table. I put my hands up to block it from crushing my ribs. At this point, the cops left the room, but not before turning the lights back up.

I sat in defiance.

I didn't lower my head. I wouldn't yield.

Later. Much later—I don't know how long—I opened my eyes. I was saturated in sweat. I thought I might have blacked out from getting hit in the head or fainted. My head felt like a sledgehammer had been pounding on me. Every muscle in my body hurt. I smelled vomit and urine. I felt wetness between my legs and realized I had peed myself. I felt humiliated, and the tears began to flow. I examined my hands. They looked the exact same way they had five days ago when we had begun our road trip, yet the blood running through my veins was different.

Inside I knew everything had changed. The world I had lived in all my life wasn't truth. I had been looking through a kaleidoscope of reality. This was the real world, where the line between life and death was a simple matter of the amount of melanin in your skin. I looked at my arms, my legs. To some I would never be good enough no matter what I did.

The door opened and a woman walked in wearing a business suit, smelling of lilac perfume. She winced, holding her nose, and forced a smile in my direction. "Hello, Zelda. Zelda, is it? I'm yere to take y'all to the bathroom and get you all cleaned up. How's that sound? Sounds good, right?"

"No thank you," I said, glaring at her.

"Honey, dere are men from the United States Army ready to take y'all out of yere, and I need to get y'all cleaned up, make y'all look presentable."

The Southern twang of her voice disgusted me. They had done this to me, and they were going to own it. Like Emmett's mother said, "Let the people see." They would not ignore what had been done to me. "No thank you."

She looked around the room, puzzled. "But it's my job, you see. Now, I know you must have to go to the bathroom. You've been in this room for a little while and—"

"What time is it?" I asked.

She looked at her watch. "It's eight o'clock."

"At night?" I asked.

"No, it's morning, of course," she said.

I knew that wasn't right. How could it be eight o'clock in the morning? How could I have been here for less than two hours? It didn't make sense. I knew it was wrong. "Wednesday?" I looked up at her. "Wednesday?" I insisted more than asked again.

"No. Thursday," she said nonchalantly.

"I've been in this room for twenty-five hours straight."

She looked around again, refusing to meet my glare. "Well, be dat as it may, I have a washrag and towel in the ladies' room. And it's the white ladies' washroom. We don't have no colored toilet. Ain't dat special? I got soap too. It's a nice new bar, smells sweet, never been used, and y'all can take it with you if you want. We'll be happy to let you keep it and the washrag too. So come on now. Git up. The army men have things to do. Dey want to see you now."

"No thank you," I said with my father's defiant tone.

"Look, y'all need to wash your body. You stink, and you're . . . um . . . there's um . . . blood smeared on your face, on your clothes and other places. I'll find a shirt for you to wear, which you can keep. And I think I can find some lipstick and maybe even some powder to make you look more presentable."

"No thank you."

"Dere are two newspapermen outside dis building," she said, anxious and nervous. "Dey'll be taking y'all photographs for the papers. Your face will be all over the country. Now, you don't want to go out there looking like this. Like you've—"

"Like I've been beaten up by the cops? Punched in the face by the cops and kicked in the stomach by the cops? It's fine with me. Let them take my photograph like this."

"Well, ain't fine with dis police department. Now, I don't want to do this any more than you do. But I have to make you presentable, and dat's all dere is to it. So don't let me have to force you."

"By all means, try and force me."

She scowled. "Y'all nasty bitch."

"That makes two of us, nasty bitches." She raised her hand to hit me. "Go ahead, make it worse."

She lowered her hand and huffed. "We'll see about dis." She turned and stormed out of the room.

A few minutes later the same two cops who had come in earlier entered. They looked at me. "You gonna git yourself cleaned up or what?"

"No thank you."

"Suit yourself. Stand up. Let's go."

When I attempted to get up, my legs wobbled and gave way. I collapsed against the table, bumping the side of my face on the edge as I fell to the floor. One of the cops hurried over and grabbed me. He helped me to my feet. I tasted blood running from my fresh wound. My whole body quivered. I steadied myself and took another step, limping and cradling my side as I walked.

"We gotta get her cleaned up," one of the cops whispered. "Dat newspaperman and photographer can't see her looking and walking like dis."

"Dem army men is waiting for her."

I stumbled and fell to the floor again.

"Shit."

The door opened.

"What the hell's going on in yere?" A man at the door yelled as he quickly closed the door behind him. He looked at me sitting on the floor. "What did y'all do? I told y'all not to touch her. Did y'all beat her again?"

"No. She fell."

"Bullshit. I told y'all to git her cleaned up. Look at her. Shit. We got dat damn Atlanta press up our asses. Dey're out dere right now. What factories are gonna want to come to this county after dey see her looking like this?"

"Tell 'em she resisted arrest. We had to subdue her."

The man at the door sneered at the cop. "This is on you. I'm not going down for y'all foolishness."

"Put a rag over her head and carry her out."

"How's dat gonna look? Shit. Look at her. There's a photographer out there too. How is this gonna look?"

"I told him not to touch her. But he wouldn't stop."

"Shut up. Come on and help me stand her up."

They talked about me like I wasn't even there. They grabbed my arms and stood me up. "Look a-here, I'm the police captain in charge, Miss Livingston. Dere are men from the US Army waiting for y'all outside this room. Dey're gonna take y'all with dem after we git you all cleaned up."

"No thank you," I said, looking at him. "They will see me as I am. I want everyone to see what happened in this room."

He looked at me as if I had lost my mind. "You're a pretty girl. We'll get you all prettied up. Go git Peggy Sue back in yere."

I stumbled and my legs gave way again.

"Shit, dis is a nightmare. If he takes her photograph looking like this . . ." He reached out and shifted my blouse to close over my bra, but since the buttons had been ripped off, it fell open again. "Dammit. Come on. Dey waiting."

I staggered out of the room. Veronica and Daphne were sitting on a nearby bench with four men dressed in army uniforms standing nearby. They let out bloodcurdling screams at the sight of me. My legs gave way, and I slouched as the two cops on either side held me up.

My eyes barely opened. My head ached and I could feel the side of my face throbbing.

A man with a camera rushed over. He stopped a brief moment, staring at me. Then he started taking photographs of me as I stood between the two cops. A reporter asked questions about my condition.

"My God, what have you done to her?" Veronica shouted.

"Did she come in like that?" the reporter asked.

"No, someone here did this to her."

Daphne snatched the mug shot pinned to the wall that showed my face when I had arrived at the station. She handed it to the reporter. He looked at it and gave it to the photographer, who snapped a photograph.

"Y'all can't have that. Dat's police property," the captain yelled.

A man dressed in an army uniform stepped up. "Miss Livingston, I'm Lieutenant Charles Smith. I am the investigating officer." He handed me a handkerchief. My hand shook. Veronica took it. "These men are military police. We're here to escort you, Miss Cook, and Miss Brooks to Fort Gordon. Please come with us."

I nodded. "Yes, thank you," I said. With Veronica on one side and Daphne on the other, we walked out of the police station. As soon as the doors opened, I saw a crowd of people standing around outside. They had been causing a ruckus but were now silent. We walked straight through them, tucked between the military police. We looked straight ahead and kept walking.

24

I EXPELLED A STAGGERING BREATH AND FORCED MYSELF to inhale deeply. I did this until I could finally breathe normally again.

At first I cried like a baby. Tears and sobs of uncontrollable grief for the innocence I once savored so preciously. I had seen racist crimes against my father and grandfather, but I had never experienced it firsthand. Not like this. Taken. Stolen. Tainted by the evil that had surrounded me like the water swirling and circling the drain at my feet. Stripped bare in the white porcelain tub, I stood with the realness and knowledge of the unjust life thrust upon me through no fault of my own. I hadn't asked to be born black. It had been gifted upon me, and I wore my skin proudly with grace and honor.

I had always known the world was harsh and cruel, but having experienced firsthand the vileness of hatred, I was more determined than ever to reign in my father's stead and to be the champion he had given his life to be. To help those who couldn't help themselves.

I scoured and scrubbed my body, trying to eliminate the muck and filth of my experience. I could still smell the stench of the police station on my skin. I stepped under the water's nominal spray. The water washed over my face and ran down my body. I washed gently around my bruises and cuts, which were covered in Mercurochrome-soaked bandages to slacken the sting. The swelling around my eye burned a little, but I paid it no mind.

I took the rock-hard bar of soap and thrashed it against the washrag. I kept scrubbing my skin until it squeaked. I didn't want anything to remain from my time there.

The water began to get cold. I had lost time standing under the flow. I didn't know where the urge came from, but I closed my eyes and said a prayer before getting out. "Thank you, Jesus. Thank you, God," I whispered. "Now please help me be strong."

I knew what I had to do.

Veronica knocked. "Hey, are you okay?"

"I'll be right there."

I quickly dried off and threw on some clothes. I greased my wet hair and pulled it back, and it sat as a thick braid at the nape of my neck. I opened the bathroom door. Daphne and Veronica were sitting on the sofa talking.

Daphne frowned in all seriousness. "They're on their way."

I stood in the tiny kitchenette with a glass of water in my hand. With the linen curtain pushed aside, I peeked out the window. It was sunny and bright, and the sky was crystal blue, but everything else on the base in my view was gray, bland, and nondescript. Fort Gordon, on the outskirts of Augusta. The place looked like a board game with a dozen matching building blocks stamped and positioned.

We were at a military camp waiting. After being seen by the doctor at the Army Medical Unit, they had brought us here.

"You look much better," Veronica said.

"For the record, I never, ever want to go on another road-trip adventure with you two again," I said, forcing an almost genuine smile.

"I don't understand how you two can just stand there and joke about what happened to us, to you, Zelda."

"Honey chile, you know this is how us black folks do. We joke about rough times. That's how we get through them—slavery, emancipation, and Jim Crow days. That's how we'll get through this," Veronica said with the worst Southern accent ever.

"There's nothing funny about this, Veronica," Daphne said sternly and then cut her eyes to me. "You can't make jokes and then expect all this to just go away. It won't. Not for me. Not for you. Not for any of us."

After that we sat in silence, each of us looking in a different direction.

"Are you worried about the testimony today?" Daphne asked.

"No. Not at all," Veronica said. "I know what to say and I'll keep saying it. I didn't see anything. We ran."

Daphne nodded. "That's right. Me too. We ran."

They looked at me. I shook my head.

"What kind of attorney kills someone?" I asked.

"It was an accident. You said so yourself."

"It doesn't matter. I did it and now everyone is lying to protect me. Everybody's life is forever changed because of what I did. I have to make this right."

"What do you mean?" Daphne asked.

"I mean I'm going to tell them the real truth and I'll face whatever justice."

"Justice? There's no such thing as justice for black people. You say that all the time. How can you even think about telling the truth?"

She was right. Blacks were killed all the time and nothing was ever done. Justice for black people was an illusion and still is. I had seen justice five years ago. I knew exactly what it looked like. It looked like nothing. There had never been justice for black people. Since the beginning of slavery we had been used, abused, trodden upon, and discarded. This country was built with our blood and on our backs, and we had never been treated equally. And nothing has changed. Freedoms were continually being eradicated and laws had been established to ensure we would never see any semblance of justice.

"Personally, I'm going to take this and push it to the back of my mind and never let it bother me again."

"How do I do that?" I asked in earnest. "How?"

"The same way you did when your father was killed," Daphne said.

"When your life changes in a way that is profoundly unfathomable, you put one foot in front of the other and keep moving. We're women. We're black women. We don't have a choice. We never did."

Seconds later, there was a knock on the door. We looked at one another fretfully. It was time.

We were driven to another building, much larger, with a lot of windows. We waited in a long empty hallway, sitting side by side on a wooden bench holding hands. My heart was pounding.

When the door opened, we jumped up anxiously. The man who had come to get us from the police station came out. He nodded curtly. "Good afternoon, ladies. I'm Lieutenant Charles Smith. We met earlier."

"Yes, we remember you," Daphne said hesitantly.

"Pursuant to Article 32, this hearing is an official investigative proceeding under the United States UCMJ regarding Private Billy Knox."

"I don't—" I began, then looked at Veronica and Daphne. "I'm sorry, we don't understand."

He nodded. "In civilian law, this is a preliminary hearing. Private Knox is being investigated under the statutes of the United States Uniform Code of Military Justice

Article 86, Absence Without Leave; Article 128, Assault; and Article 134, Conduct Discrediting the Armed Forces, and articles yet to be determined. We'll be taking your testimony shortly," he said calmly, then nodded for another man to come over with the Bible in his hand. "Please raise your right hand.

"Do you assert that the testimony you are about to give is the truth to the best of your knowledge?"

"Yes," I said. Both Daphne and Veronica also agreed.

"Thank you. We'll call you in separately."

We nodded. He turned to go back inside. I spoke up quickly before he left. "Excuse me, sir. May I please ask you a question?"

"Sure."

"How long is all this going to take?"

"Something like this can take days, weeks, even months. But this is pretty straightforward. And as civilians, your part should end today."

"Thank you."

When he went back into the room, a uniformed man stepped into the hallway. We stood up, this time more slowly.

"Daphne Brooks. Please come in."

She disappeared behind the door. A huge lump formed in my throat even though it was as dry as the Sahara. After a short while they called Veronica.

"That's me," she said, standing. She turned and looked at me, smiling. "Be right back. Save my seat."

I smiled. Veronica's dry wit with just a dash of cynicism always made me wonder what was really behind it. To be so open, she never really gave much away.

I sat alone in silence, trapped in my own thoughts. Suddenly I wished I had been more patient with my mother. She was the woman she was, and she would always be in need of a man in her life. I saw that now.

Anxious to get this over with, I looked up and down the empty corridor. Waxed and polished, the wood shined and glistened like glass. The whole building seemed to have been chopped from the same tree; the floor, the walls, the doors, even the ceiling was made of the same dark walnut wood. It smelled of musty old wood after it had been left out in the rain.

There were portraits of important men in uniform hanging on the walls, their chests filled with colorful medals and ribbons.

The door opened. "Zelda Livingston. Please come in. They're ready for you."

25

I WALKED THROUGH THE DOOR INTO A SMALL OPEN ROOM.
I had to finish this. Desks, chairs, windows, some flags—I
remembered this from when my father had taken me to
court with him on occasion. It wasn't exactly the same, but
it was close.

There was a woman sitting at the edge of the room with
a stenography machine in front of her. She looked immacu-
lately dressed. She wasn't typing. She was just sitting there
with her hands in her lap looking at me, expressionless.

Two men in uniform were seated at a long table at the
front of the room. With heads down, reading I presumed,
they didn't speak to each other or acknowledge my entrance. There were also two military policemen standing
by a door on the far side of the room. The soldier who
had escorted me in stood by the door behind me. They

all looked stiff and regimented, as if a button out of place would tumble them into sheer chaos.

I recognized Lieutenant Smith. He stood and pulled a chair out. He motioned for me to have a seat at the table next to him. I walked over cautiously, sat down, and leaned over to him. "Do I have to call them 'sir'?" I asked.

"No, that's not necessary. Just follow my lead. You'll do just fine."

I nodded, and as soon as I did, a door opened. Lieutenant Smith stood up. I did too. A third man, thin, with half glasses and a narrow face, walked in. He took a seat between the other two men at the table and opened a thick folder in front of him. He peered at me over his glasses.

"Be seated," he said.

We sat down. I looked at the three men. My heart pounded nervously. Only one looked at me, but it wasn't a look of disapproval or condemnation; it was more derivative of inquisitive scrutiny.

The man seated in the center cleared his throat roughly and then coughed loudly, which echoed briefly. "Miss Livingston, you have been sworn in."

"I have." I spoke up clearly.

He nodded his head once. I saw the woman sitting to the side begin softly typing on the stenography machine. "Miss Livingston, we're going to ask you some questions pursuant to a formal investigation. Please answer giving as much detailed information as possible. Do you understand?"

"Yes," I said.

"Would you please state your name for the record?"

"Yes. My name is Zelda Owen Livingston."

"Miss Livingston, to the best of your recollection, please tell this panel exactly what you heard and saw on the evening of Tuesday, the thirteenth of August, 1968, and the morning of Wednesday, the fourteenth of August, 1968."

"Yes, sir."

My words were calm, concise, and measured. I didn't rush. I said only what we had talked about and didn't stray from the central point. When questions were asked of me, I kept my answers succinct.

"How did you meet Private Knox and Corporal Kent?"

"They introduced themselves at a club called the barn."

"Had you ever met them before?"

"No."

"Who all was in the guesthouse on the night in question?"

"Mazie, her mother, Mr. Jackson, Veronica, Daphne, and I were on the second floor. Daniel was on the third floor."

"Where in the house were Corporal Kent and Private Knox?"

"I didn't see or hear them until the fight in the hall."

"In your written statement you allege that Corporal Kent told you he and Private Knox were AWOL and were headed to Canada. Is this true?"

"Yes. That's correct."

One of the men jumped in quickly, his voice loud and screechy. "Why would they tell you that, a presumed perfect stranger?"

I stayed calm. "They were drunk, very drunk."

"And are you drunk?"

"No, sir, I'm not," I said.

"Were you drunk at the time and misheard?"

"No, sir. I took a sip of hot, flat beer. That's it."

He glared at me distrustfully. He had tried to confuse me. He glanced down at the thick folder in front of him. "I understand you were beaten up."

"Yes, I was."

One of the men spoke up for the first time. "Are you alleging Private Knox did this to you?" His thick gray hair and matching eyebrows, stern expression, and rusty-as-nails villainous voice seemed right out of a war movie. But I was not scared or intimidated.

"No, Billy beat up Mazie. I was beat up by the cops."

"Wait, you're saying the police did this to you?" he asked, holding up a photo that had been taken when I was in the medical unit earlier. He handed it to the other two men. They looked at me, then at the photo, and back at me.

"Why would the police beat you?"

"They wanted to know who killed Rob, and they didn't like my answer, so they thought beating me would change it," I said as calmly as I could, even as my voice cracked. I kept my eyes focused on each man as he spoke to me. My father had taught me to always look your judge in the eye, to never shy away from standing up for yourself and others.

"What did you tell them?"

"I told them that I didn't know."

"Tell us exactly what you heard."

"Yelling, shouting, fighting, and Mazie was screaming. Billy sounded drunk, and he wanted Rob to give him the gun. He said he was going to kill everybody there. Then I heard a gunshot. We ran out of the house and drove away."

"Are you stating that Private Knox killed Corporal Kent?"

"I'm stating that they were fighting, then there was a gunshot. They were the only two I saw in the hall."

"So you did see them."

"Briefly, as I ran."

"These are very serious charges, Miss Livingston."

"Yes, they are. A man is dead, I'm sorry to say."

"If you were so sorry and concerned about Corporal Kent, why did you run? Why didn't you help him?"

"I was scared. I didn't know what Billy would do next. I heard him yelling hate-filled ugliness. He sounded drunk and crazed. Then the gun fired. I don't suppose anyone would have stayed after that."

"Actually someone did stay."

It wasn't a question, so I didn't respond. My father had also taught me to never get baited by comments.

"So why didn't you wait for the police?"

"Police aren't very tolerant when a white boy is dead and black people are around. I have scars, cuts, and bruises on my body right now to attest to that fact."

"Yes, yes, yes," one of the men said, obviously impatient. He sighed dismissively. "We understand you were perhaps treated unkindly. That might have been avoided had you stayed and waited for the MPs, but instead you didn't. And how are we to know if you didn't incur these marks on your body elsewhere? We have only your word to go by, and I, for one, am skeptical. I am—"

To my surprise, one of the other officers defended me. "We are not here to refute Miss Livingston's word as to whether or not she was beaten or by whom. I believe the before and after photos plainly show her atrocious ordeal. We are here to garner the truth regarding the actions of Corporal Kent and Private Knox and what precipitated Corporal Kent's death. And for the record, perhaps the police deputies of Forsyth County should thoroughly understand that the term 'Serve and protect' pertains to all citizens of the United States of America."

I didn't know what the ranks of the officers seated here were, but I had a feeling the officer with the thick gray eyebrows and villainous voice who defended me outranked the officer who didn't believe me, because the one who didn't believe me immediately shut up.

"Thank you, Miss Livingston. We appreciate your assistance in this matter," the officer seated in the center said.

"You're welcome, sir."

"These proceedings are closed," the officer in the center said, closing his file folder. The woman stopped typing and placed her hands in her lap.

Lieutenant Smith quickly stood up next to me.

I stood as well. "Thank you, sir," I said and looked at the officer who didn't believe me. He said nothing. I smiled, feeling victorious, and watched as they walked out.

"Lieutenant," the officer with the thick gray eyebrows said before leaving.

"Yes, sir." Lieutenant Smith nodded. "Stay here. I'll be right back." I watched as he walked over and spoke to the officer with the thick gray eyebrows.

Finally, with everything behind me, Daniel came to mind. I couldn't wait to see him again.

The lieutenant returned. "You did very well."

"Thank you. I hope we were of some help to your case."

"You were indeed," he said, gathering folders into a briefcase.

"So is that it for us?" I asked.

"That's it. The process will now be handled internally. Miss Cook and Miss Brooks are waiting for you on the lower level. This way." He escorted me through a different door at the back of the room.

"May I ask you a question?" I said as we walked down a long corridor with more photos on the walls.

"Of course."

"Will Billy go free?"

"Miss Livingston, I am very good at my job. I will make sure that Billy won't be bothering anyone any time soon."

"I'm glad to hear that," I said, relieved. "Thank you."

We turned a corner and continued until he stopped at the end of the hall. The nameplate on the door read in bold brass letters, COMMANDING GENERAL WILLIAM "BUTCH" MITCHELL. The lieutenant knocked and waited. An unfamiliar officer opened the door. I walked in and looked around. The room, an office, was made of the same dark wood as the rest of the building. We walked to another door, and the lieutenant knocked.

"Come."

He opened the door, and in the other room I saw the officer with the thick eyebrows who had spoken up for me seated behind a massive desk piled high with papers, folders, and books. He motioned for me to sit down in the chair across from his desk. I did. I heard the door close behind me and looked back. The lieutenant had left.

"Zelda Livingston."

"Yes, sir."

"Do you want to tell me what really happened?"

"Excuse me?"

He looked at me sternly, then rolled the nasty tip of the cigar around in his mouth. The bushy eyebrows exaggerated the fierceness of his glare. He wasn't playing around.

"A name came across my desk a short time ago. It's a name I know as well as I know my own." He didn't say anything more. He just looked at me. Then he spoke one word and my heart shattered. "Daniel."

"Is he okay?" I asked quietly, hearing my voice quiver.

"No, Miss Livingston, he's not okay. And he's not going to be okay. Not any time soon."

I started crying. A flood of unending tears spilled free like the runoff of a dam.

"I'm doing this because I served with his father and he was a good man, an honest man. And I know the son is as admirable as the father."

"I don't understand," I said.

He reached over and laid the nasty cigar in an empty ashtray. "Daniel is being charged with murder."

I gasped.

"His fingerprints were on the gun."

His words ate at my insides like acid eating through cotton. But still I remained silent. A part of me didn't trust he was telling me the truth.

"See, I happen to believe Daniel is covering for someone. Is it you? Did you kill Robert Kent?"

I didn't answer him.

"Billy is claiming it was you."

"He was drunk."

"Daniel told you to say that, didn't he?" I shook my head continuously. "But what you don't understand is that he's going to prison for a very long time and he doesn't deserve that. Now, if you want to tell me the truth, I'm listening."

There was a knock on the door.

"Come."

The door opened. A regular policeman walked into the room. At first I thought he was there for me, but seconds later Daniel stood at the doorway. He shuffled inside. He had on a blue shirt and jeans, and he was handcuffed and shackled. My heart stopped beating. He had been beaten badly. He had a black eye, bruises, cuts, and it looked like his nose had been broken. I stood up. My legs wobbled, and my heart sank into my stomach.

He looked at the general and smiled. "Thank you, sir."

"I'm listening," the officer said. "Tell me the truth."

"Zelda, no," Daniel said. "Don't."

I stared at Daniel. "I have to. I can't let you go to jail."

"Sir, the truth is Billy beat up Mazie, then Rob and Billy were fighting in the hallway. The gun went off. Daniel came down from the third floor. Billy was railing and cussing and drunk. The gun was on the floor. I picked it up to get it away from him. Billy saw me. He was malicious and vile, and he said he was going to blame us and kill everybody. Daniel stopped him. That's when we ran."

The officer nodded. "Daniel's fingerprints were on the barrel of the gun."

I nodded. "He took it from me. He didn't shoot Rob. He protected us. He still is." I took a deep breath. Yes, I had told the truth, mostly, in order to keep us safe.

"I see. Why didn't you tell the police that and why didn't you testify to that earlier?"

"I was afraid. I still am. Justice isn't always blind in this country."

The officer seemed to nod his head sadly, then stood up. "I'll give you a few minutes."

"What do you mean?" I asked the officer as he kept walking. "What does that mean?" I asked Daniel as he just stood there, silent. "I told the truth," I yelled.

"Zelda."

"What does that mean?" I asked him again.

"Nothing," he said. "It means nothing. I signed a confession. It stands."

My heart exploded. "No!" I stood and took a step toward him, then crumpled against the desk. Still my eyes were firmly set on the man who had given his life for me, for us. His dreams gone. His future gone. His life gone. There was nothing I could do but let him be the man he was.

I walked to him slowly. He smiled and reached out his cuffed hand. I grabbed it and held tight. He passed me a shiny object. It was the flask with the peach schnapps. "I need you to hold on to this for me."

I nodded. "I will. Always."

"Let's go," the man behind him said.

"What can I do?" I asked tearfully, fretfully.

"Be strong. Make your father proud. Make me proud."

"I will. I promise." I grabbed hold and kissed him as the man behind him pulled him away. Seconds later he was gone. I looked at the flask in my hand. It was all I had left.

"Miss Livingston, this way."

I turned. Lieutenant Smith was standing at the open door.

"This way."

I followed him out of the office and down the stairs. I saw Veronica and Daphne sitting in the large open lobby talking quietly. They turned, looked at me, and smiled. As soon as I walked up, they stood and hugged me.

"Ladies, on behalf of the United States military we appreciate your cooperation. We've released an official press statement thanking you for your invaluable assistance. You're free to go."

"Thank you," Daphne said, smiling happily.

I was too horrified to move. I collapsed onto the wooden bench. Veronica and Daphne each sat beside me.

"What?" they begged.

The dam broke. I cried for Daniel, for me, for all of us. I wanted to say something, to tell Veronica and Daphne what had happened, but I couldn't get the words out. Then I saw Daniel one last time, handcuffed, shackled, broken like the prisoners on the side of the road. I stood up. Veronica and Daphne turned around. They wept.

Daniel and I looked at each other, proud, strong, and loved. He nodded and smiled. I did too. What passed between us was an understanding more real than either one of us could have imagined. In the end there was nothing we could do and we both knew it. The truth didn't matter. It never did. He had given his life to save and protect me. This was reality. The world would always see Daniel as guilty no matter what.

1988

Epilogue

WE SURVIVED.

Like sand pouring through an hourglass, time, uninterrupted, flowed continuously, barely bumped by the events of that night. For years I've tried to put the haunting memories of what happened behind me, but I never quite have. The shadows still remain. They echo and reverberate, rolling in and out like the ebb and flow of the morning's tide, returning again and again, ever present, ever fleeting, ever emerging, but never disrupting the normal course of life.

When we gather together, the three of us, we laugh and talk and reminisce, but we never speak about those memories. They just hang there like rotted fruit on a dead tree in the make-believe darkness as if it had never happened. But it did.

Forever bonded by the dark secrets, we survived to see better days and to follow our dreams. Veronica and I stood by Daphne's side as she married Dr. Kimo Lee, and again when she became an associate professor at the University of Pennsylvania. Now with five glorious, delightful children, she is the happiest I've ever seen her.

Veronica dutifully married and then became a widow, all within six months. Her husband was killed by his lover and he left her all his shares in his father's company, propelling her to that coveted seat at the head of the table. Her savvy business sense has transformed the company and prepared it to face the challenges in the coming century. She married again, this time for love.

I realized my dream and became a civil rights attorney. I fight to protect those most vulnerable, the innocent, like Daniel. Never charged. Never convicted. Still sentenced and executed. He never made it to jail that day. He was killed, shot, trying to escape.

It wasn't meant to be for us, and on some level we knew it. That one moment in time was all we were given. Two souls lost in a bygone era, laid siege by hatred and cruelty. But for one night he had belonged to me and we had belonged to each other. I am forever thankful for the turbulent nine hundred miles that brought us together. He was my hero. He had saved me. He had changed me.

I turn, seeing our daughter, Danielle, walking toward me. She's got her father's piercing eyes, his warmth and heartfelt tenderness. From me, she has the fire in her stomach and the aptitude and the drive to make a difference. A lot happened to bring her into this world. She is the only evidence that he existed and that in one night we loved and lived for a lifetime. At nineteen she has graduated from Howard University and is on her way to changing the world, first in the Peace Corps and then as an attorney, following in my footsteps.

She holds her pinkie finger up, and I touch mine to hers.

This is just the beginning of her future and I know the struggle is still ahead.

I have learned to trust the God of my father and grandfather and believe that Daniel, in spirit, is with me every step of the way.

To live in the hearts we leave behind is not to die.

Acknowledgments

FIRST AND FOREMOST, ALL PRAISES TO GOD, WHO CONtinues to bless my life.

To my amazing husband, Charles, you are my love, my motivator, my best friend, and my forever shining star. Your unwavering support and steadfast encouragement keeps me focused and lifts me up every day of my life.

To my wonderful children, Jennifer, Christopher, Prince, and Charles, thank you for always bringing joy and happiness into my world. You are truly my blessing.

To my parents, Otis and Mable Johnson, you long ago inspired this novel, and I know you will always stand with me. To my loving siblings, Karen Linton and Amanda Mitchell, and my brother-in-law, William Mitchell, you stay firmly in my corner with guidance and support, and constantly challenge me to dream bigger and stay focused on the finish line. To Charles and Hattie Smith, to Roszine and Andrew Stephenson, you are my tireless supporters. Thank you.

To my dear friends Paulette and Allen Jones, Michael and Andrea Jenkins, Frances DeLoach, Renee Salnauve, Suzi White, Jeff and Theresa Coles. You have all touched my life and made it better. To my sister authors who constantly challenge and inspire me, Michelle Monkou, Maureen Smith, and Candice Poarch. I am eternally grateful for your friendship.

And finally, this book would not have happened without the diligence, patience, and dedicated hard work of my agent, Elaine English, my writing mentor, Evette Porter, and the wonderful editorial mastermind at HarperCollins Publishers, the amazing Tracy Sherrod. Your guidance, support, and insight constantly renewed my spirit.

About the Author

CELESTE O. NORFLEET IS A NATIONALLY BESTSELLING author of more than thirty critically acclaimed novels. She is the recipient of six awards from Romance Slam Jam (RSJ) as well as a lifetime achievement award. She was also honored with the BRAB, 2016 Frances Ray Lifetime Literary Legacy Award. She is a graduate of Moore College of Art and Design. She lives in Virginia.